PORTERGIRL: FOOTSTE
- By Lucy
© Lucy Bra

Lucy Brazier has asserted her rights under the Copyright Designs and Patents Act 1988 to be identified as the author of this work. This book is sold subject to the condition that it shall not, by way of trade or other-wise, be lent, resold, hired out, or otherwise circulated without the publisher's prior consent in any form of binding or cover other than that in which it is published and without a similar condition, being imposed on the subsequent purchaser.

This is a work of fiction and any resemblance of the fictional characters to real persons is purely coincidental and non-intentional.

Cover designed by Lucy Brazier

PORTERGIRL – FOOTSTEPS OF THE TEMPLAR

Lucy Brazier

Contents

BREAKFAST OF CHAMPIONS

THE MASTER'S GIFT

TEMPLAR ANTIQUITIES

A LEGEND, CLOSE TO HOME

LEAVE

NEVER A QUIET LIFE

TOMB RAIDERS

FINDING AVALON

A PLACE FOR EVERYTHING

START AS YOU MEAN TO GO ON

TEMPLARS IN THE LIBRARY

UNIMPRESSIVE QUESTING

PIGEONS AND OTHER THINGS

INTO THE CAVE

THE FAIRER SEX

STEALING THUNDER

A DUEL, OF SORTS

THE PROFESSOR'S TROUSERS AND OTHER MATTERS

A HORSE WITH NO NAME

MENAGE A TROIS

A REUNION

CATS & COFFEE

THE FAILED ASSASSIN

WHILE THE CAT'S AWAY

WHEN THERE ARE NO SAUSAGES

FAMILY TIES

THE BURSAR'S HOLE

DR MARTENS LEADS THE WAY

PORTERS & KNIGHTS

FALSE KNIGHTS

LIFE AFTER DEATH

FOOTSTEPS OF THE TEMPLAR

DUNGEON MASTERS

A REPUTATION THAT PRECEDES

THE SINS OF THE FATHER

THE PRISONER OF CHINON

HEAD PORTER'S DISCOVERY

ZOMBIE CATS & WEDDINGS

BRINGING DOWN THE BURSAR

ABSENT FRIENDS

SOMETHING OLD, SOMETHING NEW, SOMETHING BORROWED, SOMETHING BLUE

BUFFETS & PHILOSOPHY

THE MASTER'S CAT

A VERY UNLIKELY VISITOR

A HAIRS BREADTH FROM THE HOLY GRAIL

STUFF OF LEGEND

THE CHASE IS ON

VIOLENCE IS GOLDEN

GOODBYE, OLD FRIEND

CAUSE & EFFECT

ALL GOOD THINGS

SECRET DIARY OF TERRY

Part One

Part Two

Part Three

Part Four

Part Five

Final Chapter

ABOUT THE AUTHOR

BREAKFAST OF CHAMPIONS

"What? Two weeks? No, that'll never do. We'll be knee deep in dead bodies by then,."

The Dean continued to pace up and down his room, the threadbare rug testament to his particular habit. He frowned at the phone before placing the receiver back to his ear.

"I tell you – there is not a moment to lose, Professor. I need you back at Old College at once!"

Without waiting for a reply, The Dean jabbed at the handset and threw it amongst the debris on his chaotic desk. He rustled around in the bottom drawer to retrieved a bottle of rare whisky from within, he then began the inevitable hunt for his glass. One drawback of regularly imbibing rare and expensive whisky was He could never remember where he put it!

At last locating the crystal tumbler behind some neglected paperwork, he tipped out an eclectic assortment of unidentifiable objects that had gathered there, huffed impatiently at some stubborn fluff and gave the rim a cursory wipe with a grubby cuff. As the comforting glugs of the amber liquid broke the silence, The Dean frowned again. Circumstances were far from satisfactory.

The Bursar had spent the best part of the Summer Vacation excavating the once immaculate lawn of Apple Tree Court – right outside his very window! He was supposedly searching for a neolithic monastery, situated far beneath what was, in effect, The Dean's garden. So far there had been no sign of any monastery, just a monstrous great ugly hole which The Bursar had filled with Russians. He insisted that they were archeologists, but The Dean remained unconvinced. The Dean was fairly unconvinced by The Bursar in general, quite frankly. He was pretty sure he had poisoned a couple of people already and, although this was not necessarily unusual practice in the surprisingly brutal world of academia, The Dean didn't like the way he went about it. There was no *style*. No *finesse*. Far too business-like to be what you'd call proper academic murdering. Now, the previous Bursar,– there was a man who used his *imagination*. Whoever would have thought a humble kettle could be coaxed into the role of a lethal device? The Dean shook his head. This would not do *at all*.

The Dean sat himself down in his favourite high backed leather armchair and placed his whisky on top of the adjacent teetering pile of thick tomes that served as a side table. The Dean didn't think himself to be an unreasonable man. Unfortunately, he was the only one that thought this. The Dean was difficult from the top of the thick mass of dark curls on his head, to the battered brogues on his stumpy feet. In his own student days he'd been known for his prowess on the rugby fields, but a finely honed physique of youthful athleticism and long since given way to a more comfortable, if not quite portly, appearance of middle age. He was a striking man, handsome, even, in a certain light. But it was his presence that defined him. The Dean seemed to take up far more space in the universe than his physical body would allow, partly due to his unshakable - and occasionally justified - sense of self-importance. His clothes followed traditional academic fashion of being colourful and slightly worn, but he was not a traditional academic. Now a respected professor of law, he had spent most of his working life as a formidable international lawyer and so had far greater experience of the real world than most of his colleagues. However, the only reality that mattered to The Dean was the one he deemed fit, and that often, at best, had only a tenuous link to the real world.

As one of the oldest and most illustrious institutions of education in the country, Old College had seen its fair share of nefarious doings over the centuries. People often think that students are the most problematic elements of academic life. This simply isn't true. Students are just high spirited and often drunk, which leads them into silly and ill-considered situations. Such things are part of nature for young people everywhere. Whereas The Fellowship – the body of leading academics responsible for running the College – they are far more dangerous. Also often drunk, they go knowingly and with great cunning into very deeply considered situations indeed, more often than not with very clear and concise intentions. Usually these are related to the furtherance of their own positions, sometimes a malignant attempt to usurp a colleague and occasionally just because of natural insanity or homicidal tendencies.

With such machinations at play it is a wonder the College manages to operate at all. Left to their own devices, The Fellowship would quite probably have eliminated each other fairly rapidly, leaving a lot of confused students standing around waiting for someone to mark their homework. Luckily, Old College – like all Colleges of The City University – had a sure and steady backbone of College servants keeping things running as close to smoothly as is possible under the circumstances. The foremost of these are the Porters. College Porters are a rare and distinctive breed, their exact kind not found outside of University life – and then, only in the very highest echelons of educational establishments. Porters are often mistaken by the uninitiated as the types of fetchers and carriers one might find in an upmarket hotel. Such a grievous error is swiftly corrected by an arched eyebrow and quiet remonstration that 'Porters are not the carriers of bags, but the keepers of keys'. Ensconced in their Porters' Lodge, the immaculately presented team of bowler hatted, suited gentlemen serve as a port of call to students and Fellows alike, knowing everything there is to know about College life and one or two other things besides.

Old College proves quite the renegade in the Porter department, boasting as it does the very first female Deputy Head Porter. Her appointment a couple of years ago was a cause of both curiosity and consternation, but these days no one could imagine the Porters' Lodge without her. She was petite, noisy and no one could ever be quite sure whether to take her seriously or not. Her long fair hair was neatly tied in a ponytail, peeking out beneath the rim of her treasured bowler hat. Her wide blue eyes might have given the impression of child-like innocence, had it not been for the almost permanent broad grin which promised mischief. She had tried to tame the more obtuse methods of academic insanity she encountered at Old College, but more often than not had to be satisfied with just making sure no one got arrested or murdered. Both of which had to be diverted more often than you might think. No doubt following Old College's lead, one or two other Colleges have followed suit and acquired lady Porters of their own. As keen as The University is on tradition, it tends to take the attitude that tradition is all very well until something better comes along. Which is remarkably forward-thinking for an institution that is otherwise swathed in such complex layers of ancient customs and rites that no one can properly remember why they do half the things that are apparently essential to academic life.

Emerging from Old College Porters' Lodge into the watery early morning sunshine came the aforementioned Deputy Head Porter, proceeding in a half-skip and singing something unidentifiable, followed by a less enthusiastic Head Porter, a man always irritated by wanton chirpiness before lunchtime. In their bowler hats and charcoal grey suits embroidered discretely with the College crest, they would have made an impressive and solemn sight, were it not for the skipping and singing.

"Deputy Head Porter," sighed Head Porter. "Are you singing the theme tune from *Minder* again? I realise you are in a good mood, but there's no need to express yourself quite so noisily. And tunelessly."

"Well that's not very nice," Deputy Head Porter replied, abruptly abandoning her skipping to fall into step with her colleague. "It's breakfast time. And you know how I love breakfast."

And this was true. But then it was true to say that Deputy Head Porter was very fond of all mealtimes. One of the foremost reasons of her applying for the role of Deputy Head Porter was the opportunity to eat for free at a place that really knows about feeding people. And the hat, off course. She did like a good hat. A job wasn't a proper job if it didn't come with a proper hat. In that respect, she was a good fit for Old College. They both took food and hats very seriously indeed.

The Porters crossed the courtyard into the Dining Room and filled their trays from the groaning expanse of glistening grease and fat stretching the entire length of the room. Setting their hoards down on one of the huge, polished oak tables that dominate the Dining Room, they clattered their cutlery in the almost deserted hall. The unsociable hour meant that they were joined only by a couple of pale-faced early risers from The Fellowship up on High Table and a clutch of Bedders in the far corner, enjoying an illicit feast of black pudding.

"And anyway, I *am* in a good mood," said Deputy Head Porter, cheeks stuffed with half a sausage. "You know why."

Head Porter huffed.

"Yes, I know why. And it's been distracting you, I can tell."

"Are you still humpty with me for forgetting to audit the keys last week?"

Head Porter made no reply but turned his attention resolutely towards his breakfast. Deputy Head Porter looked at his plate and stifled a snigger. For his first meal of the day, Head Porter had opted for two large fried eggs and a fat, bronzed sausage which had evidently been plated up by someone with a rather saucy sense of humour.

The snigger did not remain stifled. In fact, it unstifled itself with aplomb.

"What's the matter now?" Head Porter asked, witheringly.

"Your breakfast is making me laugh."

"I don't see what's so funny about sausage and egg..."

"Ho ho! What's all this?" The unmistakeable booming voice of The Dean startled them both. "What's so funny then?"

Deputy Head Porter indicated the offending victuals with her butter knife. The Dean eyed them intently.

"Aha!" he exclaimed. "Ah yes, I see. Very good!"

The Dean slapped Head Porter jovially on the back, almost sending the poor chap face first into his plate.

"You're a sly old fox, Head Porter. Now then," and The Dean shouldered him several feet along the bench. "Shove along, I shall join you both."

Separated from his amusing breakfast, Head Porter reached out to retrieve the plate, but it was too late. The Dean had already grabbed the sausage and began absent-mindedly chewing on it.

"To what do we owe this pleasure, Sir?" asked Deputy Head Porter. "It's a bit early for you to be roaming about."

"Oh, it's those blasted Russians in The Bursar's hole outside my window," The Dean replied, spraying a little bit of sausage over the table. "I tell you, I swear he tells them to be deliberately rumbunctious. The racket they make, honestly. And at such an hour. This is his way of getting back at me, you know. Because The Master approved my recommendation for our brand new Fellow."

"Ha! Yes, I bet that has given him the pip," nodded Deputy Head Porter.

"Well, I, for one, don't blame him!" exclaimed Head Porter, not in the best of moods to begin with but now especially peeved at the loss of his sausage. "Now, I know he is an old friend of yours, Sir, but whenever that chap is about there is nothing but trouble. And Deputy Head Porter, here, well – she won't get a stroke of work done once he arrives, y'know."

"Now, now, Head Porter," The Dean adopted a cautionary tone. "You know I shall not have a rum word said about the Professor. He has been instrumental in resolving several College matters in the past, as you well know."

"Yes," agreed Deputy Head Porter. "And he has a charming hat."

"The Induction of the Fellowship ceremony is not for another couple of weeks," continued Head Porter, calmer now. "I should like to suggest that we enjoy the peace and quiet while we can, alright? Is that too much to ask?"

"Ah, yes, well about that," The Dean began, clearing his throat. "I know that *technically* he isn't due until..."

"Ahoy there and whatnot!"

All three turned as one, to the entrance of the Dining Room. The figure standing in the doorway is reduced to silhouette by the encroaching sunshine from the courtyard beyond, but is nevertheless unmistakable. The dashing fedora worn at a jaunty angle. The winsome stance. The perfect cut of his perfect suit and the honeyed American drawl.

It's him.

Professor Horatio Fox.

THE MASTER'S GIFT

"Oh, for goodness sake," muttered Head Porter

"Ho ho, my dear fellow!" exclaimed The Dean, rising to his feet to greet his friend. "You made good time, I tell you! Good to see you, old bean."

"It's definitely good to be back, I must say," replied Professor Fox, grabbing The Dean's outstretched hand and shaking it wildly. "It sorta sounded like an emergency and this Professor likes emergencies, you see."

"Head of Housekeeping won't be pleased," snapped Head Porter. "She won't have your rooms ready, of course."

"That might be a vexing matter or it might not," laughed the Professor. "I don't mind it too much. Why, if you have an extra corner at your place... I'll curl up there until she's ready with my room."

A sharp intake of breath and bulging of the eyes indicated Head Porter's horror at the prospect of having Professor Fox as a house guest. It is not so much that Head Porter didn't get along with the Professor, more that he couldn't keep up with him.

"Don't be daft," said The Dean, his face split into a rare grin. "You can bunk down with me until the old battle-axe makes up your bed. We can stay up late and tell unlikely tales."

"That sounds like so much fun, I can't begin to think on it! But we must invite the lady, too. After all, she's so very good at unlikely tales!"

The Professor shook Deputy Head Porter's hand in a furious flurry, beaming broadly and eyes a-twinkle. Deputy Head Porter felt herself flush to the tips of her ears and made a show of adjusting her hat in an attempt to mask her fluster. When she first arrived at Old College, Professor Fox had expended every last drop of his trans-Atlantic charm upon her and she'd rather taken to his sharp blue suits and dazzling smile. When he returned to the States at the end of the academic year, she felt a little abandoned, it's true. But all that was forgotten in the instant he took her hand.

"Deputy Head Porter has enough to be getting along with, thank you very much," Head Porter said quickly, eyes narrowed only slightly. "I can't have you keeping her up all night."

"Pfft!" exclaimed The Dean. "We need someone to make our tea. Or pour the whisky. Something along those lines."

"Exactly it!" the Professor agreed. "Come along too, Head Porter, if you like. Or if you don't like – come along anyway and complain about it, that's what you usually do, isn't it? But first – I need the assistance of dear DHP and quite urgently, at that. There is... a matter. Of sorts."

Professor Fox and The Dean enjoyed a somewhat unlikely friendship, getting on famously despite having absolutely nothing in common. The Dean, certainly, was not known for his warmth of feeling towards his fellow man, nor any other creature, come to that. Professor Fox, on the other hand, was an abundantly warm fellow, with a permanent mega-watt smile and an inexhaustible interest in everyone he meets. Warmth and pizazz spring and fizz from every inch of his being, barely contained by his immaculate blue suits, of which he has either only one or many; no one really knows.

It is not certain how they first met, although it possibly involved a mysterious incident in Kuala Lumpa of which neither man would ever speak. Whatever it was, it must have been an experience of some note for them to have bonded so firmly, and for The Dean to have wangled him a place among The Fellowship. But then, it never does to attempt to understand the inner workings of the mind of The Dean. It is far too terrifying a place.

***

There is little greater joy in life than doing something you shouldn't really be doing and Deputy Head Porter was now making the most of such an occasion, much to the annoyance of Head Porter, who had found that he had little say in the matter. At the very time she should have been checking fire alarms back at the Lodge, she was enjoying a refreshing lager top and steak sandwich in *The Albatross* with Professor Fox. The urgent matter about which he was so insistent amounted to little more than his desire to purchase for The Master - the aloof and vaguely terrifying figurehead of Old College - a suitable gift, by way of showing his appreciation of his new appointment to The Fellowship. Quite why this had to be done that instant, and why they were now eating steak sandwiches barely an hour after eating breakfast, was not made clear. It would remain one of those many quirky mysteries that permeated College life. Then again, it was not uncommon for Fellows – upon discovering some great emergency or other – to immediately head for the pub. Very academic behaviour, that.

Very little shopping had actually taken place, in fact, no shopping had taken place at all. Professor Fox was not only quite keen to get as many steak sandwiches inside him as humanly possible, but also very interested to hear the latest College gossip. He had been away for some time (doing what, he refused to say and people knew better than to ask) and was rather put out to have missed incidents involving missing paintings, daring midnight raids on arch rivals Hawkins College and the surprising burgeoning romance between local police officer Detective Sergeant Kirby and Old College's very own gruff stalwart, Porter (his name as well as his job title, which was handy).

"Now, that is some great news about Porter and his lady friend," remarked the Professor, brushing an imaginary speck of dust from his fedora, which had been placed with great care on a chair of its own. "I never knew he had it in him, the rascal. Especially when you consider that moustache of his. A fearsome beast with a mind of its own and I wouldn't want to know what it was thinking, ever."

"It's been a bit of surprise to all of us, to be honest." Deputy Head Porter said between mouthfuls. "They're getting married the end of next week, would you believe."

"Wowawee and then some!" exclaimed the Professor. "That's some fast moving by Porter, I say! I wonder why the rush;you don't suppose he's got her in the family way, do you?"

"Good lord. I certainly hope not." Deputy Head Porter paused her chewing to contemplate the possibility of Porter reproducing.

"And what of you, DHP?" the Professor continued. "Is there the hint of anything warm and squishy on your horizon?"

Deputy Head Porter paused again to consider the consequences of warm, squishy things on her horizon. The thought was replaced quickly by another bite of steak sandwich.

"Well, The Dean did offer to take me out to lunch one Sunday, but rescinded the offer when he noticed I hadn't brushed my hair."

"Imagine! I needs must teach him some better manners, I think!" the Professor threw back his head and a throaty, feral laugh escaped into the public house. He slapped his thigh with delight, his chair rocking precariously on its back legs. "Then again, I am certain that his manners are as they are and there is no changing The Dean."

"You're probably right, Professor. But the annoying this was, I *had* brushed my hair..."

"But anyway, let's have speaks about The Master's gift," Professor Fox scratched his chin and closed his eyes. "I am thinking of something unusual and probably old, too. Much like him, in fact. Only I don't want it to be creepy. I couldn't bear that. What do you think?"

This seemed reasonable enough to Deputy Head Porter and besides, she had no better suggestions. Before she could signal her assent, she noticed a peculiar expression playing across the Professor's face. His eyes had wandered over her shoulder and a small crease appeared on his forehead. She swung round to see that a curious-looking gentleman had appeared behind her and seemed very much like he was intent on joining them. Deputy Head Porter placed a protective hand across the remainder of her sandwich and scowled.

"Well this is an interest. Good day to you," Professor Fox addressed the stranger with his usual disarming charm. "Do you need something? Not my friend's sandwich, I hope, as I rather fear she will fight you for it. And probably win. No – definitely win."

The gentleman replied only with a smile that reached from his chin to his hairline, before taking the seat next to the Professor's hat. He was a tall chap and well built; a mane of grey hair swept down his back, held away from his strangely youthful features by a colourful bandana. All manner of eccentric jewellery adorned his hands and neck and he had draped over his shoulders a battered leather trench coat. His keen eyes darted between the Professor and Deputy Head Porter as he swept his tongue across his lips, as if smoothing the way for the words that were to come.

"Pardon my intrusion," he began, in a voice like molten chocolate. "But I couldn't help but overhear – you two are from Old College, is that right?"

"Probably and then maybe not. What of it?" replied Professor Fox, looking the fellow up and down.

"There is a chance that we could be of service to one another," the gentleman continued. "You're looking for a gift for your Worshipful Master? I know of a most unique and precious item that he is sure to adore. Something that no one else might give to him – of that I am certain."

Deputy Head Porter rolled her eyes. She could see where this was going. Old College was stuffed full of barking old boys talking in ridiculous tones such as this. Any minute now, someone was going to suggest something that amounted to a convoluted wild goose chase, when what they could actually do was just tell you in plain speaking terms what they meant and save everyone an awful lot of trouble.

"What is it, this item?" she asked. "I mean, we weren't planning on getting him anything too expensive, you know."

After a furtive glance around the pub, the gentleman places a finger to his lips.

"Not here. Follow me."

The curious gentleman got to his feet and crept slowly towards the door, never once glancing back at his new friends, as if their compliance was assured.

"What do you reckon, Professor?" asked Deputy Head Porter, her eyes resting on the departing figure. "In my experience, following strange men out of pubs brings varying results."

"That's something you probably know more about than I do," Professor Fox replied. "But I can't see how we can just let him wander off after such a great speech. Besides, there are two of us and all that steak has made me feel pretty vicious, the sudden. I say we go after him, but keep our wits about us. If he tries anything feisty... then, well... he had just better not try anything feisty, right?"

"Right, Professor."

In one fluid, sweeping motion Professor Fox deftly scooped up his hat and placed it perfectly on his head as he stood, straightened his back and rested his hands on his hips. With considerably less grace, Deputy Head Porter donned her bowler and removed most of the crumbs from her waistcoat. They headed out into the street.

TEMPLAR ANTIQUITIES

The Albatross had historically been the backdrop for the beginnings of many an interesting endeavour down the centuries. Great scientific discoveries have been excitedly announced, murders planned and solved, ghost stories born and bred – not to mention the more regular and mundane incidents that have evolved every day from perfectly ordinary people having one too many. There was no reason to believe that this occasion would be any different for Deputy Head Porter and the Professor. At least they managed to get a nice bit of steak inside them beforehand.

Squinting in the bright morning sun, Professor Fox and Deputy Head Porter tumbled out into The City streets just in time to see their strange new acquaintance slipping into a side street several hundred yards away. For someone who appeared to move so slowly, he had managed to cover an unnerving amount of ground. Clutching their hats, they made after him.

The City was a maze of winding little lanes and alleys, quite unlike anything one would expect in a modern metropolis. But then, The City did its damnedest to be anything *but* a modern metropolis, despite the best efforts of the councils and planners. Around every cobbled corner laid antiquated edifices of interest, almost organic in their feel, as if they had simply sprouted out of the ground centuries ago. Rounding a corner at some speed, a swinging door caught Deputy Head Porter's eye.

"Look, Professor. He must have gone in there."

Accompanying the swinging door was a quaint wooden-framed glazed shop front and a hand-painted sign bearing the legend 'Templar Antiquities'. Both are attached to a squat, elderly building that appeared to have muscled its way between its grander looking neighbours. The door was invitingly ajar.

"I say let's go in after him, I suppose," huffed the Professor. "What a wonder. Imagine playing a game like this with such a fellow!"

The faint tinkling of a brightly polished brass bell heralded the arrival of the two visitors, although inside there was no one to acknowledge it. Once across the threshold, Deputy Head Porter felt that they had hurtled backwards through time. The antediluvian aspects of the carefully arranged wares spilled out across the entire interior, the decor of which would not have seemed out of place in Old College itself. Furniture, jewellery and assorted nick-knacks covered every surface, neatly placed and patiently awaiting the attention of curious browsers. The place was lit by an eclectic array of wall lamps of various types, each throwing its own unique light and shadows around the room.

Underfoot were enormous rugs of every colour - although mostly faded - spread across an elderly wooden floor. The shop was eerily quiet.

"Hello and a few! Is anybody about?" the Professor called out, but no reply was forthcoming.

Deputy Head Porter felt a shudder playing along her spine,As if something was lingering at her shoulder, always just out of sight. But she convinced herself that she imagined it, as prehistoric instincts did not sit well with a tummy full of steak sandwich.

"I must have been mistaken," she said. "Maybe he didn't come in here after all."

"Well, huff-hum and a rat to that fellow, I say", exclaimed the Professor, displaying a remarkable talent for pronouncing punctuation. "However, this place looks pretty perfect to be gift hunting for The Master. This stuff is old – and unusual! And it's definitely a bit creepy, too, so just like him. Let's look!"

"There're some interesting things here," said Deputy Head Porter. "What do you suppose this might be?" She indicated a curious little item that looked for all the world like a miniature guillotine.

"You know, the sudden, I think it's used for dispatching with subversive fairies," the Professor replied. "Nah, really, DHP, it's a cigar cutter. Not at all a suitable gift, I am thinking."

"Perhaps not, Professor."

"Oooh! Now, how about this?" Professor Fox delicately held aloft a dangling, twinkly item that glittered merrily in the light.

"I think that's an earring," replied Deputy Head Porter. "Let's call it a 'maybe'. We should keep looking."

"But hey, anyway, so what if we do find something we like? There's no one to serve us. Is this a shop or a help-yourself emporium, do you suppose? It'd be dadblame difficult to check out with an item without looking like a couple of thieves. A couple of very well-dressed thieves, I'll give you that, but that'll be no defence in the eyes of the law." The Professor turned his attention back to the sparkly earring, seemingly rather taken with it. "And I never knew earrings were so nice looking. What a wonder."

"That is not the item you seek."

The sound of the dulcet, chocolatey tones were more alarming than they should have been. Deputy Head Porter span on her heels to find herself nose to nose with the gentleman from The Albatross.

"Bloody hell! You made me jump," she said, peeved. "Is this your shop? It's very nice but, I must say, I find your customer service somewhat lacking."

"What now then!" exclaimed the Professor. "Didn't your mother ever tell you that creeping up on people is rude? And creeping up on a lady, too. I should smack your nose off just for that."

"Did I startle you? I really didn't mean to. You must forgive me."

"I needs must do no such thing!" spat Professor Fox, arms folded and eyebrows forced into alarming angles. "But I might. If you explain yourself a bit."

"Over time I have become accustomed to moving quietly around my shop," the Shop Keeper replied, casting a roving eye over what was, evidently, his establishment. "I don't want to disturb the articles, you see?"

"Yes, that makes sense," said Deputy Head Porter, nodding. "I'm surrounded by elderly things all the time. They do seem to prefer peace and quiet."

"What you seek cannot be found on any shop floor," the Shop Keeper continued, ignoring what Deputy Head Porter felt was her astute and witty observation. "It is something that must be given freely and yet – at the same time – must also want itself to be taken. Do you see?"

Deputy Head Porter effected another eye roll. This is *exactly* the sort of thing she was expecting. It happened *all the time* in Old College and, more often than not, it happened to her.

"I see clearly through my eyes, I think, but I still can't make you out much," the Professor muttered in reply.

"Then I shall show you. Once more, follow me..."

A LEGEND, CLOSE TO HOME

The Shop Keeper beckoned them through to a room at the back of the shop. It was arranged a little like a drawing room – the sumptuous personal quarters of a dignified academic, perhaps – but the labels and tags hanging from the furniture and ornamental whatnots indicated that this was further stock for the unusual emporium. Dimly lit and cunningly arranged, the room felt like a staged set; darkly theatrical and other-worldly in equal measure, it had an unnerving presence about it that made the usually stoic Deputy Head Porter glad of the Professor's company.

"Please, make yourselves at home," said the Shop Keeper, gesturing to the eclectic array of seating scattered about the room. Professor Fox headed for a high-backed velvet armchair with accompanying footstool, into which he settled himself with a cacophony of satisfied gruntings.

Deputy Head Porter, upon spying a delicate china tea set sat proudly atop an elderly dining room table, pulled up one of the dining chairs in the hope that her proximity to the tea things would invite an offer of refreshments.

Deputy Head Porter never knew quite how seriously to take an offer to 'make yourself at home'. *Probably not too seriously*, she thought. *It's probably just a fancy way of saying 'sit down'.* Just as she was considering pushing the boundaries of 'make yourself at home' to 'make yourself a pot of tea', the Shop Keeper joined her at the table. She thought this rather rude as it placed him with his back to the Professor, until she noticed that he could see her eccentric colleague in the highly polished surface of a gilded mirror situated on the wall close by. Professor Fox had already spotted this and his reflection was eyeing the Shop Keeper carefully.

"Tell me, my Old College friends," the Shop Keeper began, eyes flitting between Deputy Head Porter and the Professor's reflection. "What think you of mysteries? And, for that matter, histories?" There followed a deliberate pause, during which there was some expectation that the seated guests would do more than gawp gormlessly, which is precisely what they did. The Shop Keeper tried again. "Wouldn't you wish to learn the mysteries of Nature and Science?"

"Well, here it is," the Professor replied, testily. "Riddles vex me, overall. So, let's not speak in riddles, hmm? Otherwise, if you insist on speaking in riddles, I'll need some tea and DHP would like some too."

"The Professor is right," agreed Deputy Head Porter. "But back to your question – we at Old College are fairly well versed in both history *and* mystery. If you want our help, which I can only assume that you do, then you had better start with some straight-talk. And if you have such a thing as a kettle, I should get it on, sharpish."

Much to the annoyance, but no great surprise, of Deputy Head Porter, the Shop Keeper continued as if neither of them had said a word. To add insult to injury, he made no signs of making any tea, either.

"Since I was a small boy, my interest has been held by arguably the greatest, most sublime legend of these lands – or any lands, it could even be said! A legend so well-known that it has become intangible; a mystery that has baffled and bewitched scholars and laymen alike for centuries. That is to say, the legend of the Knights Templar and their quest for the Holy Grail!"

Professor Fox sat up smartly in his chair and kicked aside his footstool.

"Deputy Head Porter – and I must be forward a bit – this guy's mad!" he cried, with no attempt at tact whatsoever. "I say if there's no tea to be had then we buy The Master that nice earring and be away with ourselves. What d'you think?"

"You would not rather present the most elusive treasure of legend to The Master of Old College? For I have reason to believe that it lay but close by." The Shop Keeper smiled, but without much charm. "In your very College, even."

Professor Fox was momentarily distracted by this announcement. On the one hand, he had developed a fierce attachment to the sparkly earring, for some reason. On the other, he was susceptible to the prospect of adventures, particularly if they happened close by. Deputy Head Porter, however, remained distinctly unimpressed. After her experiences thus far at Old College, an enigmatic Shop Keeper babbling on about the Holy Grail was barely even enough to raise an eyebrow, let alone expectations. In fact, she would go as far to say that if ever there was a likely hiding place for the Holy Grail, Old College could very well be it. Head of Housekeeping probably kept jellybeans in it, or something.

The Professor strode smartly across the room so that he was facing the Shop Keeper. He took up post behind Deputy Head Porter's chair and placed his hand on his hip – a sure sign that he meant business.

"Now, I've got a question – or a few," he fixed the Shop Keeper with his very best stare. "What makes you so sure that the Grail is at Old College and why are you so keen to tell us all this anyway, hmm? Speak up!"

The Shop Owner slid out a little drawer artfully concealed within the table's edge. He removed some carefully collected papers tied with a length of blue ribbon, handling the small bundle as one would an explosive or deadly poison, loosening the silken fastening. As he did so, he spoke.

"All my life I have researched and hunted for the truth about the Knights Templar and the Holy Grail," he said. "Along the way I have found many truths and of many things I can be certain. The Templar's connection to The City, yes, of that there is no doubt. And... the connection to Old College, well, that too is of a certainty. It is all but cast in stone, in fact..."

The Shop Keeper gently pushed the unwrapped papers towards Deputy Head Porter. As it was, there was little she could gather from them, written as they were in a form of olde English she hadn't a hope of understanding. Seeing her scrunched up face peering hopelessly at the papers, the Shop Keeper felt moved to explain further.

"It says in here, among other things, that *'the Grail sleeps beneath the dragon, watched over by minds of fire.'* It is my belief that the Templar entrusted the Grail to the College founders, so that it might be safely hidden within the construction of the building."

"The Order of the Lesser Dragon," replied Deputy Head Porter, scratching her chin. It would not be beyond the realms of possibility that the shadowy organisation behind the founding and consecration of Old College could have had some dealings with the Templar. They were, after all, powerful and influential and would go to any lengths to get one over on the Church.

"Well, I wouldn't put anything past those buggers, dadblameit," agreed the Professor.

Despite being a defunct organisation that celebrated its peak four hundred years ago, the Order of the Lesser Dragon still had quite some influence over Old College. A secretive gentleman's society of quite some standing, they were the original founders of Old College, an institution set up to directly challenge the educational methods of the Church. The initials of the Order gave the College its name and many of the ceremonies, old charges and procedures laid down by the Order were still followed to this day. Even their earliest records were still kept in Old College and their name cropped up from time to time, usually when something nefarious happened.

"I am certain that the Grail lies within the grounds," the Shop Keeper reiterated, a passion rising in him, now. "But one such as myself would never be permitted to undertake esoteric work in such secret places. But you – you! You could both hunt for me, uncover the truth and take the gift that wants itself to be taken! The gift of truth and of legend."

"Yes, I can see it now," replied Deputy Head Porter. "We do all the hard work looking for the thing, just for you to snatch it off us once it's been found! I know your type."

"Exactly!" the Professor piped up. "How do we know this isn't just a cunning ruse to snatch the

Grail for yourself? Not so cunning, actually, as we've seen straight through it right from the start! And, hey, you know what, DHP? I was right the first time. This guy's mad! Come on."

Professor Fox swept out of the shop, casting a rueful glance in the direction of the sparkly earring as he went. Deputy Head Porter marched after him, straightening her hat, which had become skew-whiff during the excitement. Turning out of the quaint little alley and heading back towards the main streets of The City, Deputy Head Porter turned to the Professor.

"What do you reckon, Professor? I mean, the chap is undoubtedly a rare one, but you know what Old College is like. I wouldn't put it past it to be sheltering the Grail somewhere, you know."

"I think that is a likely possibility and then a few," nodded the Professor. "He might be mad but then – sometimes mad people know things.

Sometimes it's the things they know that make them mad."

"Quite so. And The Bursar has been very protective over his big hole. We know he isn't really looking for a neolithic monastery. There weren't even monasteries in neolithic times, The Dean told me."

"Then he is looking for something else, the rascal. Him and all those Russians. No wonder The Dean wanted me here quick-smart. Sorta feel a bit bad now, about going shopping. Rats and a heifer."

"Right, well, it looks like another highly unlikely escapade awaits us, then," huffed Deputy Head Porter. "Head Porter's not going to be happy about this, obviously. You know his feelings on escapades."

"Are they the same as his feelings on shenanigans?" asked the Professor. "In which case, he's going to get spicy about it. But, you know, the

Holy Grail would make a really great gift for The Master."

"Oh, go *on*, then," replied Deputy Head Porter in mock exasperation. "I suppose we could take a quick look round the old place."

LEAVE

Detective Chief Inspector Thompson stood before the wall calendar in his office and smiled to himself. The complex and intricately devised document before him, carefully colour-coded and neatly noted in his own intricate hand, displayed a full block of magenta squares for the following week. The curious could cast a brief glance towards the key down the left-hand side of the chart and learn that this jaunty hue indicated 'annual leave'. And if there was one thing the Chief Inspector really needed right now; it was annual leave.

His last big case had been a protracted and dull affair involving the misappropriation of funds by an even duller member of the local council. It was not the sort of crime he found very exciting, although there had been a brief waft of satisfaction at the sense of justice being served, once his work was complete. But it was the case before *that* – and the ramifications arising thereof – that had made him particularly weary. He had been involved in a rather sad investigation at Old College, involving the initially inexplicable deaths of two young men. The case itself was soon solved, but not without the perpetual interference of the College staff. Oh, the students had been difficult enough, in their own way, as students usually are. The Chief Inspector was a student himself once, he understood these things. The Fellowship were something else entirely. In fact, on his last visit to the College he had been presented with the unpalatable vision of an elderly Fellow, naked except for a strategically placed sock – which was on fire – running past him towards the river. He had wisely decided to turn a blind eye to that incident, considering it not worth the paperwork. But wrangling with characters such as The Master and – in particular – The Dean of College had proved testing, even for a man of his considerable mettle.

On the Chief Inspector's desk at that very moment there were three letters from The Dean, which appeared to the casual observer to have been written by a very drunk, angry spider. The Dean was not usually given to the practice of writing furious letters, he much preferred to express his fury in a more direct manner, preferably face to face and with volume. Luckily his recent experience of spending a night in the cells had deterred The Dean from hunting down DCI Thompson directly and since the switchboard now refused to put through any more of his frantic phone calls, he had taken to writing letters.

The letters had been a source of mild amusement, at first. DCI Thompson couldn't quite understand why The Dean was so annoyed with him. Alright, he had arrested him twice – once for obstruction and then later for the theft of a valuable painting (a mistake the detective had apologised for at once) – but the letters gave no real clue as to the source of his consternation. They were simply rants against the police force in general and him in particular, based on nothing more than a perceived interference in College business. It's true that the Colleges abhorred any and all involvement of outside authorities and they certainly considered themselves above the laws applicable to the rest of the land, but what precisely had riled The Dean so virulently was a mystery. DCI Thompson concluded that the reason for this invented rivalry was down to some sort of mental instability on the part of The Dean. It is likely that few would argue with that.

Ah, but the magenta blocks. Allowing himself a satisfied sigh, the Chief Inspector turned back to his desk and carefully filed the three letters along with their predecessors in an ever-expanding file. There was a knock at his door.

"Come in!"

The door opened and bald, red face popped itself through.

"Ah! Inspector Harper. Come in."

Detective Inspector Harper strode into the room, looking like he had something say and he was about to stay it very urgently. An ex-military man in his late fifties, Harper was an unlikely detective. He had been far happier in uniform, serving at the sharp end of the front line and taking a very literal hands-on approach to policing, when his senior officers decided that his advancing years and forty a day habit made him an ideal candidate for something more sedate, before his over enthusiasm got the better of his heart.

"What can I do for you, Harper?" asked DCI Thompson, taking a seat at his desk.

"It's about next week, Sir. Only, I notice you're on annual leave, Sir."

"That's right." The Chief Inspector had to stop himself grinning from ear to ear.

"Right, Sir. Only, you know DS Kirby's off next week too?"

DCI Thompson raised an eyebrow.

"I did not. Does it matter? We have several other, excellent, detective sergeants on duty, don't we?"

"We do Sir, we do. Only, there's still a few loose ends from the Old College case, Sir, and I'd like to get them tied up. And seeing as it was you and her that were working on it..."

"Oh, alright, Harper," huffed DCI Thompson. "You're her Inspector, just tell her that her leave is cancelled. Or postponed, tell her to take off the following week."

"I can't very well do that, Sir, she's getting married next week, Sir."

"*MARRIED?!*" DCI Thompson fumbled his pen and it fell to the floor. "Who to? Surely not that Porter chap?!"

"Yes, Sir, him, Sir."

"But she can't marry *him*. He's a *Porter*. And then there is the matter of that moustache of his. Have you seen it? Mind of its own, I swear. It's not right."

"I'm sure he can't help his moustache, Sir." replied Harper.

"He could shave it off. Anyway, I don't mean the moustache. He is a College servant. She is a police officer. It's not the done thing."

DCI Thompson got up again, bent down and retrieved his pen. He was annoyed with himself. He hated that he sounded like such a snob. He didn't really have anything against Porters, in fact they had been of great service to him when he was an undergraduate at the illustrious Wastell College. He had a great deal of *respect* for the noble art of Portering, a much-underappreciated role in the complex machine that is academic life. He probably wouldn't go as far as marrying one, quite frankly, but then he was a Chief Inspector, after all. No. It was the fact that Porter was from Old College. He was rather hoping to keep the place at arm's length.

"You won't be going to the wedding then, Sir? She's invited half the station. They're having it at the College, Sir."

Now that Harper mentioned it, the Chief Inspector did recall seeing an elaborate envelope on his desk. Only he hadn't dared open it, in case it was another letter from The Dean, in disguise. And now he was very glad indeed that he would be safely tucked away in the Loire Valley in central France when this happy event was taking place, as it meant he wouldn't have to set foot in the blasted place and risk coming face to face with the bloody Dean.

"Very *well*, Harper. If you pass me the files I'll look over them and assign any follow-ups to DS Smart. Send him to my office for briefing first thing tomorrow."

"Thank you, Sir, much obliged." With that, Harper offered a vague attempt at a salute and left the office.

Oh, dear, DCI Thompson thought to himself. He wondered what DS Kirby could possibly see in the grumpy Yorkshireman from Old College. He might have understood it, had it been Head Porter. He was a man with authority. Although he suspected that perhaps Head Porter might be holding a candle for his Deputy. An unusual article, that Deputy Head Porter. Far too sharp to be involved with academics, that's for sure. Ex-job, too. She was the only one who had been any help at all on that last case. What on earth was *she* doing at Old College?

Perhaps she just likes bowler hats. Yes, that would be it. She seems the type to be easily pleased.

DCI Thompson shook his head. It was definitely time for a coffee.

NEVER A QUIET LIFE

Although sunlight fell like shards of gold throughout the courtyards, Old College did not share the sunny disposition of the afternoon. Exams were looming large on the horizon and a miasma of anxious tension pervaded the ancient stone walls and sun-dappled cloisters. College rivalry was at its very peak during this time, the fight for academic superiority never more fiercely fought. To make matters worse, the boat races were but weeks away and the river was cluttered with noisy young scholars practicing furiously their strokes and threatening all sorts to their rivals, often from the very onset of dawn.

The Porters' Lodge was not immune to the swirling tensions, although the pink-cheeked Head Porter had far more important things than exams and rowing at hand. Checking his watch with all the theatrics of a Shakespearian actor, his wiry hair had unfurled itself and become stuck to his dampened forehead. Babbling hordes of students swarmed about the front desk, enquiring about their postal deliveries. With Deputy Head Porter out shopping and Porter off on yet another of the seemingly endless suit fittings he was obliged to attend, the morning's post remained a papery avalanche in the dark recesses of the post room.

But Head Porter was not completely abandoned. Dr Samantha Martens, Fellow of Engineering, had been passing through the chaotic Lodge and taken pity on him. She had only really offered to make him a cup of tea, but now found herself fielding queries about packages she knew nothing about. Her trusting nature and helpful disposition had conspired to ensure that she now manned the front desk while Head Porter did what he did best, which was stand around and look a bit annoyed.

Deputy Head Porter in particular was especially fond of Dr Martens. She felt her to be a kindred spirit. Not only was she a lone woman in a field ordinarily the preserve of people with a collection of delicate objects in their trousers, she was also deemed anomalous for her personal life, too. She was an enthusiastic weightlifter and Morris dancer, although not usually at the same time. Built like an Amazonian goddess, she was surprisingly quietly spoken, making up for this with her wild mass of pink hair, which gave the impression that she was wearing a magic cloud on her head. Deputy Head Porter was particularly jealous of her hair. Porters were not allowed to have pink hair.

Professor Fox and Deputy Head Porter picked their way through the heaving throng of students, making their way towards Head Porter, who was making a good show of quivering with rage. But Head Porter didn't really have much capacity for rage, so the overall effect was more amusing than it should have been. His eyes fixed on Deputy Head

Porter and she braced herself for the stern words she felt sure were coming her way.

"Now, hold on a few, Mr Head Porter, and give me a listen!" The Professor gamely approached with a smile so amiable you would invite it to tea. "I know I've left you without your Deputy far longer than I should have. Please accept my apologies. They are great apologies, after all. And let me assure you – she has been working very hard, all for the good of the College."

Faced with the slightly vicious charm of Professor Fox and coming to the conclusion that, actually, that did sound rather like an apology, Head Porter relented.

"Well, I suppose if it's College business..." Head Porter grumbled. Then, a little smile. "So then, what did you get him?"

"Hmm?" replied Deputy Head Porter.

"The Master – what did you get him?"

Oh, bugger, thought Deputy Head Porter. *Yes. The Master's gift.*

"Ah. We haven't quite got it yet," she said.

Head Porter's little smile disappeared faster than sausage rolls at a buffet.

"Actually we're just on our way to get it now!" The Professor jumped in.

"Listen," said Head Porter. "I really can't spare Deputy Head Porter for another minute. I mean, look at it in here! And Porter's off getting measured again, as if his inside leg's changed size again since last week. No. I am sure, Professor, that you can manage the collection of a small gift by yourself."

"But... but actually no! I need the little scamp to help me with it!"

"Is it heavy?"

"Kinda not."

"Well then..."

"It's the... *Holy Grail!*" Deputy Head Porter whispered with as much gusto as she could muster. Which was quite a lot, as it happens.

"The... what?" Head Porter was rendered almost speechless. His mouth opened and closed a few times while it waited for his brain to catch up. "The Holy Grail? Really? Oh, no no no no no. I'm not having this. I just *knew* this was going to happen."

Deputy Head Porter glanced at Professor Fox, who replied with a shrug. She knew he wouldn't be happy. With a drawn-out sigh and a solemn shaking of the head, Head Porter looked her straight in the eye and continued.

"Just when things were ticking along splendidly, nice and quiet, no dead bodies, no mysterious happenings... not even a whiff of shadowy ancient organisations! Along comes Captain America here and all of a sudden, you're off searching for the Holy Grail. Unbelievable."

"Who's off searching for the Holy Grail?"

The words came as a vociferous roar, closely followed by The Dean, strutting along with a serious-looking tome tucked under his arm.

"Aha! Foxy! There you are!" he exclaimed. "I've been looking for you. I have got you this book, here. I thought you might like to read it, because I wrote it."

"Now that sounds awesome!" replied the Professor. "What's it about?"

"Well, I can't remember now, it was a long time ago. You have a read of it and let me know, there's a good chap. Now then! What's all this about the Holy Grail?"

Deputy Head Porter did her best to explain about their chance meeting with the Shop Keeper, his insistence about the Holy Grail being hidden in Old College - that it *'Sleeps beneath the dragon…'* and suchlike. The problem was, of course, was that it all sounded completely ridiculous. And it was completely ridiculous. But Professor Fox had his heart set on it and, when all was said and done, it couldn't hurt just to have a little look about the place, could it? The brief, yet spirited, account by Deputy Head Porter of the morning's endeavours left Head Porter once again shaking his head, but The Dean was delighted. His dark eyes shone intently beneath his bushy brows and he clapped his hands together with great enthusiasm.

"Well this is simply marvellous!" he boomed. "You know, I knew there was something up with The Bursar's hole. I was waiting for a corpse or something to show up, to be honest. Only this morning I was wondering when we'd get a dead body to liven the place up a bit. I was of a mind to do away with one of the Russians myself, so this is rather good timing."

"I mean, this is better than dead bodies, even!" began the Professor, getting quite excited. "The best of it is – the Grail is here somewhere in Old College grounds! We can be done and dusted in time for tea, I'll bet you. What fun this will be and not at all vexing."

"Hmm! Quite!" The Dean tugged at his ear. "Now then... what was it the Shop Keeper said about it? *'The Grail sleeps beneath the dragon, watched over by minds of fire'*. Rather makes me think it might be underground somewhere, don't you think?"

"Yes, Sir," agreed Deputy Head Porter. "And the 'minds of fire' could very well relate to academics, The Fellowship, in fact." Although, in Deputy Head Porter's experience, the minds of academics were anything but fiery. More sort of woolly. Or like something you might find at a jumble sale.

"Pah!" exclaimed The Dean. "Minds of fire are all very well but it's in the belly where you really need it. With a bellyful of fire, a chap is unstoppable!"

"But The Fellowship are about all over the place," said the Professor. "Where would they watch over anything?"

"I think it refers to the very top end of the academic hierachy," replied Deputy Head Porter. "The Masters of College. And there is somewhere quite specific where *all* Masters of College find themselves eventually. Beneath Old College."

From the corner of her eye, Deputy Head Porter saw Head Porter place his head in his hands, all hopes of a quiet life crumbling before him.

"The Crypt!" roared The Dean. "Of course! I bloody well knew it, you know. Right then! Everyone to the Crypt! At once!"

TOMB RAIDERS

The Crypt was something of an open secret at Old College. Technically, the trapdoor entrance was supposed to be hidden away from all but a select few trusted with the knowledge of its whereabouts; but most people knew it was under a bit of carpet in the neo-classical section of the Library. There used to be just one key for the trapdoor, an enormous weighty thing of esoteric ferric beauty, held under the watchful eye of the Porters. But the old trapdoor became unstable with age and had to be replaced, lock and all, before someone did themselves a mischief. Now a sturdy, modern device, the new lock had a key that was easily replicated by any two-bit key cutters and a couple of the Senior Fellows had demanded their own keys. But in practice, the Crypt was only generally accessed by the Porters (and then only really

Deputy Head Porter, just once, out of curiosity during her first term in post) and The Master.

The Master's Lodge – opulent residence of the sitting head of College, situated on the east wing – was known to have a myriad of secret passages leading all over the College, one of which led to the Crypt. The original purpose of this was so that in the old days, the bodies of deceased Masters could be swiftly interred before anyone started asking too many questions, likely as they were to have been brutally shoved off the mortal coil rather than gently shuffled. These days, The Master frequented the Crypt on occasions when he required a bit of peace and quiet to indulge his passion for sudoku puzzles. It was probably no coincidence that the Crypt is situated right next to the Old Wine Cellars, a glorious collection of catacombs that used to hold the not insubstantial supplies of beverages required by any self-respecting intellectual institution. Even in death, a true academic never wants to be too far from a decent bottle of claret.

Wedging the trapdoor ajar behind them, Deputy Head Porter followed Professor Fox and The Dean down the rickety wooden steps that led into the bowels of Old College. Head Porter remained behind in the Porters' Lodge, as 'we still have a College to run, you know.' Such a minor point had not deterred The Dean, who was eager to take the lead in events. Her eyes adjusting to the cloying gloom, Deputy Head Porter got the sense that the darkness down there was something far more tangible than a mere absence of light; it felt more like the presence of something else. She tried not to let the fact that she was surrounded by tombs interfere with a sensible and helpful mind set, although the more sinister qualities of the environment were somewhat diluted by the continual bantering of Professor Fox and The Dean.

Breathing the centuries-old air caught her throat and the resulting coughing fit caught the attention of Deputy Head Porter's companions.

"Is everything alright?" asked the Professor. "Do you need some water or something?"

Deputy Head Porter offered a thumbs up to signify the affirmative whilst a particularly vicious skirmish of dust assaulted her windpipe. The Professor turned towards The Dean.

"Now then, be a good sport and give her some water," he said.

"What? I haven't got any water," replied The Dean. Professor Fox patted himself down as if some previously forgotten source of water might appear about his person.

"Dadblameit."

"Never mind, never mind!" spluttered Deputy Head Porter, finally clearing her airways with some most unladylike noises. "I think I'm fine."

"Right then," said The Dean, beginning to pace a little (a sure sign that he was thinking). "Obviously the sensible way to proceed is to search for clues. It's a tried and tested method, searching for clues always gets good results."

This was not true. Not even nearly. Especially when The Dean searches for clues. What usually tended to happen is that he would make an almighty mess, possibly break a few things and cause all sorts of problems until someone else came along and had a proper look, not to mention a tidy up.

"I like your thinking!" agreed the Professor, with some enthusiasm. "Now, what is the usual form that these things take? I shall get both eyes to work right away."

"There's the rub, you see," replied The Dean. "They can be literally anything. Once, one of the buggers turned out to be a kettle."

"That's true, actually," confirmed Deputy Head Porter. "Anyway. Let's just have a poke about. See what we find."

Once some candles had been lit, the Crypt, in fact, did have a certain macabre charm. The artfully fashioned marble caskets were of exquisite craftsmanship and their beauty emanated still through the layers of dust. Some were adorned with delicate bouquets, infinite blooms of cold, milky stone. Others were watched over by soundless weeping angels, bent gracefully beneath their great arching wings. *There's a sort of romance about this place,* Deputy Head Porter thought. *I wonder if these forgotten Masters wouldn't rather be somewhere their resting places could be tended to and admired?* And then she thought – *Probably not, antisocial buggers.*

Progressing through the chambers of the Crypt gave Deputy Head Porter the feeling of travelling back through time as she noticed the dates on the tombs hurtle further and further into the past. Thoughts of the gravity of their task, for what they were searching, were punctuated by The Dean chortling at the more unusually named Masters and Professor Fox whistling what sounded like two tunes at once. Before long, they found themselves in a chamber that felt positively prehistoric, even by Old College's standards. The low ceiling dripped something thick and undefined and the walls had a sticky sheen of a viscous, reeking substance. The tombs here were not the elegantly carved sculptures of reverence previously seen. There was nothing aesthetic about the lichen-ridden slabs of stone that nestled stoically in the fettering gloom.

Deputy Head Porter trained the beam of her trusty Maglite on the crumbling stone to see if she could make out any inscriptions there. Running a hand along the rough and aged surfaces, the tombs felt a lot sturdier than they looked.

"Now take a look here!" Professor Fox was boisterously buffing one of the tombs with his cuff. "I've found an interest."

The Dean and Deputy Head Porter joined him at the tomb. It was just possible to make out some sort of carvings within the stone, but it wasn't in a form that either of them could recognise. There were what appeared to be a collection of symbols on the lid.

"Well!" exclaimed The Dean. "What in buggery are those things?"

"Maybe clues, my man!" replied the Professor.

Upon inspecting the other nearby tombs in the chamber, they discovered similar symbols cut into the stone, still visible after many centuries. But what could they mean? Enthused by the interesting find, the search of the chamber continued with a degree more diligence. All jovial banter subsided, a keen focus now at the fore. Deputy Head Porter was possessed by an unshakeable feeling that there was, without doubt, something to be found, even if her conscious mind couldn't imagine what it might be. And whatever it was, she was determined to find it before the chaps.

Today was her lucky day.

Near to the chamber's entrance, where the wall met the floor, was an unusual tablet-like item set into the stone. It contained three lines of symbols similar to those found on the tombs – a kind of language devised of infernal geometry – and underneath what appeared to be a translation, in Latin. She called over the other two.

"Goodness me!" cried the Professor. "What on earth is that? A bunch of gardoobling letters, looks like. What a confusing wonder."

"I'll tell you what that is," replied The Dean. "That, my friend, is a clue."

"Are they the same symbols from the tombs?" asked the Professor.

"Yes," replied Deputy Head Porter. "And this here looks to be the Latin translation."

"So what does it say?" asked The Dean.

Deputy Head Porter cleared her throat and hoped that her schoolgirl level of Latin would be sufficient. Just barely, it was.

"It says –

Remember fair Avalon, City of Harmony

Remember our Queen, the sleeping jewel

Silent in the fair City of Harmony

Or as good as, anyway."

"Awesome job, DHP!" Professor Fox clapped his hands together with glee. "As a side note, I'm wondering what sort of jewel the Queen was. Maybe an emerald. Anyways, all we have to do is find Avalon and the Grail is ours, right! Right?"

Deputy Head Porter ran her hands through her hair. She needed to think. The realisation that the Holy Grail might really be hidden somewhere in that very room was something of a distraction.

Find Avalon.

But how?

FINDING AVALON

For a fellow so seemingly devoid of logical thought as Professor Horatio Fox, he could be remarkably pragmatic when presented with a puzzle such as this. After quite some time of arguing about the relevance of jewels and queens, it was the good Professor who came up with the sensible method of thinking. Which is a surprise in itself.

"Now see here," said the Professor, firmly. "All these fancy words and phrases are just here to distract us. What's important is the symbols, see? They're the same type as the ones on the tombs. I say we discover which symbols denote the word 'Avalon' and find the tomb that has matching ones. I'll bet my hat collection that we find the Holy Grail in there."

The Dean studied intently a stray thread from his jumper. He was a bit put out that he didn't think of this himself. He rather prided himself on his handling of clues, despite all evidence to the contrary. To give him his due, his elaborate suggestion involving the Crown Jewels was brilliantly inspired, although Deputy Head Porter considered this to be a thinly-veiled excuse to break into the Tower of London. The Dean really did have a penchant for breaking into places, usually arch rivals Hawkins College and always in disguise. He had a Zorro costume explicitly for that very purpose. Deputy Head Porter couldn't decide if the break-ins were an excuse to wear the costume, or the costume was an excuse for the break-ins. Either way, he suggested both with alarming regularity.

"You are a genius, Professor!" said Deputy Head Porter. "Come on. Let's have another look at it, then."

She whipped out her battered pocket notebook – held together by curling sticky tape and willpower alone – and jotted down some notes. By carefully comparing the symbols to the text below and using a process of elimination, it was possible to identify several of the words. Eventually, she came up with three symbols which she deduced represented 'Avalon'. She circled her findings and showed them to her companions.

"It's as good a solution as any, I suppose," huffed The Dean. "Although, let us not rule out my suggestion..."

"Absolutely we won't!" replied the Professor. "Why, if this doesn't work we'll break into the Tower right away!"

"In disguise, obviously."

"Right, right, in disguise," Professor Fox nodded encouragingly. "But in the meantime, let's find Avalon!"

In a huddle, the three of them moved from tomb to tomb, the chaps vigorously scuffing away centuries of detritus while Deputy Head Porter helpfully held the torch. Head Porter would have an absolute fit if she ruined her uniform and he was hardly in the best of moods as it was.

Down there in that place outside of time it was very difficult to comprehend how time itself was passing. No sounds but those of cloth on stone (and the occasional profanity from The Dean) served to remind Deputy Head Porter that she was still in the real world and not some strange pocket of history. After what might have been a while, or longer, they found themselves a match.

On the lid of an innocuous-looking tomb, no different from the others, they saw the same three symbols staring back at them.

"In here?" said the Professor, his voice barely above a whisper.

"Let's try," Deputy Head Porter replied.

They each took purchase of the lid and together heaved and, indeed, ho-ed – a valiant crusade of flesh against stone – to slide it free.

"Buggeration!" growled The Dean, his face an unusual shade of puce. "This is no good! Let's just smash the thing up."

"Now just have a few bits of patience!" chided the Professor. "Keep at it. I think I can feel movement... come on... there!"

A sound like the stirring of an ancient beast shattered the quiet of the Crypt as stone ground against stone, yielding to the collective endeavours forced upon it. If there were any kind of poetic justice in the world, some rousing orchestral music would have burst forth and an enigmatic glow from the depths of the freshly opened tomb would have bathed their expectant expressions.

Needless to say, neither of those things happened, but instead a fetid cloud of something that many moons ago would have been air erupted right into their faces. A period of decidedly unheroic spluttering and coughing ensued, leaving everyone feeling rather peaky.

"Come on then, let's have a look inside the blasted thing," said The Dean, once he had sufficiently regained something approaching composure. "Get about it, Deputy Head Porter, you have the torch."

Brandishing her Maglite like it was Excalibur itself, Deputy Head Porter approached the open tomb. The sound of her heartbeat filled her ears and a familiar metallic taste coated the roof of her mouth, already dry from the centuries of dust. If her time at Old College had taught her anything, it was that the unexpected was standard procedure and the impossible merely part of the day-to-day running of things. But could the Holy Grail really be laying just inches from her?

Of course not.

"Bugger," said The Dean. "And bugger again. Buggering thing's empty."

"Someone's been messing around with it," said the Professor, narrowing his eyes. "That's not unlikely, you know. The Grail was always being shoved about the place. To stop people finding it, see."

"I put my money on Head of Housekeeping," muttered The Dean. "That woman is forever shifting things about."

"More likely, the Order of the Lesser Dragon," suggested Deputy Head Porter. "Perhaps the hiding place was compromised and they took it somewhere else?"

"Well, if they will go leaving clues about the place, what do they expect?" said the Professor, quite reasonably.

"Could it still be in Old College, do you think?" wondered The Dean, hands thrust into pockets and head tilted upwards in thought.

"We have to find it!" snapped the Professor, strutting up and down the chamber. "I needs must present it to The Master at my Induction feast! Dadblameit! I just knew we should have bought that earring when we had the chance. And he would've looked good in it, I'm thinking."

The Dean grabbed the Professor and held him still.

"You said we would find the Grail, done and dusted by tea time. It's ten past tea time already!"

"Listen," said Deputy Head Porter, keen to avert a kerfuffle. "If the Order of the Lesser Dragon did move the Grail, there is every possibility that it will be documented somewhere in their records. I happen to know that they are kept in a chest in the Old Library."

"Then we shall head to the Old Library!" cried the Professor.

"Didn't you hear me, old chap?" replied The Dean. "I said it's ten past tea time already. Holy Grail or no Holy Grail – that's practically a mealtime and I'm not missing *that* for anything."

A PLACE FOR EVERYTHING

Porter stood on a stool in The City's fanciest tailors, Meade & Crowmore, arms outstretched and looking for all the world like a man about to be crucified. This was mostly, of course, due to the fact that he was being measured to within an inch of his life by two firm-handed tailor's assistants, but also partly because he wasn't enjoying the experience one little bit. His fiancee, the lovely Detective Sergeant Kirby, took pictures on her phone and beamed with adoration.

It had been a bit of a surprise all round when Porter began romancing the Detective Sergeant, seeming as they did such an unlikely couple. But on closer inspection, the match was not as improbable as it appeared. Unlike her unflappable colleague, the well-bred and highly educated DCI Thompson, DS Kirby was not of University stock and despite her sharp mind and keen intuition, was far more 'town' than 'gown'. She also shared Porter's forthright manner and penchant for plain-speaking, as well as enjoying a pie and a pint and the occasional game of darts. And if she was prepared to take on that infamous moustache of his, then she was certainly the perfect woman for Porter.

"I'm sure I'm the same size as I was last week," grumbled Porter, flinching at the pinching grip of the tailor's assistant who was holding out his arm.

"I think you've got a bit fatter," replied DS Kirby, grinning.

"I haven't! Not fatter. Only more genial. I expand in your presence, my pumpkin."

"You 'ad four curries last week," Kirby continued. "We're getting wed next week and you 'aven't even looked at the wedding diet I done for you."

"I'm on my own wedding diet," said Porter. "Building strength up for t'big day. I can't be facing that half-starved, I'll never make it down t'aisle."

"Which side do you dress, sir?" A voice came from the angular and bespectacled face by Porter's groin. Porter's forehead creased and his moustache rearranged itself on his top lip.

"I dress both sides, all over," he replied. "All of me."

"No, sir, what side do you dress *on*?"

Porter thought again.

"Usually the side furthest from t'window," he said finally. "So's I don't frighten Mrs Pawley's cats opposite."

DS Kirby laughed the filthiest laugh the poor genteel tailor's assistants had ever heard in their lives.

"No, 'e means... where you put your..." and she made an explanatory hand gesture which made everything suddenly very clear.

Porter's eyes widened and he wind-milled his arms furiously before leaping off the stool, sending tailor's assistants scattering across the previously peaceful and sedate shop floor.

"Bloody cheek of it!" he exclaimed. "I'm practically a married man and he asks a question like that! I thought this was meant to be a nobby establishment, too. Bloody hell."

"Aww, come on, my love, they've nearly done with you now," cooed DS Kirby. "It's for your wedding suit, after all."

"Bugger that! Tell 'em to leave plenty of room round the middle for pies and ale and be done with it." Porter grabbed his jacket from the coatrack and wrestled it across his shoulders. "Come on, woman. We're going t'pub."

Where Porter should really have been going was back to the Porters' Lodge, where things were a good deal less chaotic than they had been, no thanks to the wilful absence of most of the staff. Head Porter leaned casually on the front counter, cup of tea in hand, contemplating another biscuit. Most of the students had cleared off now and just a couple – Hershel and Penelope – remained. Dr Martens emerged from the post room at the back of the Lodge carrying a clipboard and a brown paper package tied up with string.

"Penelope?" she said to the girl. Penelope smiled and nodded. "Right." Dr Martens reached into her cloud of hair and retrieved a pen. She made a scribble on her clipboard before handing over the package. "Sorry about that. It was filed under B for 'box' when it should have been under P for 'package'."

When Hershel and Penelope had left the Lodge, Head Porter turned to Dr Martens.

"It wasn't in the wrong place, y'know," he said, his voice dripping gravitas. "That was quite clearly a box and not a package."

"No, that was definitely a package," replied Dr Martens. "It had brown paper and string. Package."

"Yes but it was a box wrapped in brown paper and string."

"The brown paper and string make it a package."

Head Porter placed his mug firmly on the front counter and swept a stray strand of wiry hair away from his face with a flourish.

"I am a Porter of many years standing, I'll have you know," he chirped. "A Head Porter, at that!"

"I've got a PhD," countered Dr Martens.

Before this discussion of great intellectual importance could reach its no doubt illuminating conclusion, a sound of guttural malevolence like the release of a thousand demons from hell erupted from the front door of the Lodge. Across the threshold swaggered The Master's Cat, hissing and spitting, amber eyes aglow. The Master's Cat should, by all accounts, have been a magnificent creature, with its thick, lustrous smoke-grey coat and inordinate proportions. But it had the temperament of a giant furry wasp and was permanently on the look-out for unsuspecting shins to shred. The creature was referred to as 'it', partly because of its demonic disposition but also because the thing was so ferocious no one could get close enough to ascertain its gender.

Head Porter automatically leapt onto the front counter and tucked his knees into his chest, hugging his legs protectively. His shins knew all too well the potential of those claws, now neatly sheathed in innocuous-looking paws padding across the flagstones. Dr Martens, fearless in general and in possession of shins of steel, smiled amiably at the cat and bent down.

"Whodalovelypusspuss, eh?"

"Be careful! Don't go near it!" squealed Head Porter, squirming on the counter.

"Who's a lovely... er... thing..."

"Mind out for its claws! It'll have your eye out!"

The Master's Cat ceased its hissing and turned its fat fluffy face towards Dr Martens. It wasn't used to this. People didn't usually refer to it as 'lovely'. People usually fled in terror. It was confused.

"What are you doing in here, pussy cat?" Dr Martens asked, ruffling its ears.

"It's come to do a poo on top of the key cabinets!" cried Head Porter. "That's what it usually does. If it can't bite anyone."

"The key cabinets are not a litter tray," said Dr Martens firmly to The Master's Cat. "Naughty cat. Come on." And she stood up, grabbing the bemused beast under the belly as she did so.

"Merk!" said The Master's Cat. It should really be attacking with tooth and claw round about now, but there was something about Dr Martens' tone and manner that made that course of action seem impossible. And it had been hoping to do a poo, too, her firm grip on its under carriage reminding it of the fact.

"Out we go!" sang Dr Martens, gently tossing the cat out into the courtyard and closing the Lodge door behind her. "There. Outside is the place for poos."

"My gosh. I can't believe it didn't try to kill you!"

"Cats like me," replied Dr Martens. "That one has very big feet."

"Deputy Head Porter has a cat," said Head Porter, climbing down from the counter with as much dignity as he could muster. "Terry. It eats everything, but other than that it's quite nice."

"Goodness, look at the time!" Dr Martens said, glancing at the large, railway station-style clock on the Lodge wall. "I'd better be going. I've got tutorials first thing in the morning."

"Hang on, we haven't done the key audit yet!" pleaded Head Porter. Dr Martens fixed him with a beady eye.

"You do realise I'm not actually a Porter, don't you?"

"Oh but... please? Everybody's buggered off and left me." Head Porter thought for a moment. "I'll let you wear my hat."

Dr Martens raised an eyebrow. She liked hats. She liked Head Porter's bowler hat.

"I'll try it on."

To Head Porter's amazement, his hat fitted her perfectly. He had always considered himself to be quite large in the head department, so he was somewhat surprised.

"You've got a really big head for a woman," he said, before adding quickly – "It must be all those brains you've got in there."

"I think my head is mostly hair."

"Oh."

START AS YOU MEAN TO GO ON

Head of Catering was a man permanently on the edge. On the edge of what varied from day to day, but wherever there was an edge, you could be sure to find Head of Catering right on it. The demands of a hungry Fellowship, not to mention the staff, students and their guests, had taken their toll on his hairline and left him with an expression of constant panic. A fat, purple vein throbbed perpetually on his forehead, gaining pace in accordance with the situation. Today, he was as frantic as ever, in no small part due to the ferocious enthusiasm of Professor Horatio Fox.

Sat next to the Professor in the Catering office, Deputy Head Porter allowed her mind to wander a little. She was used to the whims of Fellows, changeable like the wind. Half an hour ago, finding the Holy Grail had been the most important thing on the planet. Twenty-five minutes ago it was decided that, actually, The Dean was right and maybe a spot of tea was in order before heading up to the Old Library to resume the Grail quest, which was becoming less of a Grail quest and more of a Grail meander. Then, twenty minutes ago, the Professor had noticed Head of Catering's office and concluded that the most pressing matter at hand was that of the menu for his Induction Feast.

Since then, Professor Fox had been talking ten to the dozen at an already frazzled Head of Catering, whose note-taking skills were woefully inadequate for a meeting of this nature. A constant stream of colourful ponderings and imaginings filled the air, interlaced with bursts of eccentric suggestions and quite possibly impossible demands. The Professor takes his parties very seriously indeed.

"So, I'm hoping you maybe see what I'm after. Do you?" asked the Professor. "I want it to be a little bit extravagant."

"Yes, I see what you're getting at," replied Head of Catering. "But I was just thinking... the starters..."

"You mean appetisers? My favourite!"

"Yes. I just wonder if maybe there might be rather too many of them. Usually we'd have just the one starter. We've got five here already."

"Well, start as you mean to go on, I say," laughed the Professor with a gallant flourish of his arm. "And I certainly want this gig to go on for some time, see. And on. Parties are great."

"Yes. You see, Professor, the occasion isn't so much a party, exactly, it's more of a feast," Head of Catering took brief refuge behind a huge mug of industrial strength coffee. "It's a very traditional College event. Very... er... formal."

"What?? What d'you mean, it's not a party?!" Professor Fox's mouth dropped to the floor. "Hey, you can't have mini pizzas at a formal event – what are we going to do with those?!"

"Well, this is why I thought it might be a good idea for us to just look over things one more time..."

"Hang on a minute," Deputy Head Porter piped up, a thought suddenly striking her. "Does this mean we can't have those spicy chicken things on sticks either? Because I'm looking forward to those."

"Since when do Porters go to the Induction of the Fellowship Feast?" asked Head of Catering, eyebrow arched.

"Since right about now," huffed Professor Fox. "Porters are great at eating! They should go to more feasts, I'm thinking."

"Fair enough," Head of Catering capitulated, turning back to his notes. "But we really are going to have to drop the mini pizzas and things on sticks, I'm afraid."

"Mini pizzas, for sure, they have the flavour but not the class," nodded the Professor. "But I'm pulling rank on things on sticks. Put them on the list, please and a few, but hold the thank you until I've tasted them. Things on sticks, make a note."

What remained of Head of Catering's patience stretched itself just that little bit further, as Deputy Head Porter sat on the opposite side of his desk, grinning. It was a shame about the mini pizzas, but at least things on sticks had made the cut. She couldn't help herself being completely chuffed that the Professor was joining the ranks of The Fellowship. Things would be so much more *fun* with him around. But Head Porter was right; he did lead her astray with alarming regularity. But then, a Grail quest was pretty important, wasn't it? Of course it was. Head Porter would definitely understand. Probably. A bit.

"Deputy Head Porter, are you listening?" Head of Catering's voice dragged her attention back to current matters.

"Hmm? What is it?"

"You've gone and dozed off!" scolded Professor Fox.

"No, no," she replied. "I was just thinking about something else."

"Aha! Good work, I say," nodded the Professor. "It wouldn't do if we all thought about the same things."

Head of Catering snorted a little laugh from his nose.

"No doubt Deputy Head Porter was thinking about some sort of mischief!" he said. Deputy Head Porter thought this an unfair assumption. She only ever thought about mischief if there wasn't anything food-related to think about.

"Actually, DHP and I are currently engaged in a strange and complicated matter," said the Professor, in a tone that suggested that further enquiries would not be welcome. "No doubt it is this such thing that the little cogs are turning over in that funny shaped head of hers."

"Well, in that case, I wouldn't want to keep you any longer than is absolutely necessary," Head of Catering replied, snatching the opportunity to kick them out of his office. "You have been most... thorough, Professor. I'll send a copy of the menu over for your approval."

"Right!" the Professor said, hopping to his feet and shaking Head of Catering violently by the hand. "Send samples, too – why not!"

Head of Catering closed his office door firmly behind them and left them alone in the corridor.

"We'd better get a wriggle on with finding the Holy Grail if you want to present it to The Master at the feast," said Deputy Head Porter.

"You're right, as usual," agreed the Professor. "And wriggling is, after all, quite fun. Off to the Old Library we go!"

TEMPLARS IN THE LIBRARY

The Old Library really was the hidden jewel in the crown of Old College. Situated at the top of a tucked away tower in the very oldest part of College, its only point of access was via a spindly spiral staircase that forever felt to be upon the point of collapse. Admittance to the Old Library was strictly prohibited to students and quietly discouraged even to The Fellowship. It was no wonder. There were things in there not meant for idle consumption.

Deputy Head Porter had had the importance of this esoteric place brought to her attention by an unfortunate Fellow she had befriended during her first months in post, just before he met the all too familiar fate of Fellows who knew too much and was poisoned. It was here that she and Professor Fox first discovered the grisly secrets of the Order of the Lesser Dragon, the founding fathers of Old

College, and led them to uncover even more grisly secrets, this time in contemporary times. But it wasn't only historic horrors that dwelt within the ancient walls – it was here that the secret diary of Old College's first ever Deputy Head Porter, Humphrey Babthorpe, was found tucked among some elderly floor plans. This jolly tome from the mid-1400s provided endless amusement and made the modern-day Porters seem remarkably well behaved. After reading Humphrey's diary, Deputy Head Porter was never able to look at bacon in quite the same way again. Even so. Although loftily located, the Old Library was in fact the very foundations of the College, it held the very things upon which it was built. If not the heart of Old College, the Old Library is certainly the keeper of its soul.

Climbing the swaying staircase, Professor Fox bustled behind Deputy Head Porter, seemingly oblivious to the ominous creaks and quivers of the steel spiral. They were very much at the forefront of Deputy Head Porter's mind, however, never one to be happy at any kind of height and certainly not a height that was creaking and quivering.

"If you could hurry a bit faster, that'd be awesome," chattered the Professor. "Both eyes are eager to start looking, you know."

"Alright, alright," she replied, trembling hands clumsily searching through an elderly bunch of keys. "I just need to find the right one. The lock's a bit sticky, actually."

Like many of the locks in the oldest part of College, this one required a near-balletic series of manoeuvres to persuade it to open. A complex and precise choreography of jiggles and shoves brought a satisfying *click!* from the lock and the door yawned open. Deputy Head Porter and the Professor entered, stepping carefully on the bowed and warped oaken floor.

They both slipped into an awed silence, an uncharacteristic quiet of reverence. In truth, there was nothing especially breath-taking about the functional and austere bookcases and reading tables. They were old but unremarkable. The books themselves had certainly seen better days. Spines and bindings wore their many years with solemn dignity and yet were disappointingly plain, for the most part. It was something about the ether within the place that was so intoxicating, rather than its silent occupants.

However, there were some rather special things here, it should be said. In a heavy glass case sat a first edition of Milton's *Paradise Lost* and there were a number of fascinating old medical tomes bestowed with some of the finest etched illustrations you could imagine. Closer inspection of the drab and muted bookcases revealed shelves resplendent with curious and unusual volumes, including records of the Chivalric Orders, strange recipe books of an esoteric nature and a hefty collection of surprisingly ribald poetry.

"Well I say," said the Professor, his voice dripping with wonder. "This place is even more incredible than I remember. And seems older. Which I suppose it must be – I know I am."

"This is my absolute favourite part of College," replied Deputy Head Porter. "Sometimes when it's quiet I bring a cup of tea up here and just... sit."

"Ah! That sounds nice. But we have no time to sit about just now. You must remind me where we need to be looking."

"It's over here," she said, beckoning the Professor to follow her as she made her way towards the far end of the Library. There, a huge old chest was tucked under a table. It held all the very oldest records of the Order of the Lesser Dragon.

The chest was chained to the floorboards for some inexplicable reason, although the chest lid itself was unsecured so no protection was proffered to its pertinent contents. Deputy Head Porter had wondered several times why this was, but this little conundrum would have to be pondered at another time. The slightly menacing tome was exactly where she had left it, apparently untouched since her last visit. Professor Fox helped her heave the weighty volume onto a nearby reading desk and they sat together to peruse the parchment pages.

Written as it was in olde English, the records of the Order of the Lesser Dragon were hardly light reading. A good deal of it was incomprehensible to either of them, although several glimmers of interesting information did make themselves apparent. Unfortunately, both Professor Fox and Deputy Head Porter were creatures prone to distraction and a fair amount of time was whiled away admiring obscure illustrations and darkly beautiful turns of phrase. It was an uncommonly pleasant way to pass the time and the stars were soon watching them through the windows.

Eyes sore and stomachs desperately in need of urgent attention, Deputy Head Porter and the Professor decided at length that they had scraped together enough substantial snippets to further their search. It had become apparent to them that the Order of the Lesser Dragon were, in fact, a sort of rogue faction of the Knights Templar, splitting off to dedicate their endeavours towards academic furtherance while their erstwhile brethren went about the altogether more heroic business of crusading. Perhaps that's why they were so keen on killing each other; maybe they felt that they had missed out…

"So, it seems certain that the Grail was once held at Old College," said the Professor, rubbing his eyes. "But then, rats, it was moved!"

"Yes, if we're reading it right it was taken to some sort of cave," replied Deputy Head Porter, speaking more loudly than usual in an attempt to disguise gastric rumbling. "A secret meeting place of the Templars, it seems. From the maps and diagrams it would appear to be situated just outside The City."

"Do you suppose that – if we looked really hard – we could find it?"

Deputy Head Porter nodded.

"I don't see why not. If it's still there, at least. I've got a good idea where it is, it's not far. We could go and have a look."

"Fantastic! We can go and take a look tomorrow before the feast. Then, I can present the Grail to The Master at the most dramatic point of proceedings. Why, he'll be as surprised as a bee! And won't even mind about that earring, although it was dadblame fabulous. But now, will you join me for dinner?"

"It's a nice idea," replied Deputy Head Porter. "But you're a Fellow – you have to eat at High Table and I've got to go on the servants seats."

"Oh, how horrid and dull!" cried Professor Fox. "If that's the way they are about things we shall take our food and eat it out on the bridge. See how they like that! Besides, bridges are rather interesting to eat on. All that creaking and stuff."

Quite frankly, at this point Deputy Head Porter didn't care *where* she ate her food, just as long as she got some pretty quickly. Barely able to keep pace, she followed the strutting Professor out into the evening air and across Old Court towards the Dining Room.

UNIMPRESSIVE QUESTING

Detective Chief Inspector Thompson was a man with many hobbies. Like many naturally intelligent people, he needed a lot of varied things to occupy his highly active mind, otherwise it might start suggesting unsavoury and machiavellian pursuits. Which would not do at all. This was in direct contrast to the more learned and academic mind - deliberately stuffed full of things from books until it knew more and more about less and less – which was far better off being occupied by little more than where the next meal was coming from.

The Chief Inspector knew exactly where his next meal was coming from. There was a lovely bit of sirloin gently griddling on the stove at that very moment, and would be perfectly cooked at exactly the time he would finish packing for his trip. He didn't need much for his excursion to the Loire Valley. He liked to travel light. Although, he insisted on a fresh pair of underpants for each day, also two emergency pairs, just in case things got unpredictably exciting. Other than some stout walking boots and items suitable for wet weather, all he really needed was his camera and a good map. He intended to take some moody-looking photos of some of the ancient buildings of the area, in particular the medieval chateau and the little riverside town of Chinon.

If the weather was fine (and there was nothing to suggest that it wouldn't be) then he had a wonderful, relaxing and somewhat educational few days to look forward to. He smiled and sighed happily as he rolled the final pair of walking socks into a neat ball and tucked them into his holdall. No crime. No drama. No Old College. And certainly no The Dean. It was exactly what he needed.

Also embarking on an excursion – although somewhat more locally bound – were Deputy Head Porter and Professor Fox. Following the instructions they found amongst the records of the Order of the Lesser Dragon, they found themselves in a tired-looking little town about eight miles to the south of The City. The site of the cave that once served as a secret meeting place for the Knights Templar should be situated somewhere close by, but the records were not very clear due to being being several centuries out of date. Deputy Head Porter had suggested that a bit of purposeful wandering would probably turn up something or other, with any luck a cafe or cake shop. Breakfast had been ages ago.

"The people here are funny-looking," remarked Professor Fox, rather too loudly. "There's not a smart hat to be seen, you know – and it's a bit of a wonder."

"I think, Professor, this is what normal people look like," replied Deputy Head Porter, carefully. "You've got so used to the quirks of College-types that you've quite forgotten what everyone else looks like."

"That may be true and then again probably not. There's no excuse for not having a good hat, I say."

Walking down the High Street, it was clear that they were no longer in The City. But then, it was that awkward time of day when those with something useful to do were already at it and those lacking meaningful direction were either still in bed or watching one of those ghastly television programmes where a stage full of people with about three teeth between them shout at each other for an hour. Small, slow-moving tribes of elderly people clattered about with their little wheeled trollies, deliberately frightening toddlers and kicking cats. They scowled openly at Deputy Head Porter and the Professor, pointing and muttering.

"Goodness, I wonder what those coffin dodgers are all about!" exclaimed the Professor.

"They're probably just jealous of our hats," said Deputy Head Porter, pulling him by the arm in case he was thinking of remonstrating with them. "Come on."

"I must say, it seems a bit of an odd place to have a secret hiding place. In the middle of this town."

"The town probably wasn't here when they were using the cave."

"Or – they built the town up around it so the cave would be hidden!" said the Professor, grinning. "Now that is a clever move right there."

"Very clever indeed, Professor. Now all we have to do is find it."

Professor Fox flung out an arm, stopping Deputy Head Porter in her tracks. His other arm pointed theatrically to a small, handmade sign attached to a lamp post. *Oh, really? Could it really be that straightforward?*

"Well, that little sign seems to think it's down that way!"

Deputy Head Porter squinted at the sign. It did, indeed, declare itself to be pointing to the direction of the cave. It actually said '*To The Cave*'. She considered this to be shaping up to be the least impressive Grail Quest in history. Seeing no other sensible option, they headed down the narrow side street indicated by the sign and things took an even stranger turn. The cave, if it was the cave they were searching for, appeared to be something of a local tourist attraction.

At the bottom of the side street was a twee-looking gift shop crammed full of St George tea towels and other crusade-related toot. Deputy Head Porter spotted some shortbread and, she thought, some marshmallows, making her think that it might be worth a visit, you know, all in the name of adventuring. Just past the shop was a large wooden sandwich board announcing the entrance to the cave.

"Do we just go in there, do you suppose?" asked the Professor.

"I'm not sure," replied Deputy Head Porter. "Maybe we should ask in the shop?"

"Absolutely. Let's do it."

Inside, the shop was oppressively filled with all kinds of nonsense, but was welcoming all the same. Behind a small wooden counter sat a wild-haired woman who looked like a pile of unfinished knitting. She was flicking through a pile of papers in front of her and appeared to be counting. Not wishing to interrupt, Deputy Head Porter and Professor Fox hovered uncomfortably in her eye-line whilst making half-hearted pretentions at browsing. Before too long, she scribbled on a notepad, tidied her papers and looked up.

"Yes?"

"We were hoping to visit the cave," beamed Deputy Head Porter in her friendliest manner.

"Oh," the woman replied. "Grail Quest, is it?"

"Um. Yes." Deputy Head Porter replied, not having a better answer close to hand.

"Right you are. That'll be three pounds fifty. Each. Mind the entrance slope, it gets really steep once you turn the first corner." She held out her hand for payment whilst eyeing her papers with some interest.

"Here's the thing – this *is* the Knights Templar cave, isn't it?" asked the Professor. "I'm thinking we're at the wrong place."

"Yes it is," the woman replied. "Pride of the town is our Templar cave."

"Okay then," he conceded. "I suppose so as well."

Traipsing out of the shop, Deputy Head Porter and Professor Fox passed the jolly wooden cave sign and the mouth of the Templar cave stood before them, almost inviting. But not quite.

"The odds of the Grail being down here now are longer than a Formal Hall dinner," grumbled Deputy Head Porter.

"You're definitely right," agreed the Professor, surprisingly cheery. "But we're here now and I needs must have a look about this cave. Hey, we might even find a few snails!"

PIGEONS AND OTHER THINGS

Meanwhile, back at Old College, the Porters' Lodge was once again teeming with activity, but unfortunately not with Porters. The now permanently harassed Head Porter was simultaneously checking his watch and the Lodge clock, glaring with increasing alarm at their faces, as if they were somehow responsible for his predicament. The postman, brows knitted furiously, hovered by the front desk waiting for someone to relieve him of his bulging sacks while a gaggle of students tried to recount to Head Porter a colourful tale of a pigeon being trapped in a gyp room. Both Head of Housekeeping *and* Head of Catering were already in his office, waiting to see him. Porter was off yet again on another nuptial-related errand and Deputy Head Porter was up to goodness knows what with Professor Horatio Fox. Head Porter knew this would happen. All the Fellows were trouble, but this one especially so. Especially where Deputy Head Porter was concerned. He must be doing it deliberately, there could be no other explanation.

As the spirited retelling of the pigeon episode reached its climatic conclusion, the Lodge door burst open and an unruly pink cloud scurried through, dragging beneath it Dr Samantha Martens. Head Porter spun round to face her and sighed testily.

"There you are!" he cried. "What time do you call this? The postman's waiting."

"I've been doing my actual job of teaching people things," replied Dr Martens. "I came as quick as I could. Now, where's my hat?"

Dr Martens had reluctantly been recruited as a part-time Porter on the condition that she could have a bowler hat. She refused to wear the rest of the uniform on the grounds that the trousers looked itchy, but she insisted upon the bowler hat. Head Porter considered it a small price to pay, seeing as he was shedding Porters at such an alarming rate. And Dr Martens was surprisingly helpful for a member of The Fellowship and displayed very few signs – if any – of the homicidal insanity that so typified the academic elite. She also knew how to make a proper cup of tea, which was very important, even though she didn't actually drink the stuff herself, tending to prefer a nice cup of coffee. So, she wasn't even a burden on the stocks of Assam, which Deputy Head Porter monitored with ferocious vigilance.

"Your hat is in my office," said Head Porter, glancing towards the neat little room at the back of the Lodge. "I'll go and get it. You deal with the postman. And remember what I told you about boxes and packages."

Leaving Dr Martens at the front desk, Head Porter dashed into his office, completely abandoning the students and their pigeon story in the process. Head of Catering was sat in the chair opposite his desk looking through a menu, while Head of Housekeeping was stood near the hat rack, fidgeting and emitting sharp little breaths that were intended to denote her impatience. Head of Housekeeping was a formidable woman, and much feared throughout Old College. She ruled her army of Bedders with a rod of iron – and anyone else who was unfortunate enough to wander under her beady gaze. She had a mop of wire wool hair that extended in every direction and appeared to be perpetually in motion, much like the rest of her, which twitched and crackled as if made of static. Among the static mess sat one pair of glasses, another pair hung on a brilliantly polished chain around her neck. She was an unfailingly hard-working woman and woe betide anyone who didn't share her redoubtable work ethic. She had never been fond of the Porters, considering them to be rather untidy. Head Porter decided to deal with her first, get her out of the way and out of his office as quickly as possible.

"I need to speak to Professor Fox, do you know where he is?" Head of Housekeeping didn't bother with the usual pleasantries of social intercourse. "It's about his rooms."

"I'm not interested in the Professor's rooms, nor do I know where he is," replied Head Porter. "If that's everything..."

"He's asked for another wardrobe, would you believe? Apparently, one isn't sufficient."

"Really? That's weird," Head of Catering piped up. "You only ever see him wearing that blue suit."

"Maybe he's got lots of blue suits," pondered Head Porter. "I mean, he wouldn't just have one suit, would he?"

"Surely he wouldn't have lots of identical suits?" asked Head of Catering. "That would be stranger than just having one suit."

"He might put other things in the wardrobe," Head Porter continued, evidently more interested in the Professor's rooms than he would have Head of Housekeeping believe. "Strange, terrible things."

"What even is he a professor *of..*?"

"You two are no help whatsoever," tutted Head of Housekeeping. "Just you tell him – the second wardrobe will be delivered this afternoon. Personally, I couldn't care less *what* he keeps in there, as long as he keeps it tidy. And you can tell him that, too."

Head Porter nodded but he had no intention of doing any such thing. Professor Fox made him nervous. Head of Housekeeping left the office and Head Porter and Head of Catering puffed their checks and rolled their eyes, indicating the hardship of handling their brusque colleague. Head Porter took a seat and retrieved a packet of ginger nuts from his top drawer. Head of Catering gratefully took one. He had come to discuss the things on sticks. He was worried about those.

Dr Martens waved to Head of Housekeeping as she swept through the Lodge, scattering half-asleep students in her wake. Dr Martens was very pleased with her Portering efforts thus far. She had dealt with the inordinately irritated postman who was quite put out at having to wait, it put the rest of his run out, he probably wouldn't get his tea break, and so on. Dr Martens had also dispensed what she considered to be some excellent advice regarding the pigeon. Portering had proved to be a tad trickier than she had expected, at first. It was just so unpredictable. And then there was the illogical business with the boxes and the packages. It was very different to her usual field of engineering. You knew where you were with engineering. It was built on the solid foundations of things immoveable like mathematics and physics. Mathematics and physics didn't mess about, they did what they were supposed to. It was true to say that there were occasional surprises in engineering, but they didn't usually involve pigeons.

Approaching the front desk was a twinkly-eyed older lady wearing the most magnificent purple scarf. Its velvety folds hugged her neck, then trailed off behind her, flapping cheerfully as she walked. Her demeanour was genial in general, but she looked like she meant business nonetheless. Dr Martens gave her, her best smile and clasped her hands before her on the desk in a manner that she had always thought looked suitably efficient.

"Good morning!" said the lady, returning the smile. "I do hope you are well. I've come to see The Dean of College if he's free?"

Dr Martens' smile dropped off at the corners. What was it Head Porter had said about The Dean? He didn't like visitors, certainly. Even people with an appointment usually got turned away. This lady seemed very pleasant, so she thought she had best be as helpful as she could.

"Do you have an appointment?" she asked.

"I don't, actually, I came straight here," replied the lady. "It's quite important."

"Oh well, if it's important..." Dr Martens moved some bits of paper around the desk while she tried to think what to do for the best. "The thing is, The Dean doesn't like people very much and I'm supposed to tell you that he's out or at least very busy. Sorry."

"Well, that is remarkably honest of you and I appreciate that. Perhaps if you just gave me a little clue as to where he might be, I could just sneak in without you noticing and find him myself?"

"It was important, you said?"

"Yes, very important."

Dr Martens straightened a pile of envelopes. It seemed reasonable enough. She had told the lady that The Dean was out and very busy. If she then slipped through without her noticing, there wouldn't be a lot she could do about it. And The Dean wouldn't want to miss something important, she was sure. That seemed to be the thing to do. Dr Martens gave directions to The Dean's rooms in Apple Tree Court and tried very hard not to notice as the lady made her way through the Lodge.

INTO THE CAVE

It had always irked Head Porter that his Deputy was such a naturally noisy little beast, seemingly unable to exist without an accompanying cacophony of clattering, nor open her mouth without bringing forth noises at levels offensive to the more delicately inclined. However, her racketiness paled in comparison to that of Professor Fox, who somehow managed to sound like a raging mob all on his own. It was a trait Deputy Head Porter found quite admirable and wondered, as she followed him along the path into the Templar cave, how he managed to make the echoes of his footsteps achieve the impression that a herd of hippos were stampeding.

They turned a corner and the path steepened and Deputy Head Porter found her footing less sure, despite her sturdy boots. She was soon trailing behind the Professor, who was chatting away to no one in particular, unencumbered by the unusual terrain, as if he had a four-wheel-drive setting.

"Come along now, DHP!" the Professor called back. "You have to keep up! We're nearly there, you know."

Rubber soles skidding on the loose gravel, Deputy Head Porter stumbled as best she could into the main chamber of the cave. She mouthed a silent 'wow'.

The cave was not so large, probably about seventeen feet in diameter and around ten feet high. It was shaped like a beehive, with a small aperture at the top. All around the curved surrounds were extensive and remarkable wall carvings. Her eyes adjusting to the gloom, it was some time before Deputy Head Porter could make sense of what was before her.

The carvings appeared to depict scenes of the Crucifixion and Resurrection, but also what might have been an image of Saint George, wielding his sword at a serpent or a dragon. Elsewhere, she spotted the figure of Saint Christopher, patron saint of travellers, with the child Christ on his shoulders and staff in hand. There were carvings beyond number that she couldn't begin to fathom.

"This is incredible," she whispered to the Professor, raised voices seeming improper.

"I don't believe I've seen anything quite like it!" he replied. "I bet the Knights Templar made these carvings, wouldn't you say?"

Before she could reply, a shift in the air turned their attentions towards the cave entrance.

"Some say that is so, others deny it," a honeyed voice dipped in familiarity trickled through the half-light. "But when all is said and done, the truth is what it is and cannot be silenced."

Stepping into the cavern, they immediately recognised the portentous figure of the Shop

Keeper from the strange antiques emporium in The City. He didn't seem surprised to see them in the slightest.

"My friends, we meet again!" he approached jovially, with arms outstretched as if expecting an embrace. Professor Fox stepped smartly backwards, and Deputy Head Porter fended off the over-familiar greeting with a panicked wave of her hand. "Tell me! Was I right? Was the Holy Grail ensconced within the bowels of your esteemed establishment?"

"It was..." began the Professor. The Shop Keeper's eyes lit up and he threw his hands into the air with delight. "But now it's not."

"Oh! For shame." The Shop Keeper was crestfallen.

"But your theory was, at least, correct," said Deputy Head Porter, giving the Professor a stern side-eye for building up the poor chap's hopes like that. "It was definitely hidden at Old College for a time. But then, for whatever reason, it was moved. The records we found suggested it had been brought here. What are you doing here, anyway?"

"This historic enclave is a favourite thinking place of mine," replied the Shop Keeper. "And also the gift shop does some sublime shortbread."

"You know, it's a wonder you make any kind of a living at all from that shop of yours," Professor Fox mused. "Your customer service is abominable and now you tell us you spend all your time sitting in caves. There's something wrong with you, a little bit."

"What suggested to you that the Grail was brought here?" asked the Shop Keeper, ignoring the Professor.

"There was a map," replied Deputy Head Porter. "And there are markings here that are very similar to those we found back at the College."

"So, they brought it here..." mumbled the Shop Keeper, stroking his chin. "And the markings! It can mean only one thing."

"Surely not just the one thing," said the Professor. "We don't want to overlook anything, you know. If you do that sort of thing, you can miss stuff."

"This cave holds all kinds of secrets about the Templar," the Shop Keeper continued. "See here, this figure is King David..." he pointed to a jaunty-looking chap, just below Saint Christopher and some other saintly-looking fellows. "This exact depiction of him also appears atop an illuminated manuscript of Psalm 69 which now resides in the care of Wastell College. The Wastells were a prominent Templar family, even thought they were of French origin. We know that they were once here, as here they leave their markings..." again, he pointed to the walls and there were carvings just like those found in the Crypt. "These markings are found in only one other known location. It must have been the Wastells, leaving a breadcrumb trail of the progress of the Grail!"

"I suppose it goes without saying that the Grail isn't here, then?" huffed Deputy Head Porter, disappointed despite not being entirely surprised. "This does rather bugger up our plans of finding a gift for The Master, you know."

"Dadblameit!" tutted the Professor. "I say, I don't suppose you still have that earring available for sale, do you?"

"What? Oh. Er... Oh. Earring? I'm not sure…"

"Double dadblameit! Well, that decides it, then."

"Decides what, Professor?" asked Deputy Head Porter, almost wishing she hadn't.

"We have no option but to follow the trail. I simply cannot turn up empty-handed to my own feast. We must find the Grail! Or, I'll look like a noogin."

"But the feast is *tonight!*" exclaimed Deputy Head Porter. "There's no way we can find the Grail by then."

"Aha, but hold on and a few here," replied the Professor. "The Master's gift shall be this – I shall spearhead a research mission to locate and retrieve the Holy Grail, all in the name of the glory of Old College! Now, that is a gift and a half, I should say. I mean, I'd be proud to receive it myself."

When you put it like that, it does sound rather impressive, thought Deputy Head Porter. Quite how happy The Master will be about his newest Fellow immediately jumping ship to go Grail questing is anyone's guess, but then Professor Fox had an unnerving ability to talk anyone round to his way of thinking. If anyone could pull this off, it would be him.

"We should hurry back to Old College," continued the Professor. "I needs must prepare my great revelation speech and also unpack my best hat."

"Hang on," said Deputy Head Porter. "We don't know where the trail leads yet." She turned to the Shop Keeper. "You said these markings are found in one other place. Please, tell us what you have in mind, dear chap."

"Indeed, the markings can be found in another place," replied the Shop Keeper. "The Chateau de Chinon in France's scenic Loire Valley. Many of the Templar were held in the dungeons there before being executed. It is in those sunken strongholds that the etchings can be found."

The excitement of events overtook them and when Professor Fox decided there and then that they should travel to the Chateau de Chinon at the earliest possible moment, Deputy Head Porter enthusiastically agreed. She could surely talk round Head Porter, but somehow that only occurred to her as a minor side issue. The adventure was the important thing. The logistics of the plan were at little sketchy at that point, but what they lacked in arrangements they more than made up for in enthusiasm. But time was running short and it was imperative they return to Old College at once. There was, after all, the Induction Feast that evening, apart from anything.

As they left the cave, a hitherto unnoticed carved scene caught Deputy Head Porter's eye. Three figures; a man, woman and child all holding hands. Innocuous as it looked, her interest was piqued.

"What's this?" she asked the Shop Keeper, pointing to the happy scene.

"Ah, well," he replied, a glint in his eye. "That is what they call the Holy Family. The man and the woman are Jesus and Mary Magdalene."

"And the child?"

His response was nothing more than a smile.

THE FAIRER SEX

Head Porter cantered over to the front desk where Dr Martens was not noticing as the tail of a luxurious purple scarf disappeared into the cloister.

"Who... who was that?!" gasped Head Porter.

"Who was who?" asked Dr Martens.

"That woman. That *lovely* woman. With the scarf."

Dr Martens' eyes darted from side to side, before returning to the pile of envelopes that had suddenly become very important.

"I didn't notice anyone."

"If I give you the hat, will you tell me?"

"Yes. Give me the hat."

Head Porter retrieved the bowler hat from the stand in his office and returned to the front desk. With some ceremony, he held the hat with both hands above Dr Martens' head.

"I declare you a Porter!" he announced, trying to fit the hat onto her head. Her mass of hair was having none of it. "Your hair is fighting back! My goodness."

"You have to know how to handle the hair," replied Dr Martens, taking the hat from him and wriggling it onto her head. It suited her beautifully.

"Now then. Who *was* she?"

"Actually, I don't know," said Dr Martens. "I just wanted the hat. She said she needed to see The Dean and that it was very important."

"What?! What did I tell you about people who want to see The Dean?!"

"I did exactly as you said. I told her that he was out and also very busy. Then she snuck past without me noticing."

Head Porter watched as the lady with the scarf glided elegantly along the cloister. He was looking at her the way Deputy Head Porter looks at bacon. Well, then. This clearly presented him with a very clear course of action. An unaccompanied lady wandering around College simply wouldn't do. Especially not if she was looking for The Dean. Why, anything could happen to a lady like that. There was nothing for it. It was his duty as a gentleman and a Head Porter to go after her right away.

"I'm going after her right away," said Head Porter. "You're in charge of the Lodge."

Dr Martens considered protesting, but felt it was pointless. Anyway, she had the hat now. And she was starting to enjoy being a Porter. Seeing as she was there, being a Porter, she thought she might as well change the ridiculous post sorting system. And eat some biscuits. This was a whole new side of College life she never knew existed and, quite frankly, she rather liked it.

Head Porter caught up with the scarf lady at the far end of the cloister. He angled his bowler at a slightly rakish angle. It was a look he had been privately practicing in the mirror and he thought it gave him something of a dashing quality. A little bit dangerous, even. He coughed politely and the lady turned to face him.

"Oh! Hello there!" she beamed. "You must be a Porter. I expect you must be curious as to why I'm wandering around your College."

"*Head* Porter, in fact, ma'am," he replied, smiling with just one half of his mouth in a manner he was sure made him look manly.

And then he faltered. Head Porter had been carefully cultivating a public image as a bit of a ladies' man; however, it had only been half successful. He was very keen on lovely ladies – that bit he had covered brilliantly. Unfortunately, lovely ladies did not always return the sentiment, and some were very happy to tell him so. Even unlovely ladies presented problems, at times. His mouth dried up and he stood there, smiling his manly smile and hoping his dangerously placed hat didn't slip off his head.

"*Head* Porter, indeed? Well this is an honour," replied the scarf lady. "Then you are the perfect gentleman to help me. I am looking for your Dean of College. Could you direct me appropriately?"

"Oh, you don't want to see him. Not as this time of day," Head Porter replied. "He won't have had enough whisky to be amenable. Besides, no one gets to see The Dean without an appointment and even then, it's luck of the draw."

"He will certainly see me," the lady replied. "But how rude of me – I haven't even introduced myself. I am The Headmistress at Saint Jeannine's Preparatory School on Thornback Green. The Dean's young nephew is one of our most spirited first years, as I'm sure you can imagine. It is quite important that I speak to him directly."

Head Porter had heard about The Dean's nephew, the offspring of a hysterical sister and unknown other party (possibly a sailor). The Dean had taken on responsibility for the boy's education and sent him to a variety of expensive establishments, which invariably found him something of a handful. It would seem his latest school were currently in the midst of enjoying the company of a miniature version of The Dean. Head Porter thought that he should probably escort The

Headmistress to Apple Tree Court. No doubt The Dean wouldn't be very happy to see her, but then again, he wasn't very happy to see anyone.

"If you will come with me, ma'am," said Head Porter. "But I must warn you, The Dean can be very difficult at... err... well, he's jolly difficult most of the time, actually. And very rude. Some of the words he uses I've never even heard of."

"Oh, don't worry, I know some quite rude words," replied The Headmistress, walking alongside Head Porter. "And I'm sure The Dean knows how to speak to a lady."

"I wouldn't be so sure, ma'am. The Dean views women as men with bumps at the front. He says it's called being feminist."

And that was one thing you could say about The Dean - he didn't discriminate. Gender, race, religion, social class – it honestly didn't matter to him. He considered everyone to be equally irritating and definitely not as great as *him*. It was a very even-handed kind of prejudice.

"But don't worry, ma'am," continued Head Porter, his confidence plumping itself up just a little bit. "We're not all like that, here."

The Headmistress laughed a tinkly little laugh that Head Porter thought sounded like summer rain. He then had a word with himself about thinking in such impractical and clichéd metaphors.

"I'm sure not!" she giggled. "I have no doubt you are an expert at handling women, Head Porter."

"Gifted amateur," he replied. "But getting better. Actually, I'm handling two women in the Lodge at the moment. My Deputy is a woman and so is the other one that's not a man."

"Very fascinating, I'm sure."

They had arrived at H Staircase, the dwelling place of The Dean. Head Porter directed The

Headmistress to the second floor and wished her the very best of luck.

"I would offer to accompany you, ma'am," he said, earnestly. "But there is a very important feast happening this evening."

"Oh, I expect you have lots to prepare," nodded The Headmistress.

"Well... not really, no. But last time I showed an unannounced guest to The Dean's rooms he threw a paperweight at me and I don't want to miss the feast on account of being horribly injured. Ma'am."

The Headmistress smiled and touched his arm.

"You stay down here where it's safe," she said. "Thank you. I hope we meet again."

As he watched her climb the staircase to The Dean's rooms, Head Porter hoped exactly the same thing.

STEALING THUNDER

Standing in the Wide Gallery of The Master's Lodge, a glass of something fizzy and expensive in hand, Deputy Head Porter would have to admit to having mixed feelings about the evening. The Induction of the Fellowship ceremony – an esoteric service carried out in the Chapel and conducted in Latin, a means of officially acknowledging new members to Old College's highest order – was a triumph. It passed without incident which, when you consider that Professor Horatio Fox was involved, was something of a marvel. She was half expecting mischief of sorts, but from what Deputy Head Porter managed to spy from under the curtain (a bizarre tradition dictates that Porters watch the secret ceremony from beneath the heavy embroidered curtains in the Chapel), he partook of the solemn ritual with the earnest gravitas perfectly fitting of an Old College Fellow. In his very best top hat, too, which deserved a ceremony all of its own, quite frankly.

The Dean was unusually jubilant, now that his old friend was firmly part of the academic family and Deputy Head Porter was just as pleased to have Professor Fox as a regular fixture. She couldn't quite put her finger on what was causing her unease. *Experience,* she thought to herself. *This is Old College. There's bound to be something afoot, somewhere.* Or perhaps it was the fact of being in the Wide Gallery, the scene of the previous Junior Bursar's retirement party. Goodness knows, that didn't end well. He tried to throw her off the Flag Tower, for one thing. There was something about Bursars and an overwhelming desire for indiscriminate violence. Take the current Bursar, Professor Dexter Sinistrov, for example. They had never managed to prove it, but Deputy Head Porter was absolutely certain that he had bumped off Lord Bernard, the Master of Hawkins College. And he would definitely have poisoned their Head Porter, too, if she hadn't stopped him in the nick of time. He could easily have killed last year's briefly appointed Economics lecturer, Professor Palmer, but no one minded much about that. That chap was asking for it.

Deputy Head Porter decided that there was nothing else for it but to put her misgivings to one side and have another drink. If something unlikely was going to happen, it would happen regardless of whether she worried about it or not. Instead, she turned her attentions to the things on sticks, or rather the lack of them. She was sure she had specifically requested those. *Where were they?*

Head Porter had been looking uncomfortable all evening, but the inexhaustible supply of top-notch fizz seemed to be helping. He didn't particularly savour events such as this, but Professor Fox was most insistent that he attend. He stood with Deputy Head Porter, the two of them listening to Professor

Fox and The Dean bantering with enthusiasm between great mouthfuls of colourful canapes. Head Porter wanted to ask The Dean about his meeting with The Headmistress but thought better of it. Instead, he hoped fervently that The Dean's nephew kept up his disagreeable behaviour and that further meetings would be necessary.

"Do you have your speech ready for the toasts later, dear chap?" The Dean asked Professor Fox, looking slightly worried that his glass was nearly empty.

"I think I absolutely do!" replied the Professor. "I have it, right here." He reached into the jacket of his immaculate blue suit and pulled out a veritable manuscript of chaotic scribblings that Deputy Head Porter thought looked pretty scandalous, even from where she was standing.

"Ho ho, I imagine it will be some rip-roaring entertainment, old bean!" The Dean laughed, playfully jostling the Professor and making his hat wobble alarmingly.

"Yes, that's right," replied the Professor, regaining his balance and placing a steadying hand on his hat. "I have been sure to include my greatest adventuring tales as well as some jokes I heard on a merchant navy ship several years ago. I hope they won't be too spicy for everyone."

"There is nothing, I take it, relating to... Kuala Lumpa?"

Professor Fox and The Dean held each other in the most solemn of gazes.

"Never, my friend. What happens in Kuala Lumpa, stays in Kuala Lumpa."

The Dean nodded slowly, before regaining his festive spirit.

"Oh, I remember when we inducted dear old Dr T," he continued. "By the time we got round to the speeches, the best he could muster was a ribald sing-song about a fish monger and his rather accommodating daughter. Went down a treat, I tell you. Rather like the fish monger's daughter, apparently."

"Will there be any musical accompaniment to your speech, Professor?" Deputy Head Porter asked quickly, keen to steer the conversation away from this rather unsavoury-sounding young woman.

"Well, you know, DHP, I have engaged the talents that young organ scholar – Alex, that fellow with the good hair – to tinkle out a tune or two for later on," he replied, very pleased with himself. "I thought he could strike up right after I make my announcement about the Grail."

"Aha! Great plan, Foxy!" exclaimed The Dean. "I like the theatrics of it all. And you know, I have every intention of joining you in France. I have the very talents that are absolutely essential when one is questing, certainly."

"Terrifically good, I say" the Professor replied. "I had rather hoped you might join us. I say *us* – of course DHP is coming along too, you know."

"What?!" Head Porter spluttered, champagne urgently exiting his nose.

"Bloody good idea!" said The Dean.

"Obviously she's coming," the Professor continued. "I mean, we need someone to make the tea, don't we? Plus – she's more useful than even that."

"But... but... what about the Lodge?" Head Porter's voice was something between a wail and a shriek. The corners of his mouth shot downwards and his watery eyes darkened. He had no interest in this ridiculous Grail Quest, but he didn't see why Deputy Head Porter should get a trip to France and not him.

"Oh, pah and nonsense!" huffed The Dean. "You've got Porter. And some of those other ones that work nights. She will only be gone for a couple of days, do be a chap about it, what?"

Head Porter, emboldened by three glasses of expensive fizzy alcohol, looked for a moment as if he might protest. But before he could get his words out, the great stentorian peal of the dinner gong rang throughout the Gallery.

"Excellent!" said the Professor, clapping his hands together. "It must be time for my feast."

But as they turned towards the door, they saw that is was not the waiting staff brandishing the gong's striker. Standing aloof in the doorway was none other than The Bursar. The Dean uttered a collection of words that Deputy Head Porter had never heard before but was certain they must be rather offensive.

The Bursar cut quite an extraordinary figure, with his oddly-styled jet black hair, pallid countenance and penchant for expensive Italian shoes. It is always tricky to get the measure of him as a great sweep of fringe – like a raven's wing – covers half of his face. He looks out at the world through one piercing beady eye, cold as infinity. A respected chemist from Russia, he has the disadvantage of a mangled accent and confusing patter, which makes him remarkably difficult to understand. Not that anyone wishes to listen to him for too long. There is something about his voice that fills your veins with ice. He and Deputy Head Porter got off on the wrong foot last term, after he spent the Summer Vac stalking her then tried to frame her for the murders of a student and his companion. They made it up, of course, all good japes and misunderstandings, but no one quite trusted him after that. Well you wouldn't, would you.

"I don't like the look of this," mumbled Head Porter.

"Ladies and, indeed, gentlemen," announced The Bursar, hair hanging across his face, obscuring his expression. "The feast is almost upon us. But, before we take our seats in celebration of our newest brother, I should like to offer my own humble tribute to the esteemed Professor Horatio Fox."

The Professor was scarlet from his chin to his hair, top hat quivering with rage. The Master stepped from the throng of curious Fellows to engage with The Bursar.

"This is most unusual, Bursar," he said. "It would be proper for you to hold your testimonial until the toasts, as is our custom."

"Master, under ordinary circumstances I would agree," The Bursar replied, his voice like molten steel. "But I hope to bring lively discussion to the dining table, a thing so delicious that the food itself may weep with regret."

"What sort of a phrase is that, for goodness sake?" Deputy Head Porter asked nobody in particular.

"I say what a bummer you are, the sudden, Mr Bursar!" cried the Professor. "You're keeping us from the feast. Or, more correctly, *my* feast. Away with him until the toasts!"

A rumbling of support broke out among the gathered Fellowship. No academic likes to be kept from a meal and The Bursar would surely know this. Deputy Head Porter took no pleasure in realising that she was right. There *was* something afoot.

"I have a proposal for Professor Fox," The Bursar continued, unabashed. "An unequivocal means of assuring his place in the College chronicles and a manner by which he might prove his intellectual superiority to those *lesser* persons who mingle uninvited among the academic elite."

"I'm not sure I like where this is going," Deputy Head Porter murmured to Head Porter.

"I don't think I do either," Head Porter replied. "Er... what is he talking about, do you think? He's going to propose to the Professor?! Christ, we've already got one wedding to deal with..."

"I think that would probably be the least of our worries, Head Porter."

"Well, what do you propose, Bursar?" asked The Master, testily.

"A great undertaking!" exclaimed The Bursar. "I would ask the Professor to join me in the climax of my research and share in the glory of uncovering, finally, the ultimate resting place of... the Holy Grail!"

A DUEL, OF SORTS

I should have been quicker, Deputy Head Porter thought to herself. *I could* have been quicker. *I suppose something mischievous deep inside held me back.* As her fingertips brushed against the tails of the Professor's jacket, Deputy Head Porter couldn't help feeling rather pleased that she wasn't quite quick enough to catch him.

Like a very well-dressed bird of prey, Professor Fox launched himself at a wary-looking Bursar with alarming alacrity. It was as if all around him time stood still and the assembled crowd could only watch, open mouthed, as what looked like the beginnings of fisticuffs unravelled before their eyes.

Just as it seemed he might tear the very nose from The Bursar's face, the Professor's progress was halted abruptly by The Master's flailing arm falling neatly between them.

"Enough!" boomed The Master.

"Bugger," muttered The Dean.

Professor Fox kicked The Bursar smartly in the shin, causing him to emit a most unusually high-pitched cry.

"Professor!" The Master exclaimed. "I must insist that you control yourself!"

"Huff-hum!" replied the Professor, crossing his arms to contain his outrage.

"What is the meaning of this?" The Master asked, calmer now. "Surely – this is a marvellous thing that The Bursar has discovered. Not to mention, a fine gentlemanly gesture to invite you along as well. Why ever would you behave in such a manner?"

"Sir! What this beast suggests is not a great honour, nor is it gentlemanly in any way," the Professor replied. "I shall tell you what it is – it is an effrontery to common decency, dadblameit!"

"Oh, this is very *good,*" The Dean chuckled to Deputy Head Porter. "Do you think it will come to blows? I do hope it comes to blows." He was really enjoying this. This was his kind of thing.

"You see, Sir," the Professor continued. "My friends and I are this close – that's very close – to laying our hands on the Grail ourselves. This is a thing I had planned to reveal to you, with much spectacle and amusement I might add, at the time of the toasts."

"It's all true!" yelled The Dean from his position by the canapés.

"I don't understand this at all," said Head Porter, brows knitted in confusion. "I mean, how could he…"

"This must be what his big hole is all about," said Deputy Head Porter. "In Apple Tree Court."

"Well, I shall look forward to hearing *both* of your announcements at the appropriate moment – during the toasts," said The Master, making moves to end the theatricals and proceed on to the Feast.

"You're not invited to France, you know!" the Professor growled at The Bursar.

"France?" The Bursar replied, a staged look of perplexion on what was visible of his face. "Why, the Holy Grail does not lie in France. No, no, my dear fellow, you are bewitched by falsehood. The Grail lies right here, beneath our own dear College!"

"Ha!" exclaimed The Dean in a low voice. "We're already a step or two ahead of him, the silly bugger. Ho ho! We should tell him so."

"That is tempting, Sir," Deputy Head Porter whispered back. "But I think it wise to keep our counsel for now. There's something off about all this."

It appeared that Professor Fox felt the same way as he was exercising remarkable restraint.

"I don't quite understand to what ghastly place your research has led you, Professor Fox, but my own carefully considered work shows that the Grail is inarguably ensconced within the ruins of an ancient monastery which slumbers, untouched for centuries, deep in the ground betwixt Sprockett Gate and Apple Tree Court."

Gasps and excited mumblings erupted around the Wide Gallery, the revelation igniting the interest of the assembled Fellows and staff.

"This certainly does sound exciting, Bursar," said The Master.

"How can something so totally dead wrong be exciting?" grumbled the Professor.

The Dean decided that he had sat on the side lines for long enough. Brandishing his glass of whisky like a military standard, he strode across the room and placed himself at the very centre of the action.

"Now see here," said The Dean, firmly. "The way I see it, there is only one course of action open to us that will settle the matter."

"A duel!" cried Professor Fox.

The Dean seemed to consider this.

"Well, two ways, then. But my way is better – if the proof of the pudding is in the eating, then both Fellows must undertake their own endeavours and the first chap to present the Grail to The Master is the winner!"

Watching the partially obscured face of The Bursar, Deputy Head Porter thought she saw a flicker of doubt play across those unreadable features. Only for a second, but she was sure it was there.

"So then, gentlemen!" said The Master, rubbing his hands together with delight. "The gauntlet has been thrown down! Who so of you shall pick it up?"

"I accept the challenge doubly!" declared the Professor, striking a suitably heroic stance and tipping his hat defiantly. "Bursar, what about you?"

The Bursar offered a smile so slippery you could butter toast with it. He didn't speak. Perhaps he was worried that his words might betray him.

"Then it is decided!" The Master announced. "And now, there is the Feast awaiting us. Come!"

A throng of hungry academics surging towards their first course is indeed a sight to behold. If there is one thing guaranteed to get a Fellow moving, it's a feast. Deputy Head Porter, The Dean and Head Porter joined Professor Fox by the threshold.

"This is what it is! We have been challenged! Now we have to find the Grail before that dadblame Bursar!" The Professor was so riled he was practically hopping from foot to foot. "Come on! Come on! Let's go pack right away. To France!"

"I'm right behind you, my good man!" roared The Dean.

"But... the Feast!" wailed Deputy Head Porter, the unhappy prospect of an abandoned banquet looming large on her horizon. The Dean was sympathetic.

"She's got a point."

The Professor tapped his chin and furrowed his brow.

"It does seem a shame to miss out on all this... especially since we tortured Head of Catering so," he said. "Very well – feasting now, questing... very soon. There we have it."

Deputy Head Porter smiled. That was very much her kind of plan.

THE PROFESSOR'S TROUSERS AND OTHER MATTERS

As the first pink fingers of dawn pinched at the horizon, the Grail-hunters gathered, sleepy-eyed, in the Porters' Lodge. Head Porter was there too, fussing like a mother hen while all the time pretending that he couldn't wait to see the back of them. Although, he hoped that with the triumvirate of chaos (Deputy Head Porter, Professor Fox and The Dean) out of the way for a few days, things might actually be a bit more peaceful. He still had the occasional assistance of Porter, of course, and now Dr Martens was proving to be a very competent addition to the Lodge. She had some funny ideas about packages, certainly, and she could be a bit frightening with her brutal – yet polite – honesty, but she was generally much less trouble than most Fellows. Or Porters, come to that.

Professor Fox was something of a fluster, his ordinarily immaculate hair poking out wildly beneath his fedora, flushed cheeks puffed out in an alarming manner. Deputy Head Porter wrongly assumed that his condition was due to the fact that they would be leaving College before the kitchens opened.

"Are you alright, Professor?" she asked. "Are you worried about breakfast?"

"I've had a rather vexing start to the day, I am afraid to admit," he muttered, quite clearly not his usual self.

"What's the matter, you daft bugger?" snapped The Dean, nursing a post-feast hangover of epic proportions. "I told you. We can stop for food on the way."

"Dadblameit! I'm not so sure that I could stomach it, to tell you the truth."

Deputy Head Porter gasped. This must be serious indeed.

"Goodness Professor, are you unwell?" Head Porter inquired, with some concern. "Maybe something has disagreed with you."

"The Bursar, for one thing," snorted The Dean.

"The Bursar is a fine piece of dadblamery that I must bear, but he is not enough to keep this Professor from breakfast," the Professor replied. "No. I'll tell you what happened. It happened early. It happened fast. And it's quite scary. Are you ready for it? I was just getting out of bed and thinking about which trousers – is that what you call them over here? You know how I like to go native when I can. Anyway and a few. I was thinking about which trousers to put on, when the door to my rooms was flung open by this... this... it must have been a woman judging by the way it wobbled in certain places. And so on, it came in, brandishing a feather duster and gave me quite a fright! I said to it –

'Madam, (if Madam you be)' – I'm pretty super at pronouncing punctuation, don't you think? – I said 'Madam! I am not the kind of gentleman who appreciates or condones this sort of thing!' And the thing bustled out again like a herd of wildebeest. Can you imagine? What do you think that was all about?"

"Oh, that would just be one of the Bedders," giggled Deputy Head Porter.

But Head Porter was more interested in the matter of the trousers. This proved that Professor Fox had more than one pair of trousers and, therefore, one can deduce, more than one suit. Many identical blue suits! He must share this vital information with Head of Catering as soon as he got the chance.

"A Bedder?! Goodness. What is that!" the Professor spluttered. "I say to you all, I don't want one of those things intruding on me first thing in the morning... or ever, actually."

"They are the Housekeeping staff," Head Porter explained, gently. "They come in to clean the rooms and such. She probably thought you'd be on your way already. They really are not so dangerous."

"That's a matter of opinion!" barked The Dean. "I had one appear unexpectedly once. Frightened the life out of my fish, I'll have you know. One of the poor buggers has been swimming backwards ever since. Those Bedders can be vicious creatures."

"Now, I'm just so spooked, I could hide, I think," the Professor shuddered. "I was in such a state, I couldn't begin to think about my pants – trousers – and just put on the first pair that came to hand. Pah!"

Deputy Head Porter tried to cheer him up a bit.

"I've packed my favourite tea set," she said convivially. "And all sorts of brilliant teas. Even fruit teas!"

"Even cherry?"

"Even cherry."

"Things are looking up already!"

There was an impatient *Beep! Beep!* from just outside the Lodge.

"That'll be our car," stated The Dean, somewhat unnecessarily. "Come on, chaps."

As they fumbled with their cases, Head Porter began to shift from foot to foot and his watery eyes reddened a little. He would never admit to it, but he wasn't really looking forward to their impending departure.

"Now, make sure you take good care of Deputy Head Porter," he instructed The Dean. "I need her back in one piece. Deputy Head Porters are not easy to come by, you know."

"Don't worry, old chap," replied The Dean, playfully elbowing him in the ribs. "We shall return her to you in first rate condition! Which is probably better than the condition she's in now, quite frankly. Ho ho!"

"We will be back before you know it," declared Deputy Head Porter. "Cross my heart and hope to die."

"Hope to die? Goodness. We shouldn't hope for such things," said Professor Fox. "That's rather extreme."

"Alright then," replied Deputy Head Porter. "Cross my heart and hope to get a really nasty Chinese burn. Abruise upon my knee anda splinter."

This was acceptable to Head Porter, who proceeded to bid her farewell with an unexpected, and quite squeezey, embrace. The same treatment was not afforded to her travelling companions, to their obvious relief.

"Now then, you've got everything you need for Terry, haven't you?" Terry was Deputy Head Porter's cat. He would be residing with Head Porter for the duration of her trip. She hoped that Terry would be better behaved for Head Porter than he was at home.

"Yes, yes, now don't worry," replied Head Porter. "He's a cat. I can manage a cat. We shall be the best of pals in no time, you'll see." Head Porter didn't really believe this. He wasn't fond of cats and they liked him even less. Even so, it was probably safer than storming a chateau in France.

Probably.

A HORSE WITH NO NAME

Dust and gravel were kicked up by thundering hooves and scenery shot past in a blur as Detective Chief Inspector Thompson urged his beast onwards down the country track. He had covered most of the journey to the Loire Valley by conventional methods, but never one to be satisfied with the conventional for very long, he had decided to satisfy his adventurous yearnings and complete the final leg by horseback. There was something decidedly heroic about travelling by horseback, the Chief Inspector thought. It was such an impressive way to arrive anywhere, too. It was a bit like a motorbike, but much more organic. Any old chap could master a machine, thought Thompson. But it took a special kind of man to bend the will of a wild beast to do his bidding.

In fact, it wasn't a wild beast at all. It was a slightly over-weight, middle aged mare he picked up from a friendly innkeeper further back along the Vienne river. He had been riding all afternoon and had so far managed about ten minutes of heroic galloping. The horse was lazy and very greedy. It seemed to need to stop and eat parts of the countryside on a far too regular basis. And it was disobedient. The Chief Inspector was not a cruel man, so had kept physical encouragement to a minimum, but very much got the feeling that he could have flogged the thing to within an inch of its life and it wouldn't have moved a petulant hoof until it had a mind to. It reminded DCI Thompson of one or two policeman he knew.

But for now, at least, the wheezing mare was picking up pace. Which was, ironically, a bit of a shame as the approach to the medieval town of Chinon was swathed on every side by stunning scenery, offering unmissable photo opportunities. DCI Thompson was going to have to miss them, though. He dare not put the horse off its stride in case he couldn't get it started again. Never mind. It was the quaint architecture of the towns and chateaus of the *Val de Loire* region he had really come to see. Photography was one of his more sedate hobbies and with the mild continental breeze on his face and great outdoors at his feet (or, at least, the feet of his horse), the Chief Inspector was finally starting to unwind and forget about the rigours of The City and all that came with it.

Just as he had adjusted to the increased speed of travel, DCI Thompson found the abrupt need to readjust once more. The horse had spotted a lush patch of clover by the roadside and meandered to a trot without warning. Thrown momentarily off balance, the Chief Inspector cursed as he struggled to remain upright at the same time as saving his rucksack from hitting the dust. Oblivious to the passenger's plight, the horse brought its fat self to a stop before lowering its head and chewing in earnest at the clover.

DCI Thompson rolled his eyes and huffed. He knew any remonstration on his part would be pointless. Travelling light, as always, he nonetheless had the necessary essentials for outdoor survival in his rucksack. He dismounted and slung the bag from his shoulder, seating himself on a mossy log by the side of the road. Retrieving a small camping stove and a pot of unfeasibly strong coffee, the Chief Inspector comforted himself with the thought that in just a few hours he would be enjoying the hospitality of a historic local inn, famed for its feather mattresses and exemplary local fare. After much careful research, he had found *Le Chat Noir* right in the heart of Chinon and intended to make it his base for the next few days. He glanced across at the horse. It appeared in no mood to go anywhere anytime soon. DCI Thompson sighed. As long as he got there before they stopped serving food, he would be happy enough.

MENAGE A TROIS

Deputy Head Porter couldn't help feeling that escaping the confines of Old College was both exhilarating and unnerving at the same time. Shed got used to the all-encompassing existence of College life that it was quite possible to forget that there was a whole world out there, going about its business with little or no regard for the academic alternate reality. Once she had breathed the last of the fusty, didactic air from her lungs she started to relax and enjoy herself. The same could not be said of The Dean who, despite his hauteur and bluster, felt tetchy and diffident away from his usual stomping ground. This did nothing to quell his typical opprobrious behaviour, however. If anything, it only made him worse.

Professor Fox, of course, was a renowned traveller and adventurer and was rather disappointed that the French scenery did not appear so very differently to that of Great Britain. Although, he remarked that it was 'much tidier', to Deputy Head Porter's consternation. She had become accustomed to the grand tattiness that typified much of the green and pleasant land and felt rather defensive at this remark. She couldn't deny that this rural Gallic example was simply gorgeous. The wild hedgerows and rolling fields flaunted their sleepy charm before them, clearly showing off to the foreign interlopers. *Our scenery might be tattier, but at least it doesn't show off like that,* thought Deputy Head Porter. And there had been no sign of a stiff upper lip since they arrived. Nor a pothole, neither. She had to give the French credit for that. It was an unusually delightful experience, to travel by road without the onset of sciatica threatening every hundred yards.

The weather had been kind to the questers and the scenic journey had been punctuated by several stops for refreshments of breads and cheeses, pastries and buns and even a sneaky crepe or two. Deputy Head Porter had brought little from Old College, except her trusty Maglite and a small but well-stocked tea set. She was pleased to have brought along her own tea set as the local offerings simply couldn't compare. The coffee was quite wonderful, though, and good enough to have kept The Dean from his whisky for the entirety of their travels. Evening was well established as they reached the picturesque Chinon, resting by the banks of the majestic Vienne river.

The Dean had made overtures of announcing their arrival by immediately storming the Chateau, but was soon persuaded otherwise by the mortal requirements of refreshment and refuge. The decision was made to find lodgings for the evening.

Chinon was really not that dissimilar to The City, aside from its size and prominence. It was of a similar era and shared a quaint, haphazard design. Little shops, inns and cafes jostled for position along the winding streets which led up to the chateau, themselves cobbled with elderly stones dating back to near on the fifteenth century. Timber houses of comparable age added to the impression of a town caught in a bygone era, which Deputy Head Porter found a comfort, away from home.

"This place is a wonder and a few," remarked the Professor as they made their way over to a likely-looking inn. "It is so like Old College it's like we never went anywhere at all! Humdinger."

"The Templar obviously had a liking for places of this ilk," agreed The Dean, looking around appreciatively.

"I'm not sure that they were here entirely by choice," said Deputy Head Porter.

"I like the look of this inn," said the Professor, nodding towards their destination. "'*Le Chat Noir*'. It's kinda mysterious sounding. And it smells sorta good too and this Professor is famished."

"And I could do with a drink," said The Dean. "A proper drink. They had better not make me drink wine, you know."

"Come on," sighed Deputy Head Porter. "Let's see if they can put us up for the night."

The inn was an unostentatiously historic building, its timbers well maintained and paintwork humble yet immaculate. Inside, the warm glow of candlelight and delicious aromas of roasting pork were as welcoming as the red-cheeked young lady who stood behind what passed for a reception desk. The faint sounds of a badly played accordion and voices raised in song tapered invitingly from a place beyond.

The Dean approached the pretty girl at the desk with what must be assumed to be his attempt at a charming smile.

"*Bonjour!*" he offered, gamely. "We are looking for lodgings for a night or two, can you assist?"

"*Monsieur*, we have only one room left," the girl replied with a voice as pretty as she was. "But it is a very large room and maybe you can all share, *oui?*"

Deputy Head Porter didn't like the sound of this. She imagined that The Dean snored terribly, and goodness only knew what Professor Fox got up to after dark. The Dean turned to his companions.

"Well, I'm tired and hungry and interested to find out more about that singing going on through there," he said. "So I think we should take the room."

"That doesn't make any sense, I fear," replied Professor Fox, puzzled.

"A few stiff drinks and it soon will, my good man! I say, let us have the keys, *madame*."

The girl blushed to the tips of her ears.

"In fact, monsieur, it is *mademoiselle!*" she coyly twirled a thick curl of chestnut hair between her fingers and regarded The Dean with a manner that Deputy Head Porter would reserve for a sausage sandwich. She slid the room key slowly across the desk.

Oblivious to this amorous display, The Dean snatched up the key with one hand and his suitcase with the other.

"Come on, chaps!"

The inn was a higgledy-piggledy place comprised of narrow staircases and crooked corridors, making Deputy Head Porter feel that she should be doing some Portering while she was there. The journey to the room was an adventure in itself.

"My goodness, this reminds me of Old College!" exclaimed the Professor. "Now then – you don't suppose they have those Bedder things here, do you? I'm not sure my constitution will stand up to another vision of that kind. I think I nearly had two heart attacks – at once."

As if in answer to this question, they were confronted suddenly by an elderly, stout woman who looked a little like a baked potato. With her dusters and polish she did in fact resemble a Bedder. Professor Fox shuddered at the sight of her.

"*Mon dieu!*" she squealed. "You have startled me! So many strange-looking guests arriving today, *zut alors!*"

"I will have you know that we are not strange-looking," retorted The Dean, although not entirely convincingly. "I myself am very handsome. And anyway – what do you mean by that, exactly?"

"About an hour ago a very strange-looking gentleman arrived," she replied, her English excellent although heavily accented. "He went straight to his room also. He spoke English, but I am sure he was anything but. In your hats and clothes you look very like him. Maybe it is your English custom, *non?*"

"Actually, I'm American, and that's the truth," Professor Fox pointed out. She shrugged.

"It is all the same."

"Listen, we're not interested in your strange guests," said The Dean, losing patience a little. "We are looking for our room."

"All three of you? In the one room? You English are much bolder than we think! It is here," she replied, indicating the door closest to her. "I am just finished cleaning it. Enjoy!"

The room was indeed large and much more comfortable than they were expecting. There was an enormous bed at the far end, preceded by a plush sitting area consisting of an over-stuffed sofa and an elegant chaise longue huddling around a low table. Deputy Head Porter sat down and began to unpack her tea things.

"I say, look at the size of that bed!" gasped The Dean. "I reckon we could all get in that. What do you say, Deputy Head Porter?"

"Absolutely not, Sir."

"Well, we all have to sleep somewhere and it seems a shame to waste it."

"We have the reputation of Old College to uphold, Sir," she replied, quickly. "We cannot very well go jumping into bed with each other that the drop of a hat."

"Pah! You Porters have no sense of adventure."

This was one adventure Deputy Head Porter could probably live without.

"I'll take the chaise longue!" announced Professor Fox, leaping on it and making himself comfortable, legs deftly propped up on one of the cushions. "This will suit me very well indeed! It's kinda bouncy, a little bit."

Deputy Head Porter was thinking of making a claim on the sofa before The Dean brought up the subject of the bed again, but several loud thudding sounds abruptly interrupted proceedings.

"What could that be?" wondered the Professor, sitting up, smartly.

And then, a guttural scream like some sort of awful beast followed.

They leapt to their feet. Glances were exchanged. They headed back out into the corridor.

A REUNION

The receptionist at *Le Chat Noir* placed her elbows on her little desk and rested her head in her cupped hands. As the sounds of jocularity spilled over from the bar, she thought how delightfully quaint were the English. With their hats and their accents and their curious hairstyles – she thought that England must be a truly magical and quirky country. Of course, anyone who hasn't actually been to England always thinks this. Anyone who has spent any time on a high street of a Midlands town on a Saturday night tends to take a different view. But, it is true to say, that there are still plenty of examples of those charming British anachronisms shuffling about the place, nowhere more so than at Old College and the likes of The City. And one of them was just about to walk through the door.

The miniature brass bell tinkled, announcing the arrival of another visitor to *Le Chat Noir*. The receptionist turned her round, pink face upwards to greet a tired looking but nonetheless dashingly handsome man. His clothes looked rather dusty and he was walking with a slightly odd gait, but other than that appeared positively charming. He came up to the desk and let his backpack drop to the floor. Wearily, he smiled at the receptionist.

"*Bon soir, mademoiselle,*" he said. "I hope you can help. I have heard excellent things about your establishment, and I am looking for a room for a few nights. The name is Thompson."

"*Je suis desole, Monsieur Thompson,*" she replied, a little heartbroken at having to disappoint the attractive stranger. "I have just given away the very last room!"

"Oh, dash, that's a damned shame," said DCI Thompson, making a bit of a face. "I was really looking forward to staying here."

"If it consoles you, *monsieur*, the room was taken by Englishmen such as yourself."

"That really doesn't console me much, to be honest." DCI Thompson sighed. He was tired, hungry and aching in his softest places from the afternoon's unpredictable ride. "Perhaps you could recommend somewhere nearby?"

"It is high season and the town is very busy, *monsieur*, but I will make some phone calls on your behalf. I will find you somewhere, I promise."

"Thank you. Much appreciated." The Chief Inspector caught a whiff of the roasted pork emanating from somewhere among singing voices and, no doubt, flowing drinks. "Perhaps while you're doing that, I'll grab a bite to eat. Would you..."

A hideous scream from the floor above stunned them both into silence. The receptionist threw her hands to her mouth and her sable eyes shone with terror. DCI Thompson raised an eyebrow.

"I ought to look into that," he said, before rushing past the desk and towards the uneven, twisting staircase beyond.

Taking two steps at a time, he shot up the stairs and launched into the maze of antiquated corridors that, had he not been in so much of a hurry, he would have thought were quite charming. DCI Thompson burst onto a carpeted landing and was about to head towards the door ajar at the far end when he was stopped in his tracks by something that would, quite frankly, stop anything in its tracks.

"Oh, for goodness sake."

"YOU!" roared The Dean, pointing at the Chief Inspector.

Great! thought Deputy Head Porter. *At last someone sensible has arrived on the scene.* She was fond of DCI Thompson, despite his unwelcome meddling in College affairs, which, really, was only him doing his job, when you think about all the dead bodies and whatnot. Although saying that, he did make her a bit nervous. It was something about those broad shoulders and naturally authoritative tone. Made her feel like she should behave herself.

"Yes, it's me," DCI Thompson replied, hands on hips. "I would like to say I'm surprised to see you, but following that bloodcurdling scream, I can't say that I am. What's going on here?"

"That's exactly what we were about to find out!" retorted The Dean, also placing his hands on his hips, and jutting his chin for good measure. "And I can't say I'm surprised to see you, either, considering this is our business and, yet again, here you are with your nose. Sticking it in."

"Well, I, for one, *am* quite surprised to see you, Chief Inspector," said Deputy Head Porter. "I mean, of all the places. Are you investigating some nefarious international crime of great importance?"

"No, I'm here on holiday."

"Who is this?" asked Professor Fox. "Is this a policeman? Just the fellow we want, if so."

"I tell you, this is exactly the fellow we do not want!" countered The Dean. "And why haven't you replied to any of my letters? That's what I want to know."

"I'm a senior detective with The City police force," replied DCI Thompson, witheringly. "I'm not your pen pal. Listen, we haven't got time for this – there was an awful scream. Someone should probably find out if anyone needs assistance. Someone – meaning me."

Before The Dean could launch into another tirade, the Chief Inspector strode down the corridor towards the yellow light seeping out from the room at the far end. The Dean looked to Deputy Head

Porter and the Professor, and motioned for them to follow him.

"Stay close, chaps," he said, under his breath. "This could be grisly."

"Thank goodness I am still wearing my travelling trousers," remarked Professor Fox, glancing at the garments identical to every other pair of trousers he wore. "I would hate to get grisliness on my best trousers. Then, they wouldn't be the best."

This sartorial remark got Deputy Head Porter thinking.

"D'you know, I really should think about wearing something other than my Porter uniform, occasionally," she said. "We're not even in Old College. Yet here I am, bowler hat and waistcoat."

"You were at Old College when we left this morning," pointed out The Dean. "Besides – you are representing us! You shall keep that uniform on until I tell you otherwise, do you understand? But anyway, your attire is hardly at the forefront of current events. Follow me."

And so, Deputy Head Porter and Professor Fox followed The Dean, following the Chief Inspector, towards the room at the far end of the landing.

CATS & COFFEE

The last golden rays of evening fell lightly through the great glass windows of the Porters' Lodge, gilding the ancient flagstones and polished oak counter. It was one of those rich autumn evenings that made one feel as if summer was still in full bloom and would never end. A much-needed calm had befallen the Lodge and Head Porter and Dr Martens sat quietly looking out across the courtyard at the river beyond. Before them was a squat circular table, upon which Dr Martens had placed two very small cups and a plate of very thin biscuits. Head Porter leant over and inhaled the rich aroma from the steaming cups.

"We usually only have tea in the Porters' Lodge," he said. "Tea is very British. I'm a bit nervous about coffee. Isn't it a bit... continental?"

Dr Martens rolled her eyes.

"Tea comes from China. And India," she replied. "And all sorts of places. It isn't very British at all. And it tastes a little bit like wee. Just try the coffee."

Head Porter was aware of coffee, of course. Head of Catering drank the stuff by the bucket load, for a start. But Head Porter had always played it safe and stuck with tea. And what about those biscuits, eh? They weren't proper biscuits, to his mind. They might be wafers, of a sort, but not biscuits. Mind you, those brightly coloured 'party ring' things of which Deputy Head Porter was so fond couldn't really be called biscuits, either. Hey ho. Never let it be said that he didn't have a sense of adventure.

"I bet Deputy Head Porter is drinking coffee," said Head Porter, savouring exotic sips of the thick brown liquid. "Over in France. Ooh! It's got a bit of kick to it, hasn't it?"

Just then, the front door to the Lodge sprang open and in walked a beaming DS Kirby and Porter, arm in arm and both beautifully flushed with the distinctive pink of the newly in love.

"Oh, hallo stranger!" said Head Porter, smiling.

"Aww, I'm sorry I've kept 'im away from work so much just now," said DS Kirby. "It's 'is blummin' wedding suit – it don't matter 'ow many fittings 'e 'as, the blummin' thing never fits 'im right!"

"Could be wedding stress," said Dr Martens. "Stress and anxiety can play havoc with the metabolism."

"You might be onto something there, ma'am," replied Porter. "You'd be stressed an' all if you had blokes with cold hands nipping at your inside leg three times a week."

"Well, we think we're almost there now, don't we darlin'?" DS Kirby said to her beloved. "As long as you don't eat anything between now and the wedding you'll be fine."

"It's only a few days now, isn't it!" trilled Head Porter. "I'm quite excited. I think everything's ready."

"Yep, Head of Caterin' has got all the buffet sorted," replied DS Kirby. "I've got me dress and all them lot from the nick have got their shifts sorted so they can all come to the knees up after. There's just the one thing we wanted to see you about, 'Ead Porter."

"Oh?"

"We was wondering – 'ave you got anyone to 'and out the shots before we go into the Chapel?"

Head Porter almost choked on his very small biscuit.

"Shots... *before* we go into the Chapel?"

"Yeah - we thought it might 'elp relax people an' that."

"I'll do that!" said Dr Martens, brightly. "I've got a lovely big tray that will be perfect. What shots do you want?"

"Pernod."

"Pernod?"

"Yeah, it's a bit of a family tradition," DS Kirby explained. "In my family, we always have a few shots of Pernod before a special occasion."

"Pernod it is, then!"

"Awww, thanks hun, you're the best."

DS Kirby took Porter's pudgy paw in her hand and whispered something in his ear. He gave no visible reaction, but the bristles of his moustache became very erect. DS Kirby giggled.

"Right you are then, Head Porter, ma'am," he said, a hint of breathlessness in his voice. "We'd best be getting off. Er... I mean... we'd best be... on our way. I'll see you in t'morning."

As they left the Lodge, a familiar visitor slunk in through the door in their wake. Head Porter's hands automatically flew to his shins. Dr Martens squealed with delight and jumped to her feet.

"Whoooooosealovelypussycat, eh?"

Dr Martens leant down and scooped up a perturbed Master's Cat, its eyes bulging and hackles on end. Once again, it didn't know what to do. It had come in here for a malicious poo and to perhaps injure someone, and now it was being squeezed like a child's teddy bear. It narrowed its eyes into glowing slits, curling its lips back across needle-sharp ivory teeth... but the demonic hiss it had prepared in its throat stayed exactly where it was. Firm fingers were working the fur behind its ears, knuckles kneaded pleasingly on its head. Its mouth closed and whiskers like fencing foils, drooped. And then – horror upon horrors – a thick, oscillating sound began to build from the place where the hiss should have been. What was that? It was something that tugged on a vague memory from kittenhood. Something it definitely didn't do anymore. It had a reputation to maintain... it didn't do this... it...

It.

Was.

Purring.

"Hahahahaha!!" shrieked Head Porter, u n e x p e c t e d l y. "L o o k a t t h a t! TheMaster'sCatispurring... heeheehee!" His words came out with the staccato effect of a Gatling gun and at a good octave higher than they should have b   e   e   n   . "OhgoodnessmeIdon'tknowwhyI'mquitesoexcited."

To the relief of The Master's Cat, Dr Martens promptly dropped the feline on the flagstones, and it made for the door, partly confused, mostly shamed.

"How many coffees have you had?" she asked, head cocked to one side.

"IhadmineandthenIhadyoursbecauseminewasverysmall!" Head Porter stopped and drew a big breath. "Whyisthiswhatissupposedtohappen?"

"You're not used to the caffeine," replied Dr Martens. "Oh dear. I'd better get you some milk."

"Youlikecatsdon'tyouDrMartensIcanseeyouliketh em..."

"Just calm down, Head Porter."

"I'vegotacatwellit'snotmineit'sDeputyHeadPorter'sandit'sstayingwithme..."

"Sshh!" Dr Martens handed Head Porter a glass of milk and rubbed his back. She wasn't sure if this would help, but had seen it done in films. As it happened, it did seem to calm him down a bit.

"Sorry about that. Look, I've got Deputy Head Porter's cat staying with me while she's away. He's called Terry."

"That's nice," replied Dr Martens, eyeing him carefully for signs of heart attacks.

"No it bloody isn't!" said Head Porter, cheeks red. "He eats everything. Even my food. *Especially* my food. I haven't got the knack you've got."

"I think I see what you're getting at," Dr Martens nodded. "Not only to you want me to run your Porter's Lodge, you would like me to look after the cat too?"

Head Porter adopted his very best pathetic look that always worked on Deputy Head Porter.

"Alright then," replied Dr Martens. "I've already got three. Another one won't make any difference. I shall come and collect Terry tomorrow evening."

Head Porter smiled gratefully and breathed a sigh of relief. Now all he had to worry about was the irregular heart palpitation brought on by that blasted coffee. But for a day in Old College, this was most definitely a result.

THE FAILED ASSASSIN

The door slammed shut just as DCI Thompson reached it, the sliver of warm yellowy glow from beyond abruptly torn from the gloominess of the corridor. Tutting, he grabbed at the handle but it rattled uselessly in his hand as a faint *click* informed him that the lock had been engaged.

"What's going on in there?" yelled the Chief Inspector. He had to resist the urge to shout 'this is the police, open up' as, strictly speaking, in this foreign land he wasn't the police.

"Ukhodi!" came a gravelly cry from behind the door.

"What was that?" asked The Dean.

"Sounds a bit Russian, to me" replied Professor Fox.

"*Aidez -moi!*" came a second, frightened voice.

"Listen, if you don't open this door right now, I'm going to kick it in," said the Chief Inspector, firmly. The Chief Inspector was fond of kicking in doors. He didn't get nearly as much opportunity for such things these days. He was going to make the most of it.

Some muttering could be heard from behind the door and perhaps it could be assumed that deliberations were taking place within. There was not time to discover either way, however, as DCI Thompson made the decision for them with a well-placed foot and a convincing amount of brute force. Shocked cries greeted him as he strode into the room, quickly followed by the eager Old College contingent. Inside, the scene was not quite as dramatic as one might have expected. The room itself was not dissimilar to that recently occupied by The Dean, Deputy Head Porter and Professor Fox. It was comfortably furnished with fat-looking furniture and several twee rural scenes occupied quite ugly frames on the painted walls. Sprawled on a worn but clean umber rug in the centre of the room was a small man, neatly dressed, one hand reaching out for a green felt hat that appeared to have been knocked from his head. Standing over him was a swarthy brute of a chap, with fists clenched and bunched eyebrows like enormous fighting caterpillars.

"I say!" exclaimed The Dean. "That big fellow's biffed that little fellow, there! What's all that about?"

"This is probably none of our business," said Deputy Head Porter, conscious of the unpredictability of The Dean in situations of violence. "I'm sure you said you wanted a drink, Sir..."

"The small one is right," said the swarthy chap in a thick, Eastern European accent. "This is none of your business."

"We're sorta known for other people's business," replied Professor Fox. "We take a communal attitude to business. Especially if that business involves loud screams and things like that."

"You are English?" swarthy chap continued, knotting his considerable brow and turning towards them, eyeing each in turn.

"Not me," the Professor replied hastily. "Don't let the language fool you. I'm American."

"I am looking for the English, with their smart clothes and their little hats." He glanced down towards the stricken man on the rug, who was rubbing his chin and wiping his streaming eyes. "This one is French. I have made a big mistake."

"Well, let's hope you don't make another one," said DCI Thompson, squaring his broad shoulders and moving closer to the confused pugilist. "Tell me what you want with the, as you say, 'English'."

The swarthy chap scratched his head and muttered to himself. The small Frenchman scrambled to his feet and gathered what remaining dignity he could muster.

"This man is *insane!*" he cried, pointing at his attacker. "He burst in here, speaking bad English, demanding I solve a puzzle! Or he would *kill* me! A puzzle for my life! But, his English is so bad - I did not know what he was talking about. I told him - speak the beautiful French or leave! Then he hit me! *C'etait terrible!*"

"I imagine so," said Deputy Head Porter. "No one likes being hit. No one likes puzzles that can cost you your life, either." She turned to the swarthy chap. "Why are you threatening to kill people over a puzzle? It's a bit of an odd threat. Either kill them, or don't kill them. I don't see what puzzles have to do with it."

"I'm feeling that someone should call the police," said DCI Thompson. "But I doubt the local constabulary would thank us for it, quite frankly."

"Leave the flat foots out of this," snapped The Dean. He thought for a moment. Then, "Or, the *pied plats!* Ho Ho!"

"Oh, my" sighed the little Frenchman. "Your French is worse than his English..."

"Quiet, you. No. Listen. If anyone is going to be making threats around here, it's going to be me," retorted The Dean. "So I say to you, my strangely aggressive friend, tell us what is going on right now, or *we* will kill *you*."

"Just to be clear," the Chief Inspector interjected "No one is going to be killing anyone. At all. Do you understand?"

The swarthy chap exhaled deeply and dragged himself over to the chintzy settee nearest the rug, before dropping down onto it, exhausted with life in general.

"This is bad," he mumbled. "This is very bad." He reached into a pocket and withdrew a battered and tarnished hip flask which, upon opening, emitted a strong waft of something akin to paint stripper. Taking a generous gulp, he swept his hair from his sweaty brow and turned his large face towards the others. "I make a big mistake. The boss will not be happy. He said to me, 'Vladimir,' he said, 'Vladimir, you must find the English visitors. You will know them by their neat clothes and their little hats. You will make a bargain for their lives. If they do not solve the puzzle, you will kill them. If they do solve the puzzle, you will kill them anyway. Whatever you do, you must kill the English."

"Your boss sounds very peculiar," noted Deputy Head Porter. "Not to mention, fond of the dramatic.

And the unnecessary. Hang on, you don't suppose..."

"This is clearly an English matter and nothing to do with me," announced the Frenchman, retrieving his hat and making for what remained of the door. "I do not know what you foreigners are about and I do not want to know. I shall bid you *bon soir*."

With that, he scurried out into the corridor, no doubt hoping to find a stiff drink and a sympathetic ear somewhere quite far away.

"Who is this boss of yours?" asked DCI Thompson. Vladimir shook his head.

"He is nameless to me, faceless also. I only spoke to him on the phone. He hired me for this job and I've failed." His face fell into his hands and, to the surprise of all, faint sobs could be heard from behind the massive hands.

Professor Fox hurried over to the settee, face etched with concern, and began to stroke the heaving shoulders of the would-be assassin.

"Hey there and a few, there's no need for that, my good man!" he said in his most soothing voice. "You didn't do so badly, when you think about it. You gave that Frenchman a good biff - even though he was the wrong fellow! I say that shows willing, you know. Maybe your boss won't be so cross after all."

"The main thing is, nobody got hurt," said DCI Thompson. "Except the other chap. But he seems mostly alright."

"The main thing, surely, is what about this puzzle?" The Dean boomed.

"Yes! Hey, maybe if we do the puzzle thing, that will make up for the lack of killings!" exclaimed the Professor.

"I'm thinking that the main thing should be trying to find out who wants us killed, actually," said Deputy Head Porter. "Now, if you think about it, there's only really one..."

"Oh, do be *quiet*, Deputy Head Porter," snapped The Dean. "If there is a life-threatening puzzle at hand, I want to solve it."

DCI Thompson sighed and pinched the bridge of his nose. This really was the worst possible start to his holiday. And he hadn't had anything to eat yet at all.

"Look. If we do the puzzle, can we please just go and get something to eat?"

"But... what about my boss?" Vladimir looked up at the Chief Inspector with red-rimmed eyes. "If he finds out I have been such a fool..."

"We won't tell him!" snapped the Chief Inspector. "I promise, we won't tell anyone. Let us please just have this over and done with."

"And then you can make tracks yourself," said Professor Fox. "I mean, you definitely shouldn't kill us now. Or we'll tell everyone about you crying."

"I swear, I will return to my homeland. You will never hear of me again. I will go now."

"The puzzle!" roared The Dean, as Vladimir got to his feet.

"Oh yes. The puzzle." Vladimir called over his shoulder as he made for the door. "If you have me, you want to share me. If you share me, you don't have me. What am I?"

His heavy footsteps retreated down the corridor as The Dean muttered the words over and over to himself, tapping his chin and gazing at the ceiling. DCI Thompson clapped his hands together.

"Right. You lot can do what you want. I'm going to the bar."

"I'm going to the bar, too," agreed Deputy Head Porter.

"Wait! We should solve this puzzle first," declared The Dean.

"We can solve it in the bar," replied the Professor. "This Professor is hungrier than a stoat."

"Anyway, I've already solved it," grinned Deputy Head Porter.

"You wily old goat!" The Dean said. "Tell me what it is this instant."

"Shan't," she replied. "It's a secret."

And she winked.

WHILE THE CAT'S AWAY

"Terry! Terry! Bloody hell. Where are you, you furry bugger?"

Head Porter stood on his back step, looking out through the misty dawn that fell like a shroud across his small and hectic garden. A little paved pathway peeped out through a thick, unruly lawn and led down to the organised chaos of the vegetable patch beyond. Bell-headed hollyhocks nodded in the soft breeze and early morning dew glittered in the long grass. It was a beautiful morning and all in the garden was bathed in the peach-gold glow of the rising sun. All, that is, except Terry the cat.

It had been an eventful twenty-four hours as a feline guardian, for Head Porter. His Deputy had assured him that Terry was a friendly and docile beast and would give him no trouble at all so long as he was fed and told he was handsome on a regular basis. This was a theory applied by Deputy Head Porter to relationships of all kinds. And, it was true, Terry had not attempted any acts of violence upon his person, unlike the fearsome and nameless Master's Cat. But he had turned his nose up at the wobbly tinned food Head Porter had put in his bowl, although he couldn't really blame the little chap, it smelled dreadful. Instead, Terry had set about either stealing or walking in almost everything Head Porter had prepared as his own. He wondered what on earth Deputy Head Porter was feeding the fellow for him to assume that a cut of rump steak could possibly be for him. And, despite the provision of a perfectly serviceable cat bed, Terry had insisted on sleeping on piles of freshly laundered clothes or - horror or horrors - Head Porter's own bed.

He was spoiled, that's what it was. Deputy Head Porter was clearly far too soft on the creature. And her bed must be full of cat hair, it stands to reason. Head Porter wrinkled his nose at the thought. No wonder she was single. But anyway. Terry was now gone. Head Porter knew this for certain because he had absent-mindedly left half a tuna sandwich on the side in the kitchen last night and it was still there. Whilst he himself would not miss the greedy little beast one bit, he knew that Deputy Head Porter would be devastated. Dr Martens was due to collect him this evening as well - another twelve hours and this wouldn't have been his problem. Head Porter shuffled uncomfortably and shook the jingley mouse toy Deputy Head Porter had told him was Terry's favourite. It was hopeless.

Head Porter sighed. He didn't know the first thing about cats or where they might go when they went missing. But Dr Martens might. She was a remarkable woman, dealing with The Master's Cat the way she did. If anyone could find Terry, it would be her. He had to leave for Old College very soon anyway, a wandering cat was no reason to be late for work. And, you never know, the furry bugger might turn up again later. That would be a very cat thing, Head Porter was sure. Closing the back door behind him and heading into the hallway for his coat, Head Porter consoled himself with the thought that The Dean's nephew might misbehave himself again soon and that lovely Headmistress would have to come back to Old College. Yes. He would concentrate on that and not the missing cat. Things were looking up already.

The positive trajectory did not last long. When he reached the Porters' Lodge, Porter was already in situ, having an animated discussion with the usually immaculate and charming Night Porter. Despite his advancing years, Night Porter was something of an expert on the art of romance and had several girlfriends, dispensing his affections on an intricately devised rotational basis. His continued success with the fairer sex was attributed to his impeccable sense of style, beautiful manners and knowledge of naughty poetry. He was kind enough to share the benefits of his wisdom and experience with his colleagues and Porter's success with DS Kirby was thought largely to be down to this. Night Porter was looking what can only be described as ruffled, by his ordinarily polished standards. His College tie was askew and one solitary bead of sweat clung to his forehead, unsure whether or not to proceed with the business of dripping.

"Ah! Porter! How nice to see you!" said Head Porter, trying out a bit of gentle sarcasm. With Deputy Head Porter away, someone had to maintain standards. "Don't tell me you'll be joining us for an actual shift?"

Porter broke off his conversation with Night Porter and turned a round, expressionless face to Head Porter. The moustache appeared indignant.

"With respect, sir, I'd leave t'sarcasm if I were you. It don't suit you, sir."

Head Porter pulled a face. He was hoping to use sarcasm as a starting point, then slowly build up to wit. Never mind.

"What's going on here?" Head Porter took his more usual tack of the blunt, verging on the downright rude. This seemed to sit better with his staff.

"There's been trouble in The Bursar's big hole," replied Night Porter.

Ah, yes. The much-maligned big hole that supposedly contained an ancient monastery and the Holy Grail, no less.

"What d'you mean, 'trouble'?" ventured Head Porter, immediately knowing he didn't want to know where this was heading.

"There was fighting," Night Porter continued. "Drunken fighting among the Russians."

"Oh no! What was it about?"

"I don't know, they were speaking Russian! Anyway, I shone my torch at them and threatened them with The Dean. They soon settled down. I hope they don't find out that he isn't here."

"What were they doing in the hole in the middle of the night?" Head Porter pondered. "Drunk, at that. Why didn't you go and get The Bursar? They're his chaps, after all."

"As to what they were doing in the hole, I have no idea," replied Night Porter, the weariness of the night shift beginning to show around his eyes. "And I did try to find The Bursar. I took the liberty of letting myself into his rooms when my knocking received no response, but they were empty. No sign of him at all."

"Well, that's strange," said Head Porter, head cocked to one side. He folded his arms. "Maybe they knew he was out of College, that's why they got drunk. While the cat's away, sort of thing." *Cat! Cats going away... bugger...*

"You'd think t'Bursar would be keeping a close eye on that hole," said Porter. "What with that competition between him and Professor Fox. Somethings not right here, you mark my words."

"Consider them marked, Porter." Head Porter huffed and shoved his hands in his pockets. "Well, there's not a lot I can do this minute. Not at this hour, anyway. I tell you what I'll do - I'll have a cup of tea and think on it."

"I'll put t'kettle on, sir."

"Thank you, Porter." Head Porter thought for a moment. "Actually, Porter, make that a cup of *coffee,* would you?"

WHEN THERE ARE NO SAUSAGES

If there was one thing of which Deputy Head Porter was particularly fond, it was a proper breakfast. She was fairly open-minded about the form taken by the most important meal of the day, just so long as it left her tummy rounder than it was when she woke up. Sausages, for example, could make a tummy splendidly plump - not least when accompanied by their close relation, bacon. Toast is acceptable, but only as an aside to the main event. And always with proper butter. A fried slice or two (or three) is better and eggs are practically essential. There is often some debate about the suitability of tomato as a breakfast food; Deputy Head Porter was generally in favour, as tomatoes are cheerful looking. Baked beans, however, have no place on a breakfast plate. The bean juice interferes with the other items and that simply won't do.

There was no such fare on offer at *Le Chat Noir* that morning, but the continental spread laid out in the dining room was delectable nonetheless. The Dean took some convincing, at first, perhaps because the sight of so much fruit first thing in the morning unnerved him a little. But once he was ushered towards the pastries (which absolutely *are* a breakfast food) he perked up somewhat. By the time he reached the cured meats and cheeses he was verging on jubilant.

The dining room was half empty by the time Deputy Head Porter, The Dean and Professor Fox finally made their way down, the excitement of the previous evening no doubt the chief cause of them oversleeping. Also, the Professor had taken an inordinate amount of time to decide which trousers to wear and Deputy Head Porter is incapable of appearing in public before her third cup of tea. The urgent evacuation of the small Frenchman meant that Detective Chief Inspector Thompson had a room after all and he was finishing up his coffee and reading a book as the Old College contingent seated themselves noisily at the next table.

"Good morning, Chief Inspector!" chirped Deputy Head Porter, flaky pastry already stuck to her chin. Well, it was a long walk from the buffet to the table and she was hungry. Also, there hadn't been quite enough room on her plate for the second Danish pastry and she was forced to consume it in transit.

The Chief Inspector looked up and offered a thin smile, deciding there and then that he should really be getting on with his day.

"What-ho Thompson," grinned The Dean, uncharacteristically amiable. "What are you up to today? Meddling in other people's affairs, I expect?"

"Not today, Dean, I'm on holiday," replied the Chief Inspector. "Sorry to disappoint you. I try to restrict my meddling to when I'm on duty."

"Pah!" scoffed The Dean. "Don't believe a word of it. If I didn't know better, I'd say you were trying to elbow in on our great adventure."

DCI Thompson sighed and placed his cup carefully on the table before him. The whole point of this holiday was to get *away* from College-related nonsense.

"And what great adventure would that be, Dean?"

"Aha! You see, I told you," said The Dean. "Can't help himself. Nosy bugger." And he deliberately turned his back to the Chief Inspector to focus his attentions on wrapping bits of cheese in slivers of cured meat.

"I'm sorry about him, Sir," Deputy Head Porter said to DCI Thompson in a low voice. "You know what he's like. I find it best to ignore him most of the time."

"I don't understand what possible appeal working for Old College could hold for you," replied DCI Thompson, a hint of pity evident in his voice. "You are almost normal. You should get out while you still can. Before you end up... like that." He nodded in the direction of The Dean and Professor Fox, who appeared to be arranging their food in alphabetical order.

Deputy Head Porter nodded solemnly.

"You're probably right, Sir. But I'm a bit worried they might hunt me down if I try to escape. Might be best to sit tight and just enjoy the hats and the free food."

"Well, if you change your mind..." whispered the Chief Inspector. "I mean, don't worry about The Dean... things could be done, you know. It would look like an accident..." With a grin and a wink, he stood up and tucked his book into his jacket pocket. As he headed towards the door, Deputy Head Porter wasn't sure if he was serious or not.

"...It's just as well I brought my Zorro outfit!"

The tail-end of this statement from The Dean caused Deputy Head Porter to turn her attention sharply back to her colleagues. The appearance of the Zorro costume was always a bad omen.

"Sorry, what was that, Sir?" asked Deputy Head Porter. "What about the Zorro costume?"

"I was just saying, how we will need disguises for the next part of our mission."

"Yes!" exclaimed the Professor. "Wait. Why?"

"In case we are recognised, man!"

"Who on earth is going to recognise us?!" asked Deputy Head Porter, genuinely confused. But then again, The Dean found it impossible to comprehend that he wasn't instantly recognisable to absolutely everyone, everywhere.

"More to the point," the Professor continued, "What would we be disguised *as?*"

"Not the Zorro costume!" Deputy Head Porter held up a hand and closed her eyes. "Definitely not that. Look. We are foreign. We are tourists. If we go up there being foreign tourists no one will pay us the slightest bit of attention. Then we can see about sneaking into these dungeons."

"Aha, so you mean to fool the buggers by hiding in plain sight?" The Dean replied, stroking his chin. "Clever, Deputy Head Porter, very clever."

"Well, look, if that's the case, I kinda think I oughta change my trousers," said Professor Fox. "These are my attention-grabbing trousers, see. And that won't do."

"And I must insist upon wearing my jumper draped across my shoulders," said The Dean.

"Like a cape?" asked Deputy Head Porter, narrowing an eye at him.

"No! Not a cape. It's my casual look. Like I might look if I was just, say, casually looking around a chateau without any untoward intentions at all."

"We-ell... okay," said Deputy Head Porter, after a moment's thought. "Come on, then. We've wasted enough time already."

FAMILY TIES

The Chateau de Chinon loomed before them, a grand and breathtakingly imposing structure, as one might expect of the preferred residence of Henry II. Deputy Head Porter was expecting it to be something along the lines of Old College, but fancier. This place looked as though it could eat Old College for breakfast and still have room for Hawkins and Saint Samantha's. It would be an absolute bugger to Porter, certainly. It was *huge*. Standing on a rocky outcrop above the Vienne River, the chateau had natural defences on three sides and a large, man-made ditch dug on the fourth. It was divided along its length into three enclosures, each separated by a deep moat. The easternmost enclosure was the Fort St Georges, built by Henry II in tribute to England's patron saint. The central enclosure, the Chateau du Milieu, was known as the Middle Castle. On the westernmost side was the Fort du Coudray, a round keep of typical 14th century French design. Turrets and towers of the great stone leviathan soared above them, bringing about a feeling of sudden insignificance. Probably not in the case of The Dean, actually, but Deputy Head Porter definitely felt it.

"Do you suppose we just go in?" asked Professor Fox, eyeing the main entrance with suspicion.

"I expect so," replied Deputy Head Porter. "That's what it's there for - it's a tourist attraction and we are tourists. Let's just go in like ordinary sightseers and see what we can find out.

The Dean grumbled to himself. The idea of doing anything in the manner of ordinary people gave him the pip. He just wasn't used to it. He stroked the sleeves of his jumper that were tied around this neck. It looked very much indeed like a little cape.

Inside, the Chateau de Chinon was just as impressive, if not more so. Extensive restoration work ensured that the magnificent columns and vaulted ceilings retained their ancient glory and lovingly recreated tapestries and artworks adorned the great stone walls. There were groups of enthralled tourists scattered about; excitable school children clustered around artefacts encased in glass, families posing for endless photographs and lovers drifting dream-like through the halls, lost in the romance of the castle.

"In fact, this is very interesting," announced The Dean, his eyes shining as they took in the grandeur. "It reminds me of Old College, but without the students, or The Fellowship. So, in that respect it's much better."

"It's a feast for the eyes, there's no doubt," agreed the Professor. "Maybe a four-course feast. Five, even. With eight types of wine and a chocolate mint at the end."

"It is amazing," Deputy Head Porter gasped, slightly breathless and overwhelmed. "But something's bothering me."

"There's bound to be a cafe, Deputy Head Porter," said The Dean, irritably. "We'll get something to eat soon. You've only just had breakfast, you know."

"It's not that," she replied (although the thought had occurred to her). "Are neither of you even the slightest bit concerned about that business last night? With the Russian chap?"

"He was a vexing fellow," nodded Professor Fox. "Punching that small man and then crying about it. Very strange, I'd say."

"Yes. It was more the fact that he seemed to have instructions to kill us," Deputy Head Porter replied, patiently. "That's what sticks in my mind."

"Aha, but he didn't kill us, did he?" said The Dean. "That sort of thing is important. One cannot worry too much about chaps that *don't* kill one. You'd be worrying all day if you did that."

Deputy Head Porter crossed her arms and tried her best not to huff. She could see that she was going to have to spell it out.

"He said he had orders to kill some well-dressed English visitors," she began, speaking slowing as if to a small child who was particularly slow on the uptake. "Very obviously us."

"Me especially," interrupted The Dean. "I'm notoriously well-dressed."

"Well, quite. Not only that, he was Russian."

"This is no time for racial prejudice, Deputy Head Porter..."

"Sir. Who *else* do we know who is Russian and tries to kill people?"

"Oh, man!" exclaimed Professor Fox, slapping his palm against his forehead. "Dexter Sinistrov!

That dadblame Bursar. He doesn't want us finding the Grail before him, that's what it is. But hey - isn't that what his big hole is all about? What a wonder."

"Now, a thought strikes me," remarked The Dean, shoving his hands in his pockets and beginning to pace. "That big hole must be just a diversion. If he actually believed the Holy Grail to be under Old College, he wouldn't be sending murderous henchmen after us. Stands to reason."

"But a diversion from *what?*" Professor Fox muttered, tapping his chin. "What's the point of digging a big fat hole if he knows there's nothing in it? No one likes holes that much, I'm thinking."

"I know what it is!" The Dean abruptly ceased his pacing and glared at the world in general. "His hole is clearly a device to enrage me. It is right outside my rooms, after all. Apple Tree Court is practically my garden. He means to provoke me by defiling my personal space. It is a molestation of my private life."

Deputy Head Porter eyed The Dean carefully. This was an interesting train of thought, but one that should be derailed fairly swiftly.

"Sir, I've no doubt that The Bursar is enamoured with neither your good self nor the Professor," she said. "But a chap such has him has rather more *direct* ways of dealing with people he doesn't much like. Digging up their gardens seems a little out of character, to me."

"And, you know, he announced to everyone that the Grail was down there," said Professor Fox. "So, maybe that's what he wants people to think. Maybe he knows where it really is, after all."

"Yes," nodded Deputy Head Porter. "And now he's worried we will get it first!"

"This still doesn't explain the hole," said The Dean, shaking his head.

"You know what I'm betting? I'm betting The Bursar's realised his big hole has nothing in it. probably not even a monastery, now I come to think about it. So, he knows he is wrong, but doesn't want to look like a noogin in front of The Master, see. And so again - he sends the Vladimir fellow after us. After us and the actual Holy Grail. He was going to kill us and get the proper Grail for Sinistrov. Then maybe sneaks it back and pops it in his hole, claiming he was right all along. That explains it." Professor Fox took a deep breath and grinned to himself, very pleased with his deduction.

"Seems like a lot of trouble, just for the Holy Grail," sniffed The Dean. "I still think it's more likely this is all about me."

"You may well be right, Sir," Deputy Head Porter replied, carefully. "But the Professor makes a good point. The Bursar gets some serious brownie points with The Master by discovering the Holy Grail in Old College."

"You're right, DHP. Right in saying I'm right. That's what it is." Professor Fox tapped a foot. "But, hey, we don't need to worry, because the henchman chap has gone away to hide or something. By the time that dadblame Bursar realises his plot has been foiled, we'll be back with the Grail and treated like heroes! Or, at least, The Master won't be too mean to us for a while, which is even better. Things are going so well, we'll definitely have time to visit the gift shop."

"First we need to visit the dungeons," said Deputy Head Porter.

"Dungeons, *madame?*"

Deputy Head Porter swung round at the sound of the unfamiliar voice. Behind her stood a beaming and immaculate woman in a red uniform with matching silk neckerchief tied artfully around her slender neck. Her chestnut hair was scraped back into a neat bun and bright red lips parted in a wide, dazzling white smile.

"Madame? Er, actually, I'm a..."

"Yes, yes, madame, exactly," The Dean broke in, returning the tour guide's smile with his own terrifying offering. He stepped forward and placed his arm heavily around Deputy Head Porter's shoulders. "You see my... wife, yes, my wife... has been researching her family tree and it turns out she is descended from one of those Knights Templar fellows. Seems he might have been held prisoner here and she is just desperate to see where he was probably tortured and killed. As one might, you know."

Deputy Head Porter winced. This wasn't the first - or even the second - time she and The Dean had posed as a couple in the course of an investigation. The supposed 'affair' had caused quite a stir in the Porters' Lodge at the time. Goodness only knows what they would make of a marriage. Deputy Head Porter was suddenly very pleased to be a long way from Old College. The Zorro outfit was not involved, at least.

"Ah, but the dungeons are not accessible to the public, *je suis desole*," replied the tour guide, sounding not sorry in the slightest. "But the Tour du Coudray, that was used as a prison also and the names of prisoners are scratched into the walls even now. It may be of interest to you?"

"That does sound very interesting," said The Dean. "But it's really the dungeons we came to see. We've come a long way, you see. Far flung foreign lands."

"Forgive me - I thought you were English?"

"I'm American," piped up the Professor. "That's pretty far flung. And I've flung myself all the way over here to see dungeons, you know."

"It is impossible," replied the tour guide, her smile widening. "It is only The Curator and his staff who can access the dungeons. And he is not a hospitable man."

"I'm thinking this is not a friendly country," said Professor Fox. "Most people here are unhelpful or try to kill us."

"Well, thank you anyway!" The Dean grinned manically at the tour guide and yanked Deputy Head Porter away. "We will be sure to visit that tower!"

They scuttled away from the tour guide feeling rather miffed.

"Look at it this way," said Deputy Head Porter. "At least we know that the dungeons are still there. What's more, they can be accessed."

"Yes, but only by some blasted Curator," muttered The Dean, darkly. "And his staff." A brief pause. "I say we acquire the uniforms of the staff and..."

"No! No..." Deputy Head Porter stopped him in his tracks. *Come on, there must be a way...* "Sir, I believe this is a situation very much up my street. It's at times like this that we should stop thinking ordinarily. Now is the time to think like a *Porter.*"

THE BURSAR'S HOLE

Detective Sergeant Kirby took a deep drag of her cigarette and leant back against the wall of the east cloister in Apple Tree Court. Squinting in the afternoon sun, she observed the activity on the lawn with icy interest. Next to her, Dr Samantha Martens coughed politely. Smoking wasn't really allowed on College grounds and, as she was currently in her unofficial role as a Porter and wearing a bowler hat, she felt she had to mention it.

"You know, you shouldn't really smoke here," she said.

"I know," replied DS Kirby.

"Well... as long as you know, that's alright."

"Yeah. Anyway, The Dean's not 'ere, is 'e, so I won't get told off."

"That is true." Dr Martens thought for a moment. "I don't suppose you've seen a quite fat black and white cat around, have you? It's Deputy Head Porter's. Head Porter has lost him. His name is Terry McCann."

"That's a funny name for a cat," said DS Kirby, taking another lungful. "I'll keep an eye out. 'Ere, what do you make of that hole over there?"

"We-ell... The Bursar says he is excavating an ancient monastery with the Holy Grail hidden in it," Dr Martens replied, doubtfully. "But I'm not so sure. Because Deputy Head Porter is looking for the Holy Grail over in France. So, I think there's something suspect about that hole."

"D'you think it'll be filled in for the wedding?" DS Kirby asked. Dr Martens shrugged.

"I don't know. Probably not. There's only a couple of days to go. I'd ask The Bursar for you, but no one's seen him."

"'E might've fallen in there!"

"I don't mind if he has. He has a very odd haircut." Dr Martens self-consciously placed a hand on her own wild mass of hair. It was behaving particularly badly today and appeared to be trying to oust the hat from her head.

DS Kirby expelled a final cloud of blueish smoke and ground the remains of her cigarette into the flagstones.

"I'd better go and see 'Ead of Catering," she said. "Got to look over the final menus for the buffet. You still alright to hand out the shots of Pernod outside the Chapel?"

"Oh, yes!" nodded Dr Martens. "I've put aside one of best trays especially. I'm looking forward to that."

"Brill. I'll catch you later."

Dr Martens watched DS Kirby head along the cloister towards the bridge and thought about what to do next. She was worried that Head Porter had overdone the coffee as he had seemed rather manic this morning. He was clearly worried about the disappearance of Terry and had deployed her in the quest for his immediate return. Dr Martens had been to Deputy Head Porter's house, in case he had a mind to return home. She had searched all the side streets around Head Porter's house too, with no luck. There was a chance he could have come to Old College. He might have followed Head Porter or even looked for the scent of his mistress. She thought about what DS Kirby said about The Bursar falling in the hole. Cats were naturally curious creatures and a big hole like that would be a temptation. Perhaps she should take a look.

As she approached the mouth of the hole, she was aware of an ominous quiet from within. She had always imagined excavating to be quite noisy work. Peering in, she saw a couple of workmen drinking tea, another handful playing cards and one that was asleep. This didn't seem right. If The Dean was here they wouldn't be lounging about like this.

"Ahem! Excuse me..?"

Several mucky faces looked up at her with lazy-eyed indifference, before returning to their previous occupations.

"Oi! You lot! Listen to me!" Dr Martens placed her hands on her hips and drew herself up to her full height, which she somehow managed to give the impression of being considerably more than it actually was. "What are you all doing? More to the point, what are you *supposed* to be doing? There doesn't seem to much going on here *at all.*"

Dr Martens took a proper look into the hole. It was a pretty big hole, it had that going for it. There were a couple of ladders leaning against the sides and a few ropes strung about the place. But other than that, there was nothing but dirt and ambivalent Russians. There certainly was no evidence of ancient monasteries or anything of any interest whatsoever. She didn't like the look of this.

"Where's The Bursar?" she demanded. The Russians looked to one another without a word, before shrugging their shoulders at her. Dr Martens thought about giving them a piece of her mind, but instead fired a few well aimed tuts at them before turning on her heels and striding back towards the Porters' Lodge.

DR MARTENS LEADS THE WAY

Porter gave the impression of gazing out through the great glass windows of The Lodge and admiring the bridge, quietly going about its business of spanning the river, glittering in the sunshine. But really, he was focused on his own reflection and feeling quite critical about it. He was very aware that in a few short days he would be a married man. He hadn't had extensive experience with the fairer sex, particularly not in more recent years. He had generally thought of them as being a bit soppy a lot of time, but at least they smelled nice. Detective Sergeant Kirby was not soppy. She swore like a sailor and drank like one, too. She was fond of darts and a closing time scuffle and had buttocks you could use to crack walnuts. In Porter's view, these were all excellent attributes in a woman. And she didn't nag or mither him in that way women do. But she was very keen on bringing her handcuffs to bed and she had mentioned several times now that he was to 'do something with his hair' for the wedding.

Porter surreptitiously looked at his hair in glass, while at the same time pretending to watch the passing punts. He thought it was *good* hair. Alright, so it was greying now, but there was still plenty of it, at least. He kept it short on account of its tendency to acquire the attributes of a broom if left to its own devices. He would have to ask Night Porter about the hair, he decided. Night Porter, unfeasibly popular with local ladies, had already given him some excellent advice regarding the handcuffs and other related matters. He was bound to know about the hair.

Just as Porter was withdrawing from the window, wedding nerves settled for now, he noticed a very determined-looking Dr Martens striding across the bridge towards The Lodge. He wasn't sure he liked the look on her face. It was a look that signalled trouble for someone. Hopefully not him. Porter decided to tactically retreat to the little Lodge kitchen out the back and get the kettle on. He was safely ensconced among the crockery when Dr Martens flung back the Lodge door and marched through.

Head Porter poked his head round the door of his office. He didn't have much experience with women, either (not for want of trying) and was dangerously inept at the subtle skills required to navigate their nuanced tempers.

"Everything alright, is it?"

Dr Martens rolled her eyes.

"It's just you did rather slam the door just then," continued Head Porter. "I'd rather you didn't do that, thank you."

"Things are not alright!" Dr Martens announced, confident in her statement. "I've had a look in The Bursar's hole."

"Oh? Oh! What's in it?"

"Nothing, that's what! Nothing except mud and Russians."

"Really?" exclaimed Head Porter. "And to think he told us all there was a monastery down there. I wonder why there are Russians buried under Old College..."

"No... look... oh, never mind. The thing is, we should speak to The Bursar about this. Something's not right."

"Oh, well, that's easy enough for you to say," said Head Porter, jutting his chin. "But we Porters can't go around 'having a word' with members of The Fellowship, willy-nilly. They take offence very easily, do Fellows. They don't like back-chat from us lower orders."

"*I* am a member of The Fellowship!" Dr Martens, exasperated, thumped her chest with her fist. "You keep forgetting."

"You look so super in the hat," replied Head Porter. "It must be that."

"It is a good hat," Dr Martens conceded. "But never mind that. We should go up and see him. Bring the keys to his rooms. I shall get to the bottom of his hole one way or another."

"Haha! Good one!"

Dr Martens was on the verge of effecting another eye-roll when Porter bustled through from the back carrying a tray, upon which were two large steaming mugs and some very thin biscuits. Head Porter's eyes gleamed as he sniffed the air.

"Ooh!" he said. "Coffee!"

Dr Martens eyed the mugs doubtfully.

"They are very big mugs for such strong coffee," she said, mindful of Head Porter's low tolerance of caffeine. "I'm not sure you should drink that, Head Porter."

"But why? That's the way Head of Catering drinks it."

"Yes, but... Head of Catering... well. He's a man on the edge!" Dr Martens replied. "Probably because of all the coffee, actually."

"Rubbish! It perks me up."

"Shall I do a pot of tea instead?" asked Porter, looking ruefully at the very thin biscuits. They didn't look like proper biscuits to him. They looked like bits of sugary cardboard.

"No, no, the coffee will do nicely, thank you," Head Porter insisted. "Put the tray there, that's it. And go and get me the keys to The Bursar's rooms, there's a good chap."

Porter did as he was told, absent-mindedly running his hands through his hair as he considered the benefits of conditioner and mousse.

Quarter of an hour later, Head Porter and Dr Martens were standing in The Bursar's rooms, which were distinctly unoccupied. All rooms belonging to members of The Fellowship were curious affairs, often reflections of the eccentricities of their owners and always complete chaos. All except for the rooms of Senior Tutor, which were immaculately neat and devoid of personality. He had been a military man in his youth and his softly spoken manner belied what was rumoured to be a fairly violent past. Deputy Head Porter was fond of his rooms as it was always easy to find things and there was little chance of being buried by an avalanche of books and papers every time she walked through the door.

The Bursar's rooms could be best, and aptly, described as menacing. Thick velvet curtains swathed the windows and the heavy lacquered furniture loomed ominously in the cloying gloom. There was an over-large desk over to one side, the surface of which was smattered with unusual stains and patches of corrosion. There were several steel boxes fastened with sturdy padlocks crouching on the desk beside an angled lamp. Metal shutter-type arrangements had been fitted to the bookshelves, all also secured by padlocks. The antique rug beneath the desk - one that had belonged to the now absent Junior Bursar and no doubt other Bursar's before him - was pockmarked and singed in places.

Dr Martens flicked the light switch, and repeated the motion several times when it had no effect. She glanced up to the ceiling to see that the bulb had been removed. Frowning, she made her way carefully through the darkness to the desk lamp, and switched that on. Instantly her eyes were seared by a powerful white light, burning blue flashes across the inside of her eyelids. Head Porter headed for the windows and threw back the heavy velvet drapes.

"A h ! T h a t ' s a b i t m o r e l i k e i t . . . cheertheplaceupabit!"

Dr Martens rubbed her eyes in order to fling him a reproachful look.

"You've had too much coffee again."

"What? NooooI'mfinehonestly."

"Hmmm. Alright then." Dr Martens looked around the room. Everything was fastened tight with industrial-looking padlocks. There were no personal items to speak of and only one spindly chair that accompanied the desk. "It doesn't look like he does a lot of entertaining."

"Wellheisprettyterrifyingyouknowprobablytryto poisonpeopleanyway."

Head Porter fumbled with one of the padlocks attached to the shuttered bookcase. His jittery fingers danced around the metal and he frowned.

"NotCollegeregulation... notallowedyouknow... notgotkeysforthese..."

"Are you sure you're alright, Head Porter?"

Head Porter had gone quite pale and developed a sort of nervous tic in his left eye. His breathing was shallow and fast and he reached out a hand to steady himself against the bookshelf.

"ActuallyI... I... feelabitweird..."

Head Porter made a series of hollow burping sounds and keeled over sideways onto the floor.

PORTERS & KNIGHTS

Without doubt, Deputy Head Porter's biggest mistake when first joining Old College was trying to apply her hard-earned real-world logic and thinking to the academic environment. It took her a long time to tuck away the reasoned thought so highly developed in her previous existence and finally wrestle her mind towards the Machiavellian and contrived thought processes that govern the internal workings of College life. She learned that she almost had to approach thinking as if she was a person who had never thought at all. Having considered this matter at some length, she concluded that academics had heads so full of dusty nonsense that there was little room for much else. Porters, on the other hand, have plenty of room inside their heads. That's what makes them such a wily and adaptable breed.

Having ascertained from the Shop Keeper that the Templar carvings in the cave resemble the markings found in the dungeons of the Chateau, the next point of progress seemed clear. It would be gaining access to the buggers that could prove difficult.

"If The Curator and his staff are the only people who have access to the dungeons, then there must be a key or device that controls entry," said Deputy Head Porter to her captive audience of Professor Fox and The Dean.

"Or guards," said the Professor. "I'll bet they have guards, you know. It is a castle, after all."

"If they have guards we shall have to use force," The Dean stated. "It's the only language they understand. And little more than they deserve."

"I'm thinking they probably understand French," replied the Professor. "French and violence. bi-lingual guards. What a wonder."

"In which case I shall say to them - '*vous-avez* some of this, you buggers,'..."

"I'm fairly certain there won't be any need for any of that," Deputy Head Porter cut in, although she wasn't convinced herself.

"You know, that nice lady with the scarf said something about a tower where they kept prisoners," said Professor Fox. "With markings on the walls."

"Yes, but that's a tourist-y bit," replied The Dean, waving a hand dismissively. "There'll be no guards and no Holy Grail there, I'm sure."

"And the Shop Keeper was pretty certain about the dungeons," Deputy Head Porter continued. "So - assuming, for a moment - there are no guards, we will certainly need the keys."

"Then it is clear. We must tackle this Curator chap and beat him until he gives them to us."

"Well, Mr Dean, I like your style... but no," said the Professor. "That sort of behaviour could land us on the wrong side of the *gendarmerie,* I'm thinking. And I have heard that those fellows don't have a right side. Imagine going through life with no right side, too. Poor chaps."

"For once, I don't think violence is the answer," said Deputy Head Porter.

"If not violence, then what?" asked The Dean, genuinely perplexed.

"A place like this must have hundreds, if not thousands, of locks," replied Deputy Head Porter. "And that means lots and lots of keys. They must be kept somewhere. There must be a sort of equivalent to a Porters' Lodge. Keys can be difficult articles and they most definitely demand a place to be kept.

"Wowawee, you're right, DHP!" exclaimed the Professor. "Genius! Of sorts. I imagine, though, it'd be kinda hard to find that place, you know."

"Well, yes, my thoughts exactly." Deputy Head Porter paused. There was something that she felt simply could not go unsaid. "This is exactly the sort of thing that should not be attempted on an empty stomach. Breakfast was hours ago. A couple, at least."

"If it's not breakfast time anymore then it's definitely time for a whisky," said The Dean, nodding.

"And that means there is definitely time to go to the gift shop," agreed Professor Fox. "If there's time for food and whisky. Let's do it."

While the Tour du Coudray lay neglected and unheeded by the Old College Grail Quest, it was at least receiving some low-key appreciation from Detective Chief Inspector Thompson. You would think a man in his position would have enough crime and punishment during his working life, but his interest in such matters certainly stretched to the early fourteenth century keep of the Chateau de Chinon. He carefully photographed the graffiti-covered stone walls, carved centuries before by luckless prisoners, captured the stunning views from the thin, unglazed windows and even managed a couple of arty shots of some rusted manacles. Feeling rather pleased with himself, as he often did, he decided to next explore the grand La Tour de l'Horloge and set off with his camera once more, enjoying himself immensely.

Knowing that the most important part of any adventure is the food and drink, the intrepid trio of Deputy Head Porter, The Dean and Professor Fox spent quite some time and thought on their purchases and had decamped to one of the breezy courtyards for an impromptu picnic. The cafe had furnished them with a delightful array of crusty breads and a formidable selection of cheeses but had been little help where The Dean's whisky was concerned. Luckily, the gift shop had a selection of over-priced scotch that wasn't too terrible and, The Dean declared 'better than nothing'. Professor Fox had picked up some postcards and a rather fetching tea towel that he intended to present as a wedding gift to Porter and DS Kirby.

The afternoon air was fuddled by a warm breeze, skipping its way from the Vienne river and they watched happily as children played about the courtyard, exploring the corners and crevices and no doubt imagining themselves to be knights of old. It was a perfect accompaniment to their early lunch, and the best thing about an early lunch is that there might be time to squeeze in a late lunch as well.

"You know, I've been thinking twice over," announced the Professor, between mouthfuls of Brie. "With the crypt, the cave and now the dungeons, it strikes me that the Templar spent quite a lot of time underground."

"Well, they were greatly persecuted, after a time," remarked The Dean. "If you were accused of heresy and threatened with execution you would hardly be strutting about the landscape, would you."

"Oh, I bet so," retorted the Professor, defiantly. "I would strut about proudly, then accuse *them* of heresy and threaten *them* with all sorts of horrible things..."

Deputy Head Porter hopped to her feet to shake off the inordinate amount of crumbs that had accumulated about her person. The saddest truth about crusty bread is that far too little of it finds its way into the mouth. As she performed her little jig, she was startled by something walking into her flailing elbow.

"Mind out!" She swung round to find herself facing an unfortunate young man who now looked absolutely terrified.

"*Je suis desole!*" he wailed, holding both hands to his stricken cheek.

"Oh." Deputy Head Porter struggled to come up with something suitable to say, other than - "Sorry about that."

"Now what's up here?" Professor Fox leapt to his feet and gave the young French gentleman his best hard stare. "You can't go about walking into young ladies, you know. It's not appreciated."

"Oh, he's French," said The Dean, cramming another wedge of cheese into his already bulging cheeks. "The things they do to young ladies are unmentionable."

"It's probably my fault," Deputy Head Porter smiled kindly at the lad. "I wasn't paying attention. Thinking about something else."

"Yes, knights," agreed the Professor.

"You are interested in knights?" the lad asked.

"Oh yes!" replied Deputy Head Porter. "We're sort of on a bit of a quest. Following some other knights who came before us a long, long time ago."

"Very famous knights, no less!" said the Professor. "They were kept here in the dungeons, back when the castle was brand new. And before you ask - yes, I'm kinda like a knight myself, you could say."

"Oh!" exclaimed the French lad, suddenly enthralled. "Of course, I know the knights you mean. I know where they were kept - for their repeated trials and approbations."

"You do? Well, my man, do you think you could show us?"

Clearly impressed by the Professor's claim to knighthood, the young lad turned his pink little face towards him, nodding furiously.

"But of course! *S'il vous plait* - you will follow me!"

FALSE KNIGHTS

It turns out that the fey young fellow inadvertently assaulted by Deputy Head Porter was in fact the nineteen-year-old son of the elusive Curator, which was a stroke of luck, even by Old College's standards. He looked much younger than his years, with his wispy golden hair and delicate features. His pale, pointed chin was doubtful to have seen a razor and he had wrists a sparrow could peck in two. His name was Pascal and they were all becoming rather fond of the little fellow.

Pascal was of a jittery, nervous disposition which was not helped by the presence of The Dean, who, in the traditional manner of Englishmen abroad, insisted on speaking to him very loudly and slowly. It was a terrifying way to be questioned, even for the most robust of persons, let alone a young man with no experience of The Dean. Nevertheless, Deputy Head Porter and Professor

Fox were able to extract from him a little interesting information. Pascal had practically grown up in the Chateau de Chinon at the heel of his father and knew a great deal about the history of the place. He had a particular fascination for the Knights Templar and babbled on about them with great enthusiasm, especially the legend that they would one day return to seek restitution for the souls of their long-departed comrades. Deputy Head Porter was concerned that Pascal had taken the Professor's knightly claims rather too seriously and he, in turn, was doing everything he could to enforce these claims, confident it would encourage the lad to help them into the dungeons.

As well as the Knights Templar, Pascal also shared a few scant details about his father on the winding journey through the maze-like back passages of the Chateau. He seemed to be a curious character, a chap of whom Pascal was apparently a little afraid. But then, Pascal was probably a little afraid of most people. Pascal never knew his grandfather, who died when the Curator himself was very young. But his grandmother apparently wore her widow weeds right up until the point of her own death. The Dean noted this, remarking that a widow's son would face many challenges in life, if he knew anything about it. Which he seemed convinced that he did. The Curator shied away from public appearances on account of some kind of deformity which was the result of terrible injuries received during a vaguely-described military career. An eye patch is mentioned. Professor Fox is quite taken with this and passes the remark that The Curator sounds very much like a pirate.

"He just needs a skull and crossbones, I'd say!"

"Oh, but you must not tell him that he looks like a pirate!" squealed Pascal, horrified. "He will not like that at all."

"How about a Viking?" suggested the Professor. "Vikings are better than pirates, even. Since they ride in the longest boats."

"What? What do you say?" bellowed The Dean, causing Pascal to twitch involuntarily. "I'm not sure that you are correct, there. Vikings better? Pah. Pirates are feisty fellows, you know, with super hats. They say 'Aaagghhh' a lot and I like that."

"But Vikings had better swords, you must admit," the Professor retorted. "And, plus, they didn't smell as bad, which is probably something close to a fact."

"This is an interesting and useful conversation," said Deputy Head Porter, patience personified. "But I think perhaps that Pascal's father should be afforded a little more respect, especially if we want him to show us the dungeons."

"Papa will not show you the dungeons, never!" Pascal exclaimed.

"They why the buggery are we following you about?" asked The Dean, a bit put out.

"Because... I want to help you." Pascal looked about uncertainly and lowered his voice. "You are knights from England! I know of the legend... that one day, the Templar will return..."

"Oh, but we're not..." The Dean was cut short by a swift foot in the shin from Professor Fox.

"Our mission is, of course, top secret," the Professor continued, winking knowingly at Pascal. "Which is why I can say no more than that we appreciate your help very much. Why, you might even be a knight yourself, one day."

A rosy flush erupted across his wan cheeks and Pascal emitted a small, excited sound and his eyes shone with delight. Quickening his pace, he beckoned them onwards across a grand but dusty and unused flagstoned hall and towards a small door at the far end.

"I think you may have deliberately misled our young friend, Professor," whispered Deputy Head Porter.

"Maybe just a bit, but then again kinda not. I mean to say, who's to say I'm not a knight? Some knights are secret. Maybe no one would tell me if I was. And, you know, The Dean is sorta like a knight. Violent, anyway."

Deputy Head Porter shrugged. It was a reasoning that didn't make any sense, but at least it was delivered with style.

They followed Pascal through the little door and down a cobwebby and somewhat neglected staircase. At the bottom, there were a few twists and turns along what appeared to be seldom-used corridors before they finally emerged into a dimly-lit wood panelled room. At the far end was an elderly door and on the nearest wall were some badly hung paintings.

"What is this place?" asked The Dean, looking around and pulling a bit of a face.

"Through there is the way to the dungeons," replied Pascal, pointing towards the door. "I can take you no further! If Papa finds out..."

"Hush and a few, don't worry," Professor Fox soothed, bending down a little to bring his mega-watt smile level with the boy's troubled face. "We shan't breathe a word about any of it. In fact, I shall deny to my dying day that I ever met you. Alright?"

"*Monsieur*, you are most kind. But now I fear I am of little help. The door, it is locked. My father has the only key."

"Only one key?" asked Deputy Head Porter, raising her eyebrows. She would have liked to have raised just one, enigmatic, eyebrow, but it was a skill that eluded her. "Are you sure?"

"*Oui,* I am sure. Papa trusts no one else with the dungeons. There is not even one locked away in his office. I know this."

Deputy Head Porter nodded.

"Probably very wise of him. You get along now, if your father catches you with us he will be quite cross, I imagine. Thank you for your help."

Pascal smiled weakly and scurried off, grateful to have been of assistance, but equally pleased to be released from any impending danger. The Dean sighed. He began to pace, his focus fixed upon the door.

"I see what you're about," said the Professor. "You're going to break that down, aren't you?"

"Well of course I'm going to break it down!" snapped The Dean. "How else are we going to get into the dungeons?"

"That won't be necessary," said Deputy Head Porter.

"You heard the boy, there's only one key!"

Deputy Head Porter shook her head.

"I'll guarantee you there isn't," she said. "There's obviously something down there our friend The Curator doesn't want anyone else messing about with. Something important. Something he himself likes to keep an eye on. What if his one and only key breaks? Or he loses it? There's got to be another one. He might not feel confident about keeping it with the other keys, but there'll be one. Trust me. I'm a Porter."

Deputy Head Porter cast her eye around the room. It was empty apart from the three crooked paintings on the other wall. It was obvious from the state of the passages and the room itself that very few people came down this way. She walked over to the doorframe and started to feel with her fingers along and around it. This achieved nothing but a splinter in her thumb. Sucking the stricken digit, she went over to the paintings and stood before them, looking thoughtful for a moment. All three were covered in dust and cobwebs. But the middle one had a small pile of detritus on the floor beneath one corner. Deputy Head Porter smiled.

She tilted the painting and looked behind.

"Aha!"

She returned, grinning, brandishing a key.

"Wowawee, DHP! But how did you..?"

"It's impossible for there to be only one key. Far too risky. But if The Curator *tells* everyone there's only one key, no one will look for a spare, will they? So he pops it down here, where no one ever comes, because no one else has got a key to the door and there's nothing else in the room anyway. You can see where the dust and whatnot has been knocked off the painting where he checks every so often that the key is where it should be."

"That's using your noodle, DHP."

Deputy Head Porter tapped the side of her head.

"No, Professor - that's thinking like a Porter!"

LIFE AFTER DEATH

Through a swirling fog that looked like white noise and above a thin roar that sounded like grey, a wisp of something that was once Head Porter thought to it itself:

Oh. So this is what it feels like to die. Rather disappointing, I wasn't expecting that. I suppose most people aren't. Oh. Well, I'll miss Porter's wedding, then. Shame. I'd got new socks for that.

I wonder what happens next? How soon 'til I can start haunting people, d'you think?

Don't ask me, I'm you.

Good point.

Well. It feels a bit like velvet, this. Not so bad. And at least now I am free from all worry, ills and pain...

Allowing its face to sink deeper into the velvety warmth, the wisp became concerned. It was pretty sure it shouldn't have a face, for a start. And, actually, it wasn't so sure about being completely free from pain. In fact, some bits hurt quite a lot. The shoulder, for example. And one knee was throbbing with some insistence. It couldn't really say that it was free from all ills, either. Certainly not in the stomach. Surely death shouldn't be quite as bilious as this. Very bilious, in fact...

"Stand back! Oh, no..."

"It's gone all over your lovely scarf, Headmistress."

"You're treading in a bit, Dr Martens."

"Bugger."

Head Porter's eyes snapped open, red rimmed and streaming. He coughed out a little bit of carrot. He made a feeble attempt to lift his head from its resting place of The Headmistress' purple velvet scarf, before it was carefully forced back by a gentle hand.

"Am I dead?" he asked.

"You will be, if The Bursar sees what you've done to his floor," replied Dr Martens, looming over him, but at a distance that allowed sufficient room for the unpleasantness to go about its business of oozing.

Head Porter turned his head and, for a moment, thought that he must have surely passed through the pearly gates. Gazing back at him were two pools of glittering blue, set in a the most beautiful face, radiant in its loveliness despite the creases of concern. Concern - for him! Had he not just reincarnated his breakfast; this would have been a very romantic moment. Head Porter at once wanted to open his heart to The Headmistress, having been so close to death he wanted, now, to live - live with every fibre of his being!

Instead he burped. The Headmistress stepped back.

"I'm going to fetch Nurse," said Dr Martens.

"Nooo!" implored Head Porter, his voice a broken squeal. "I'm feeling much better now, I promise."

This was something of an overreaction from Head Porter, as the Old College Nurse was a kindly if direct woman, although she had little sympathy for patients who had anything less than a limb hanging off. The Headmistress took hold of his wrist and concentrated.

"His pulse has settled down. And he has got a bit of colour back in his cheeks."

"Yes! That's right! I've just had a funny turn."

"You've had too much coffee!" scolded Dr Martens. "I did warn you. Now see what's happened. Look, there's a bit on my boot."

Dr Martens had plenty more to say in relation to this incident but satisfied herself with the narrowing of an eye and some expert tutting.

And in fact, Head Porter did feel quite a bit better. Senses regained, he sat himself up and wiped his chin on the cuff of his jacket.

"I'm sorry about your scarf," he said to The Headmistress. "What are you doing here, anyway? Were you looking for me?"

"Well... in a way," she replied, with the kindness one reserves for the simple or infirm. "I was just having a wander about your beautiful College!"

"She wasn't here to see The Dean," Dr Martens said quickly. "So I didn't have to tell her to go away. That's right, isn't it?"

Head Porter's face split into a toothy, lop-sided grin.

"Oh, yes, Dr Martens, that's right," he replied, dreamily. "You must never tell The Headmistress to go away."

"It was lucky I was here, wasn't it! Although I'm sure Dr Martens was absolutely in control of the matter. I just happened to be passing when I heard the most awful thud. And here we are."

"Well, if you're sure you're feeling better..." ventured Dr Martens.

"Yes! Yes, quite better, thank you."

"In that case, there's the other thing."

"What other thing?" Head Porter asked.

"The Bursar thing," Dr Martens replied. "His big hole has nothing in it and he clearly isn't here."

"If he's not here, that's good!" Head Porter said.

"No it isn't," Dr Martens shook her head. "If he's not here, then he must be somewhere else."

"Very good reasoning. I can see why they made you a Fellow."

"The place he probably is, is wherever the Holy Grail might be."

"You mean... the same Holy Grail Deputy Head Porter has gone looking for?" Head Porter creased his brow.

"Unless you can think of another Holy Grail - yes."

"You've gone pale again, Head Porter..."

"No, no, Headmistress, I'm fine, I promise." Head Porter did not look fine. "I mean, she'll be alright though, won't she? I mean - Deputy Head Porter can look after herself. And she's got The Dean and Professor Fox with her."

Dr Martens raised an eyebrow and folded her arms.

"Oh my God, you're right." Head Porter swallowed hard. The remnants in his throat made him regret this instantly. "They're completely and utterly done for, aren't they?"

FOOTSTEPS OF THE TEMPLAR

Thunk-thunk Click!

The lock released and with some trepidation Deputy Head Porter placed an unsteady hand on the gnarled surface of the ancient door. It was almost as if the heartbeat of a thousand years of history could be felt through the elderly wood, prickling her fingertips in a desperate attempt to make itself know. In a fleeting moment she felt the forlornly discarded liberty of the many unfortunate souls who'd passed through this portal before her, on their final journey to the Chateau's dungeons; the last vestiges of hope clinging still to the oaken frame.

Hope does not die. No matter how much darkness surrounds it, it is the last spark of light that refuses to go out.

The realisation that she'd be treading the very path taken by the Knights Templar so many years ago filled Deputy Head Porter with an overwhelming sense of grim veneration and it was clear that she was not alone in this. Professor Fox laid a reassuring hand on her shoulder and even The Dean wore an expression of solemn reverence. No words were spoken. There was no need of words.

Placing her weight against the door, Deputy Head Porter found that it opened with surprising ease into a dark, stone walled passage about eight feet wide. Her hand fumbled for her trusty Maglight, a familiar thing of comfort in this foreign place. Once illuminated, she could see that the path ahead sloped downwards and slightly off to the left. The surface integrity underfoot appeared good yet proceeding with caution did seem to be prudent. And so they proceeded.

After several minutes of walking, the passage became significantly narrower and the ceiling bore down upon them. The subtle change of air as they progressed deeper was unnerving; the cloying dampness clinging to skin like spider webs. Deputy Head Porter felt a tiny voice at the back of her mind telling her that it was becoming difficult to breathe.

Now is not the time to start listening to voices in my head.

Deputy Head Porter was very aware that not one of them knew where they were headed, nor what they would find when they got there. There was a feeling in the pit of her stomach that she struggled to identify. It couldn't be described as fear, exactly, nor could she swear to it being excitement. It was not entirely pleasant.

"Professor?" she called out, softly, her voice sounding alien and remote.

"Yes, DHP?"

"Um. Do you mind... do you mind if I hold your hand? Just for a bit. I feel funny."

"Well, sure you can!" the Professor replied, reaching out and tucking her sweaty paw into his own. "You should know, The Dean and I have been holding hands for the last five minutes."

"That's only because I can't see where I'm going!" The Dean shouted back, curtly. "It's very dark back here, you know."

"You would be very welcome to be at the front with the torch!" Deputy Head Porter shouted back. There was a pause.

"A sturdy rear defence is of the utmost importance, Deputy Head Porter! Onwards, if you please!"

"Give me that dadblame torch," Professor Fox suggested, kindly. "I shall go at the front, since monsters usually take the people from the middle.

Just kidding. Besides, someone needs to keep an eye on The Dean back there and you, Deputy Head Porter, have far more experience in that field than I do."

They switched places and Deputy Head Porter did her best to suppress the growing nausea that threatened the back of her throat. *I cannot imagine what is wrong with me. I'm usually quite brave in these situations.*

"Let's sing a song to lift our spirits!" said the Professor.

"Splendid idea!" The Dean replied. "I suggest *Paradise By The Dashboard Light* by Meatloaf."

"That's not very appropriate, given the circumstances, Sir," Deputy Head Porter said quickly, before he could break into song. "Surely something like *Onward Christian Soldiers* would be more like it?"

"Does it have a guitar solo?"

"It could have!" the Professor chimed in. "It could go something like... oh hey, now, what do we have here?"

Deputy Head Porter walked straight into the back of Professor Fox, who had planted himself stock still in the centre of the passageway. In turn, The Dean crashed into her, creating a sort of Porter sandwich. Peeking around the Professor, Deputy Head Porter could see a squat, arched porchway or entrance into what could only be the dungeons.

This is it!

The Professor strode forward with confidence, only slightly perturbed that he had to crouch a little to pass through the archway. There was a mumble of discontent as he took off his fedora. Deputy Head Porter followed through with no such hinderance, being only slight larger than a small child (or slightly smaller than a large child). Rather unexpectedly, The Dean made a strikingly dramatic entrance involving a combat roll and a rallying cry.

Struggling to his feet, The Dean appeared to have over-done it somewhat and treated the world in general to some of his more colourful expletives. Clutching his back, he hobbled about in a circle, accompanied by a series of cracks and twangs. Sighing, Professor Fox sadly knocked dust off his hat.

"It's a sad day when a gentleman has to involuntarily remove his own hat," he said to himself.

Deputy Head Porter looked around her, her eyes slowly adjusting to the gloom. They were standing in a cavernous room, the ceiling concealed somewhere high above in the murk. She thought there might be things hanging there but shut down her imagination before it ran away with her. It was certainly a dungeon. They were in the right place - in so far as, they were exactly where they wanted to be. But very little felt *right* about it.

"Well, then, gentlemen," she said, hands on hips and upper lip stiffened in the traditional fashion. "Here we are."

"And seeing as we are here," continued The Dean, "I expect we had better make ourselves useful and start searching for clues!"

Ah, The Dean's love of searching for clues is unshakeable, thought Deputy Head Porter. *Although, often ineffective. It's a good job these chaps have me with them, I tell you.*

DUNGEON MASTERS

It is interesting to note that even the grimmest of situations can be greatly improved by the business of having something practical to attend to. Searching for clues had become something of a favourite pastime of The Dean and he now engaged himself in this endeavour with cheerful aplomb. He had some early success, it must be said, with the discovery of a switch that, when pressed, revealed the presence of some ineffective - yet very welcome - lighting.

The dungeons seemed far less ominous when bathed in the grubby orange glow of badly installed synthetic lighting and parts of the stonework even appeared rather beautiful, in Deputy Head Porter's opinion. There were some curiously shaped holes scattered about the walls which her logically thinking brain told her that, at some point in history, may have hosted instruments of nefarious means. The fact such instruments no longer remained was of little comfort.

Professor Fox had vanished into the gloom, but his manic humming could be heard from further along the chamber. The Dean was strutting up and down a segment of wall, occasionally thumping a selected area with his fist. Deputy Head Porter observed this and dreaded to think what purpose it served, but he seemed so intent on his work that she thought it better not to ask. There was a strange atmosphere down there, certainly. The undertone of residual sorrow from centuries past was tangible still, but there was something far more recent hanging in the stilted air. Deputy Head Porter couldn't quite put her finger on it. It was something far less distressing than she expected. Perhaps the dungeons had seen happier times since their macabre heyday.

"AHA!" a triumphant cry from deep within the chamber came from the Professor. "Hey goodness!

You won't believe me if I tell you, but I'm going to tell you anyway - I think I've found something!"

"Well done, that man!" cried The Dean. "Come on, Deputy Head Porter, look lively!"

Increasing the pace of his strut significantly, The Dean headed towards Professor Fox, Deputy Head Porter trotting obediently behind. There was a thumping in her chest and ringing in her ears as the prospect of moving closer to the Grail fuelled her fervour.

The Professor was crouched down in a little enclave within the wall, poking excitedly at something. He turned his face upwards to deliver a mega-watt victorious grin.

"Look-y here!"

Deputy Head Porter moved to take a peek but was shoved unceremoniously out of the way by The Dean.

"Well, bugger me!" exclaimed The Dean.

"I'm sure you don't mean that, Sir."

"Are those not the same carvings we saw back in the Crypt? A clue illustrated by symbols!"

"Exactly right!" replied Professor Fox. "And the ones from the cave. They're everywhere over these walls, can you believe."

"That's the symbol of the Wastell Templars," gasped Deputy Head Porter. "They really did make it all the way to Chinon!"

"Yes, and got themselves captured," remarked The Dean, bluntly.

"Then the Grail was definitely here!" squealed the Professor, hopping to his feet and doing what could be described as a small dance. "I'm so excited I can't even say how much."

"This is brilliant!" replied Deputy Head Porter. "Come on, keep looking."

She turned on her heels to continue the search and her boot connected with something sort of squishy. From beneath the boot, a hideous screech emerged, and the squishy thing made a sharp exit. Deputy Head Porter glanced down just in time to see a large rat careening off into the gloom beyond. *Ick!*

"Mind how you go, Deputy Head Porter," said The Dean, frowning.

Suddenly, there sounded an almighty *CRASH!* followed by the gentle tinkling of breaking glass. Eyebrows raised, the three exchanged curious glances and headed together towards the noise, the sounds of their footsteps echoing off the dungeon walls providing a suitably tense soundtrack.

"Well! Would you look at that?" exclaimed Professor Fox. "What is it, do you think?"

The scene before them was most unexpected. The rat, in making its escape, appeared to have collided dramatically with what Deputy Head Porter recognised as a rather elaborate home-brewing set-up. Smashed demijohns laid despondently among the tubes and bungs and a strong-smelling sticky liquid.

"No wonder the Curator is so particular about who visits the dungeons," she said. "He seems to have a little moonshine venture going on down here!"

"Enterprising," said The Dean, allowing himself a little smile. "I'll say that for him."

Before further comment could be passed, Professor Fox held up a hand to hush them into silence. Placing a finger to his lips, his eyes wide, he indicated furiously back towards the way they came.

And then they heard it.

Footsteps.

Someone knows we are here.

A REPUTATION THAT PRECEDES

As the sound of approaching footsteps grew louder, Deputy Head Porter held her breath. Which was an unlikely thing to be doing, when she might need the extra oxygen for running or fighting at any moment. It is a perfectly natural human reaction to such things, but a remarkably stupid one.

"I bet things are going to get pretty spiced up in here," whispered Professor Fox. "I'm thinking I should put down my hat so it will be safe."

"Never mind your blasted hat," replied The Dean. "We need a plan. Whatever it is that comes for us, I say we attack it all at once. I shall go for the head, since I am the tallest."

"I'll go for the neck, since I'm almost as tall," said the Professor. "Plus, it's a soft target. You go for the head, if you must. Maybe the arms? They're more lethal than the head, after all. DHP should concentrate on the knees."

"Might I propose an initially non-violent approach?" suggested Deputy Head Porter. "We are British, after all."

"Well, I'm something of an American, overall," replied the Professor. "Violence is a past time where I come from."

The Dean looked set to put forward his case for unfettered ferocity but there was no time. The pursuer was upon them.

The footsteps came to an abrupt halt as their owner stopped dead, an initial look of surprise soon replaced by an eye-roll of resignation.

"Oh. I might have guessed."

"Buggering hell!" exclaimed The Dean.

"Hello, Chief Inspector," said Deputy Head Porter. "This is a surprise."

"No, it really isn't," sighed DCI Thompson. "Any sign of trouble and it's bound to be you lot. What are you doing down here?"

"Don't tell him!" cried the Professor. "It could be a trick."

DCI Thompson shook his head, exasperated. He would have liked to have said that his holiday had been going so well up until that point, he really would. But save for a few blissful hours taking photographs, Old College had managed to blight almost every waking moment.

"More to the point, what are *you* doing here?" asked The Dean.

"Well, would you believe, I was having a look round the chateau, taking photos, when I spotted a very distressed young fellow darting out of a corridor. He looked in quite a state. He was off before I could grab him, so I thought I'd see where he'd come from, perhaps ascertain the source of his distress."

"Oh, that would have been Pascal," replied The Dean, airily. "Dreadfully delicate lad. Shook like a leaf every time I so much as spoke to him."

"Hmm..." DCI Thompson examined The Dean with his best detective stare before continuing. "So anyway, I went along this little warren of corridors and arrived in the dusty room back up there. I was about to give up the thing as a bad job all round, when I heard a smashing noise and general commotion, so I kicked in the door and headed down here."

"There was no need to kick in the door," said Deputy Head Porter, reproachfully. "I'd already unlocked it."

"Well I realised that, obviously, but only after I'd put my boot through it."

"Kicking in doors is kinda what you do in times like that," remarked Professor Fox. "I don't suppose anyone'd mind. Except people who like really old doors."

"That was MY really old door!"

All four swung round to be met with a vision significantly more surprising that Detective Chief Inspector Thompson. A shiny white dome of a head was decorated dramatically with a black leather patch that covered his left eye. An angry-looking purple scar snaked from the socket down towards a jaw that looked as though it had been fashioned from granite. The right ear was missing. He stood at over six feet tall.

"Could it be... the Curator?" Professor Fox barely managed to say.

"GET HIM!" roared The Dean and at once there was a fearsome rush of air as he and Professor Fox charged headlong towards the Curator, watched open-mouthed by Deputy Head Porter and the Chief Inspector. The element of surprise served them well and their adversary came crashing to the ground beneath a flurry of fists and expletives. But the Curator was clearly a man well-versed in the art of war and it was not long before he was thrashing around on the floor, viciously fighting back.

DCI Thompson watched with interest; this was one of the more unusual fights to which he had been witness. Deputy Head Porter felt that she should be doing something to help, but the maelstrom of flailing limbs was somewhat off-putting. The Professor's hat rolled off into the spilt moonshine, so she scooped it up before it got too sticky. No doubt he would thank her for that, later.

"For goodness sake, Deputy Head Porter, DO something!" shouted The Dean, wrestling with an arm the size of a tree trunk and evidently losing.

"Yes, blind him in his eye!" Professor Fox yelled. "The thing about being blinded is... you can't fight... what you can't... see."

Well, thought Deputy Head Porter. *I don't think I've ever blinded a man in my life. And he's only got one good eye as it is, so that seems a bit unfair. Perhaps a temporary blinding is in order.*

Now, it is well documented that in times of stress and excitement, the human brain does not function as well as it should. Which may go some way to explaining what Deputy Head Porter did next. With the intention of temporarily blinding the Curator at the very forefront of her mind, she gamely bounded over to the seething mass of human flesh, locked in mortal combat, and placed her posterior squarely on the face of the adversary, making sure to completely cover his one good eye. This obviously came as quite a surprise to the Curator, who let out a very unusual sound before attempting to bite the offending behind.

Deputy Head Porter deftly manoeuvred herself so that her cheeks remained unchomped, but it quickly became apparent that this was not a very good idea, overall.

"I just think this is making matters worse, to be honest," she said. "Are you sure a non-violent approach wouldn't be better?"

The Dean, red-faced and panting, turned his face to that of the Curator's, the part which wasn't obscured by buttocks.

"What d'you say old chap, have you had enough? What say we talk this through like gentlemen, hmm?"

"I shall agree to whatever terms you suggest, *monsieur!*" rasped the Curator. "But please remove this woman from my head!"

Deputy Head Porter leapt up, pleased that her role in the action was at an end. The chaps seem to have exhausted themselves with their tussling and gingerly clambered to their feet, watched by an increasingly amused DCI Thompson. Once breath had been caught and balance restored, a degree of more refined discussion could begin. The Curator regarded them warily with his one remaining eye and wore an expression of unease.

"Before anyone says anything, I'd just like to point out that this is absolutely nothing to do with me," said DCI Thompson. "Whatever this lot are up to is entirely their business. I'm just here on holiday. Trying to be on holiday, anyway."

"But it was you, was it not, that broke my lovely door?"

"I think we may have all got off on the wrong foot," said Deputy Head Porter, in her best diplomatic voice. The one she used on The Dean when he was especially animated. Sometimes it worked.

"*Mon dieu!* If you interfere with a man's winemaking, then what is it that you expect?!"

"That was *wine?*" muttered The Dean, eyeing the remains of the stricken brewery.

"What are you doing with wine in a dungeon?" asked the Professor, accompanying his words with his second-best smile. "Too good for prisoners. But, here's the thing - we didn't do anything. It was a rat that did it."

"Do not take me for an imbecile!" spat the Curator. "I know that you are here to steal the secrets of the finest wine in France. You English winemakers cannot compete. You know it! You three ruffians..."

"I've never made wine once, let alone in a Dungeon," protested Professor Fox. "Plus, I'm not English. Promise. Double promise. We are adventurers!"

"You may be the widow's son, but we are not three ruffians. We are academics," The Dean chimed in, trying to add some gravitas to proceedings. "From Old College, in England. What we seek certainly isn't wine..."

"Although, if you happen to have a bottle to hand, I wouldn't say no," said Deputy Head Porter. *Well, you never know. Besides, I'm parched.*

"Old College? Old College?!" the Curator's reaction suggested that he might have heard of that esteemed establishment. Although, the clenching of his fists and the protruding of the veins on his neck implied that whatever he had heard, wasn't good. "You filthy, English pig-dogs!"

"You know, I may have brought this up before, I'm Ameri..."

"*Silence!* You - you people take from me the most precious thing that exists and now, all these years later, you return! And destroy my wine! I hoped I would never again hear the name of your cursed College as long as I lived!"

"Someone from Old College has obviously rubbed him up the wrong way," said Deputy Head Porter. She turned to The Dean. "Have you been here before, Sir?"

"Not me," replied The Dean. "But we're certainly missing something, here. What could it be?"

THE SINS OF THE FATHER

"Now, wait there just a minute!" The Dean was on fine form and displaying his preferred expression of outraged indignation. "You say someone from Old College has been here before?"

"*Oui,* it is true," replied the Curator, glaring as furiously as a chap can, when he only has one eye. "It was many years ago when I was little more than an *enfant.* My father was the Curator then and I helped him in his work as best I could. *Mais,* he was a difficult man to please and the weighty burden of his disappointment was laid upon my shoulders each and every day..."

The Curator was lost for a moment in a bitter reverie and it was almost possible to see the shadow of the hurt little lad behind the leathery crags of a face that showed a life hard lived.

Deputy Head Porter thought of Pascal and wondered if history was not repeating itself.

"Yes, yes, never mind about that," continued The Dean. "What about our mysterious predecessor?"

The Curator spat on the floor and muttered something unintelligible in his mother tongue. Deputy Head Porter sniffed. She couldn't help thinking that, although providing a suitably dramatic backdrop, the dungeon might not be the very best place to continue this form of verbal intercourse. There was a funny smell - either from the rat or the spilt wine - and the place was generally starting to feel oppressive.

"Must we really stand around here in the dungeon?" she asked, annoyed at how whiny her voice sounded. "I mean, surely there is somewhere nicer we could have a chat?" *Somewhere with some tea, maybe cake,* she didn't add out loud.

A wicked smile cracked the Curator's face and a sinister little chuckle echoed around the *oubliette*.

"Hehe! But you forget, *jeune fille,* perhaps I have good reason to keep you here in my dungeon!"

"Goodness!" exclaimed Professor Fox. "Haven't you ever heard? It isn't nice to threaten people, you know. Once one starts threatening, one begins to be in danger of getting a bop on the nose. And now that you bring it up, I can't think of any good reason to be kept in a dungeon. Perhaps only if you're hunting rats."

The Curator shrugged.

"The reasons are good for me, perhaps for you they are not so good. *Pas mon probleme.*"

The Dean was an interesting shade of puce and the Professor flexed his fists in the manner of one who is absent-mindedly livid. Even DCI Thompson had adopted a serious-looking stance. Deputy Head

Porter flicked her gaze between them. If she wasn't careful, fisticuffs could resume at any moment.

"I'll have you know I am a very senior and highly respected member of Her Majesty's Constabulary," said the Chief Inspector, chin jutting and finger wagging ominously. "Any attempt to detain me unlawfully will be met with dire consequences, I assure you!"

"Okay, okay," Deputy Head Porter spluttered. "Let's just keep this friendly, shall we? Now, as far as dungeons go, this really is not a bad one. Let's stay in the dungeon, then. But can we please come to the point of this expeditiously as I am rather in need of a cup of tea. And, as it happens, a wee."

This thinly-veiled threat moved things on a little. Reluctantly, the Curator recounted an amazing tale. It would appear that decades ago, an unidentified Fellow from Old College did indeed come to the Chateau de Chinon. They, too, were searching for the Holy Grail and also found themselves in the very same dungeon. What's more, the Curator said, bitterly, they were successful!

"You mean to say that the Holy Grail really was sequestered here?" The Dean exclaimed, a mixture of disbelief and triumph fighting for space on his face.

"*Oui,* it is so," the Curator replied, nodding sagely. "The Knights Templar hid cunningly the Grail in these very catacombs before they were executed. Your foregoer must have had such esoteric knowledge that none before could call upon as he found the Grail and stole it away, back to your cursed College! The swine."

"Goodness me and then some!" Professor Fox was somewhere between astonished and bewildered. "I can't believe - not for a moment, mind you - that the Grail isn't here, but rather back at Old College! I just tired my legs for no reason, it means."

"But who was it that came here?" asked Deputy Head Porter, wondering if they were still among The Fellowship.

The Curator shook his head.

"I do not know, I myself never saw him. My father refused to speak of it again, such was the shame that this thing had happened. Not even he knew exactly where the Grail was hidden and for it to be taken by an outsider... an Englishman at that... the dishonour was too much for him."

"Then what happened?" Deputy Head Porter continued.

"My father took to the wine and was never the same again. His passing followed quickly, leaving my mother a widow." replied the Curator, melancholia dripping from every word. "Soon after, I left this place to join the army and become a man."

"I can't believe it... were you once a woman?" asked the Professor, innocence personified. Deputy Head Porter tried to prevent his words coming out by deploying a sharp elbow to the ribs, but she was too late.

"That is of no interest to me," snapped The Dean. "What we need to know is - who took the Grail and where is it now?"

"I'm thinking, you know, that overall, we really should have got that earring."

The Curator fell silent. Whether the morose memories of sad times held his tongue, or the unusual dialogue of Professor Fox, it is hard to say.

A sudden icy zephyr cut through the dank air.

Deputy Head Porter felt the hairs on the back of her neck prickle, and she felt his presence before she saw him.

What the devil is HE doing here?

When it came, the voice was darkly familiar; the undertones of malice unmistakeable.

"That is precisely what I intend to uncover..."

THE PRISONER OF CHINON

Emanating grim mordacity from the top of his raven-haired head to the very tips of his elegant Italian shoes, The Bursar emerged from the gloom. A mirthless smile clung spitefully to his lips as he appeared to bathe in irascible delight at the collective consternation in the dungeon.

"Well, this isn't entirely a surprise, Sir," said Deputy Head Porter, arms folded defiantly and a frown firmly in place.

"And even if it was, it wouldn't be a good one, neither," muttered Professor Fox.

"Deputy Head Porter, you disappoint me," The Bursar replied. "Have you not missed your Bursar during your Gallic gallivanting?"

"Who is this ridiculous-looking man?" asked the Curator, notably unimpressed by the new arrival.

Deputy Head Porter leaned towards DCI Thompson and whispered - "You see? I told you ages ago that chap was creepy. You should have listened."

"Being creepy *still* isn't a crime, Deputy Head Porter. Mind you, I do take your point."

"I say to you now, *garçon,* that you must be careful how you form your subsequent utterances," purred The Bursar. "For it would be distressing to me if you were to embarrass yourself in the presence of your betters."

The Curator furrowed his brow in concentration. His English might well be perfect, but The Bursar's curious communication style is baffling even to a native.

"You know," said Professor Fox "Don't pick on him too much. For one thing, he doesn't like Old College a whole lot as it is. For another thing, those shoes are going to get ruined if you're not careful."

"He is another filthy pig-dog," The Dean pointed out, helpfully. "Like us, from Old College. Although what the bugger is doing here is anyone's guess, quite frankly."

"Searching for the Holy Grail, just the same as you, The Dean."

"Hold on for a few," said the Professor, raising an eyebrow. "So you really are admitting we were right all along? That digging up Mr Dean's garden was all dadblamery? Yeah. I just knew it. Even DHP knew it, you know."

The Bursar exulted a cheerless chortle. DCI Thompson huffed and turned to Deputy Head Porter.

"This is all rather irritating, to be honest," he whispered. "I mean, who does he think he is? Some sort of arch-villain or something?"

"Perhaps he is," shrugged Deputy Head Porter. "He's certainly got the haircut for it."

"Can it really be ruminated that I would postulate the presence of the Grail beneath Apple Tree Court?" The Bursar paused for dramatic effect, which was helpful as it gave everyone a chance to gather what he was saying. "That was an aberration of devilish design. You see, I have no intended persuasions of allowing a thing as inestimable as the Holy Grail to remain in a rancorous hovel such as Old College."

"I say. That's a bit harsh!" remarked the Professor.

"You stinking great *bugger!*" roared The Dean, purple with rage. "How dare you. I've a bloody good mind to smack you one, I tell you."

"Silence, pig-dog!" The Bursar retorted.

"Yes, hush," said Deputy Head Porter. "With any luck, he might just reveal the intricacies of his fiendish plan before vowing to kill us all. Things seem to be heading that way, at least."

"How predictable," sighed the Chief Inspector. "What these arch-villains really lack is a sense of originality. No imagination."

"Hmm, that seems something of a risk," replied The Dean, stroking his chin thoughtfully. "I am not in the mood to be killed. But I am rather interested to hear about the plan."

"I say we hear about the plan," suggested the Professor. "After that, we'll follow our noses, sort of thing. Definitely avoid getting killed."

"There is absolutely no way I am ending my days at the hands of a third-rate Bond baddie," said the Chief Inspector. "For goodness sake. Let me deal with this."

"For many years I have been assembling my wits for this occasion," continued The Bursar, as his reluctant audience effected a collective eye-roll. "Even forging partialities that stretched for decades, spent in order to find the true resting place of the Holy Grail. But it is not for the glory of Old College that I do this, nor even the sublimity of my own person - no!"

"Is he doing it for his shoes?" The Professor asked no one in particular.

"Oh, your snivelling Master will receive a Grail from the very bowels of his paltry brain factory, a thing to satisfy his lust for dignity. As they dig the ground now, my men will place such an article in a place to be found - like a trinket in the sand!"

"Do you mean to say that you have been digging up the lawns knowing full well that the Grail isn't even there?" huffed The Dean. "Head Gardener is going to be absolutely furious about this, you know. There's a man who knows how to handle a rake, I warn you."

"He will never know a thing about it," sneered The Bursar, really getting a feel for the situation. "The tongues to tell him shall be silenced this very day. The authentic Grail shall immediately be dispatched to my superiors in my motherland while the illegitimate bauble shall be lauded by the asinine thinkers of your fatuous institution."

The Bursar finally drew breath and stood, arms outstretched, and head thrown back, posing theatrically and awaiting the expected horrified response from the room. There was a brief flurry of whispered discussion as those gathered tried to get to the bottom of what, actually, The Bursar's monologue had been about. Eventually, The Dean gamely had a stab at it.

"I think I see what this is," he began, nodding. "You are going to have an imitation Grail placed among the diggings at Old College, whilst sending the real Grail back to some unspecified country - although not too hard to guess which one, as presumably you have come from there as a spy and purveyor of other such nefarious duties?"

"Also, I am going to kill you all."

"Very cunning," said Deputy Head Porter, unfazed.

"Like I said. Predictable." DCI Thompson folded his arms and felt quite smug.

"The only problem is," continued Deputy Head Porter "is that we haven't actually got the Grail. Sorry about that."

"What?"

"*Oui,* it is true," agreed the Curator. "The Grail, she was taken from here many years ago, stolen away to your confounded College."

"Curses!"

"Now, now Bursar," said Deputy Head Porter. "No one actually ever says 'curses'."

"Silence, wench. There is no further recourse left open to me but to slaughter you all where you stand."

"I am sure - if you had a good many thinks on the matter - you could come up with another option" - but the Professor's words fell on deaf ears.

The Bursar advanced.

But he didn't get very far.

DCI Thompson strode towards the murderous academic and launched his fist squarely at his face with such ferocity that it seemed, for a moment, that The Bursar no longer had a nose. He fell to the floor, out cold.

"Apologies for that," said DCI Thompson, inspecting his reddened knuckles. "That fellow is absolutely infuriating. Deputy Head Porter, you were right, being creepy should be a crime. Mind you, it isn't, and I rather fear I've landed us in a bit of a pickle, here."

"*Mes amis,*" the Curator said, his voice soft and low. "I do not know who this man is, but he is a dangerous lunatic, certainly. He must never lay his crazy hands upon the Holy Grail. I bring to you now an offer. I shall keep him here in my dungeon until we have forgotten all about him. You shall return to England and say nothing of this matter."

"That's jolly good of you," said The Dean, affably.

"But in return you must make me a promise," the Curator licked his lips and his voice cracked just barely. "You must swear to return the Grail to Chinon if ever you find where in your College it is hidden. *Convenu?*"

The Dean held out his hand and fixed the Curator with a hardy gaze.

"I shall level with you, sir. You have my word."

The Curator accepted his hand and shook it vigorously.

"Very well. It is done. Hurry now, from this place, return with speed to merry England. But -

never forget the bargain you have made with me here this day."

"I shouldn't think we'll be likely to forget anything about this day in a hurry" replied Deputy Head Porter.

There was little else for it but to do as The Curator had said. The four of them hastened from the dungeons and the Chateau itself, minds reeling from the day's events, unlikely even by the standards of Old College veterans. It would all make for interesting conversation on the journey home, at least. And home had never felt so very far away.

HEAD PORTER'S DISCOVERY

"Are you sure you're feeling alright, Head Porter?"

"He should probably have a bit of a lie down."

Dr Martens and the Headmistress struggled to keep up with Head Porter as he strode manfully from The Bursar's rooms, out the staircase and into the cloister. The remnants of his recent and mercifully brief period of ill-constitution were still visible on his jacket cuff, but on his face sat a resolute visage of renewed vigour. Bowler hat at a rakish angle and fists flexing, he piloted himself with uncharacteristic determination towards Apple Tree Court.

"What is he going to do, do you think?" the Headmistress asked Dr Martens, breathless, as they scurried along in Head Porter's wake.

"I'm a bit worried he's going to take on the Russians," replied Dr Martens.

"The Russians?"

"The Russians in the hole in Apple Tree Court."

"Oh I see." The Headmistress paused. "This is a remarkably unusual College."

"Yes, it's definitely that," Dr Martens replied.

"I shall see to it that more of our very best pupils come here, in that case."

Head Porter erupted from the cloister into the blazing sunshine that glared relentlessly onto Apple Tree Court. The solemn majesty of the Chapel bore down from the left and the tapering tower of the Old Library loomed from the right. In the very centre, right in the middle of the once immaculate lawn, The Bursar's hole gaped into the very bowels of Old College, overlooked reproachfully by The Dean's rooms high above. Head Porter straightened his bowler and loosened the perfectly knotted College tie around his neck.

"Right, you buggers."

Marching like a one-man army towards the crest of the hole, Head Porter filled his lungs and prepared to launch into the little speech he had been hastily putting together in his head. He wasn't going to put up with this nonsense any longer. Big holes in College. Sinister Fellows stalking his Deputy. Drunken Russians making the place look untidy. He was the Head Porter of Old College, was he not? These were not the sorts of things of which College approved. And he had had *enough.*

Polished boots planted firmly on the pit's edge and hands on hips, Head Porter drew himself up to his full height, which was not inconsiderable. In his bowler he was well over six feet tall and when not adopting his usual gait of slouched despondency, his shoulders were broad and indurate. Flinging his hardest Head Porter stare into the abyss below, he curled his lip and drew breath to release the opening roar of his announcement.

And stopped.

His snarl unfurled and slackened his jaw, while eyebrows huddled together in puzzlement.

The Bursar's hole was empty.

Well. Not *completely* empty.

Dr Martens and the Headmistress scrambled to join him by the hole and followed his gaze.

"Where are all the Russians?" asked Dr Martens.

"And what's *that?*" the Headmistress pointed.

"Bugger," said Head Porter. "I'd got a really stern speech all worked out. I was going to order those bloody drunkards out of College and have this thing filled in. I've had it up to here with that bloody Bursar. He's a wrong 'un."

"Oh, why don't you do your speech anyway?" suggested the Headmistress, as if offering encouragement to a small child. "I'd love to hear it."

"No. I'd feel silly. I want to see what that is down there, can you see it? Dr Martens, fetch a ladder."

"You can't go ordering me around like that," replied Dr Martens, although kindly. "I'm a Fellow, remember. I'm not a Porter. I'm only helping."

"It's a little known fact that Porters actually out-rank The Fellowship," remarked Head Porter. And in fact this was quite true. It's just that The Fellowship didn't know it. And, frankly, no one dared tell them. "Alright. I'll nip along to Maintenance and borrow one. You stay here and watch the hole."

As Head Porter bounded off in the direction of the Maintenance sheds, Dr Martens turned a careful eye towards the hole. It didn't look like it was about to go anywhere or do anything, but she couldn't be sure. Anything involving The Bursar was not to be trusted. Presently, Head Porter returned, swaying unsteadily beneath a set of enormous aluminium ladders.

"These should do the trick!"

Before long, Head Porter was wading through debris towards the pale-coloured item peeking out of the mud, its once glittering sheen now dulled, yet still able to catch a little of the sunlight. It came free with a couple of good tugs and Head Porter buffed it unceremoniously on his trousers. His mouth fell open and his eyes were the size of dinner plates.

"What is it?" the Headmistress called down. Head Porter turned his beaming face towards her, his brow glistening with sweat and wonder.

"I think... I think... Oooh!"

"It's an 'oooh'," said Dr Martens. "How exciting, I like an oooh. Bring it up, then!"

In his excitement, Head Porter almost fell off the ladder twice on the way back up, but eventually he managed to drag both himself and his tarnished find to the surface. They passed it between them, turning it over in their hands curiously, examining every dent and crevice. Dr Martens even sniffed it.

"Do you think this could really be it?" gasped Head Porter. "Was The Bursar really right all along? Is *this* the Holy Grail?!"

"I don't think so," replied Dr Martens.

"What? Why not?"

"It's got 'Made in Taiwan' on the bottom." She handed it back to Head Porter, who turned the thing over.

"Oh."

"But, if it's any consolation, I think someone wanted us to believe it was the Holy Grail," Dr Martens continued. "Although, someone who obviously thinks we are very stupid."

"The Bursar," Head Porter said, stiffly.

"I say, isn't this fun," trilled the Headmistress. "I never knew anything like this during my university days."

"I wonder if Deputy Head Porter has found the real Grail yet," mused Dr Martens. "Have you heard from her?"

Head Porter fumbled in his pocket for his phone. Since a recent ill-advised foray into the murky world of social media, which involved him assuming an unlikely online identity which backfired spectacularly, Head Porter had been very nervous of his phone. Even switching it on brought him out in a cold sweat.

"Oh. Yes. She's sent a text. They're on their way back, apparently. Doesn't say anything about the Grail. But at least we know they're alright."

"I think we should keep this... whatever it is... safe until they get back," suggested Dr Martens. "There's obviously something afoot."

"Good idea," agreed Head Porter. "I'll lock it in my desk. Come on, let's go back to the Lodge."

ZOMBIE CATS & WEDDINGS

They say that when you leave a place, a part of you stays behind so that there is always a little piece of you remaining. On the journey back to The City and the comforting confines of the walls of Old College, Deputy Head Porter wondered who it was that said that. *Probably the Greeks* she thought. *They were always spouting notions of that sort.* But whoever it was, it got her thinking about what she had left behind in Chinon, and whether she would ever return to collect it again. *If it's my sanity I shall probably leave it be. There are little bits of that scattered around all over the place as it is.*

One thing they certainly did leave behind was The Bursar. Deputy Head Porter was rather unnerved by what the Curator had said - about leaving him in the dungeon until they had all forgotten about him. *I'm not sure what happens after that. Will he let him out, do you think? How does that work? Something tells me that The Bursar will become a rather angry, highly educated Schrodinger's Cat.* Deputy Head Porter made the unwise decision to share her musings with with The Dean and Professor Fox, who immediately launched into a spirited debate. Whilst The Dean seemed intent on steering the conversation towards theories of quantum superposition, the Professor was much more interested in a cat that is both alive and dead at the same time. His mind translated this as a zombie cat. *Of course. What else?*

Speaking of cats, I am missing Terry very much. I do hope Head Porter has been taking good care of him.

"Now you must answer this question," said the Professor to The Dean. "If the cat is both alive and dead all at once, do you think the same thing will happen to The Bursar? Or is it just cats, do you suppose? I mean, if it did happen to The Bursar, I would be forever scared. I might die, even. Or at least, not sleep at all for a whole night. Maybe two."

"I wouldn't put anything past that sly bugger," The Dean replied. "Following us about, pouncing on our Grail and whatnot. Even if he did die, he would stay alive just out of spite. The bugger."

"Do you really think the Curator will just leave him down there in the dungeon?" asked Deputy Head Porter.

"I expect so, he gave us his word."

"I'm not sure I like the idea of a zombie Bursar," remarked the Professor, unable to shake the idea from his mind. "Are you sure we shouldn't go back? And... do something!"

"And you gave your word that we would return the Grail to Chinon, if we ever find it," continued Deputy Head Porter, ignoring the Professor. This was because she was also troubled by the thought of a zombie Bursar. "And you know, someone at Old College definitely has it."

"And, of course, that is what we shall do," replied The Dean. "We gave our word to the Curator. Of course, it had occurred to me to cross my fingers behind my back. But once the old boy showed his true nature, that he was on the level, my mind was set."

"That is very gentlemanly, Sir."

"Sometimes a chap must be a gentleman, Deputy Head Porter. Even just once or twice."

"Speaking of gentlemen - and not any more of zombie Bursars, I hope - what happened to that policeman fellow?" asked Professor Fox.

"That blasted man is no gentleman!" snapped The Dean. "Did you see the way he punched The Bursar? Like a common knave, he was. And he kicked in that lovely door, too."

"But The Bursar *was* trying to kill us," Deputy Head Porter pointed out. "And you yourself, Sir, are not averse to the kicking in of doors. Actually, you attempt it all the time and I have to stop you."

"Now what about this phoney Grail The Bursar said was hidden in the hole?" asked the Professor, keen to move on from such aggressive undertones. "Since he's not coming back, how do we explain that? Now Old College has two Grails. Rats and a heifer."

"I say we deny all knowledge of absolutely everything," The Dean replied, portentously. "At least, until we can get a feel for the waters back at College. I dread to think what has been occurring since we've been away."

"Well, at least we'll make it back in time for Porter's wedding!" Deputy Head Porter said, cheerfully.

"Awesomeness!" exclaimed the Professor. "Maybe there'll be a fight. I hope so. I could always start one, if not."

"There will be a lot of rozzers there," warned Deputy Head Porter. "That might not be a good idea."

"We should give careful thought to what we might wear," said The Dean, rather unexpectedly. "What is it they say? Something old, something new, something borrowed, something blue?"

"I think that is for the bride, Sir." Deputy Head Porter was duly ignored.

"This will be a good opportunity to give my blue trousers an outing," continued The Dean.

"Blue trousers? I am, the sudden, quite jealous. Blue is the best colour for trousers. Or anything."

"You should borrow my blue trousers, old chap - kill two birds with one stone, that way."

"I tried that once - killing two birds with one stone. I missed. Probably hit a gnat or something."

With conversations as diverse as zombie cats and wedding attire, the journey back to Old College passed as swiftly and pleasantly as one could hope. Deputy Head Porter was sure she must have nodded off once or twice as she struggled to keep track of discussions, which, to her, appeared to veer wildly from one topic to another without warning. But, of course, this could have just been typical of the eclectic communications of her travelling companions. Before it was dark, but long after her stomach had decided it was dinner time, Deputy Head Porter and her colleagues found themselves traipsing through the welcoming doors of the Porters' Lodge. There to greet them was an exasperated Head Porter, his wiry hair sticking out in all directions and a purple vein throbbing gently on his forehead.

"Head Porter, my man! What have you been about?" the Professor flung his arms wide by way of a greeting and flashed his famous smile.

Head Porter looked back at him, hoping this was not an invitation for a hug. He pulled a bit of a face. Undeterred, the Professor continued.

"You know, I should mention, you look a bit... puffy about the face. I bet this is because DHP wasn't here to take care of you. I am so sorry for taking her away that I can't even begin to say how sorry."

"I'll have you know, Professor, that I have been considerably up against it!" Head Porter attempted indignant but didn't have the energy. "There has been... there has been... Russians! And the wedding preparations! And... and..."

"You poor thing," cooed Deputy Head Porter with as much sympathy as she could muster. Which, admittedly, wasn't much, considering her own trials and tribulations. "I'm sure it's been dreadful."

"What? What?" spluttered The Dean. "We've been nearly killed! More than once! And had a fight. These things are much more dreadful, I assure you."

"Oh yes, did you find the Holy Grail?" Head Porter asked. "I've got the Grail locked in my desk."

"You have been busy, Head Porter," smiled Deputy Head Porter. "And on top of all that, you've had to take care of my Terry. I do hope he hasn't been too naughty."

Head Porter opened his mouth once or twice, but no words came out. His left eyebrow began to quiver.

"Oh, has he been really naughty?"

"I'm afraid there is... something I need to tell you about Terry..."

BRINGING DOWN THE BURSAR

Deputy Head Porter rushed through the back streets of The City, her feet stumbling once or twice on the ancient cobbles, hot little acid tears blurring her vision and stinging her cheeks. She hadn't eaten for several hours and the journey had tired her, but a crackling bundle of nervous energy propelled her along the winding alleyways and away from the Porters' Lodge. She wasn't sure where she was going. Somewhere she could hide her tears.

The tears were, she knew, unhelpful at best and at worst, melodramatic. The sharp words she had spoken in anguish to Head Porter had been uncalled for. It really wasn't his fault. Cats were a law unto themselves at the best of times and moving Terry from his own stomping ground to Head Porter's cosy terrace perhaps wasn't the best of ideas. But she was just so *upset*.

She stopped by the low wall in Scholar's Passage and sat down. She wiped her eyes and took a few deep breaths. Terry would be alright. He was an alert, nimble little fellow and resourceful, too. He certainly wouldn't be going hungry. Terry was an excellent hunter, if the numerous sticky gifts brought back to his mistress were anything to go by. Sometimes half a gift, twice as sticky, dropped onto her face while she was sleeping. No, he would be alright. Terry would turn up again when he was ready, she was sure of it. Where else was he going to get scrambled egg for breakfast at weekends? She would just have to be patient. And wait. And try not to cry again...

Deputy Head Porter was tired, and she was hungry. It had been a long day. A long few days, in fact. There was nothing else for it but to head home for a substantial dinner and a good night's sleep. She would apologise to Head Porter in the morning, when everything would seem much better.

***

A decent dinner and a proper sleep cure a lot of things. The new day did not see the return of Terry, even though Deputy Head Porter had stood out on the back step for half an hour, wafting a couple of slices of crispy bacon in the morning air. In the end, she had eaten the bacon herself and dragged herself to work, glum but trying to be hopeful. Besides, there were pressing matters at hand at Old College.

Head Porter was bustling about the Lodge first thing and had obviously got in early as he had already had at least one cup of tea before Deputy Head Porter arrived. She noticed the stained and still warm mug on the front counter. She also spotted a packet of expensive-looking coffee shoved with some force into the bin and wondered what it was doing there. Perhaps best not to ask.

She dropped her bag on her desk. Head Porter scuttled out of his office?

"Any news?"

Deputy Head Porter shook her head.

"He will turn up."

Deputy Head Porter nodded.

"Do you want to see what we found in The Bursar's hole?"

Deputy Head Porter trotted after him and over to his desk. With all the ceremony and reverence of some shamanic holy man conducting an esoteric rite of great importance, Head Porter slowly drew the battered, tarnished object from the drawer. He placed it with care upon his desk.

"We don't think it's the real one," he said. "It's got 'Made in Taiwan' on the bottom."

Deputy Head Porter picked it up and turned it over in her hands. She snorted.

"Anyone would be an idiot to think this was the actual Holy Grail," she said. "That's just typical of The Bursar. He really thinks everyone is completely stupid. A fake Grail, eh? So that means he must want to keep the real one for himself…"

"Have you seen The Bursar, by any chance?" Head Porter asked, wringing his hands. "It's just... I was searching his rooms. There was a certain amount of unpleasantness. I've got the Bedders working on it but... it still smells a bit."

Deputy Head Porter screwed up her face and all at once felt that she didn't want to know anything about this but at the same time needed to know everything.

"The most unpleasant thing about The Bursar's rooms is the fact they've got The Bursar in them!" Professor Fox sauntered through the door, teeth gleaming and blue fedora at a jaunty angle. "Well they did have. Now they don't. That's a win for our team."

"I'm no fan of The Bursar," said Head Porter. "But I much prefer it when we've got him where we can see him. He's been gone for days and I don't like it. I thought perhaps he might have gone after you..."

"We need a proper debrief about all of this," said Deputy Head Porter, putting the Terry matter to the back of her mind. "Where's The Dean?"

"He's on his way down now," replied the Professor. "Grumbling, of course. This is practically the middle of the night for The Dean."

"I've asked Dr Martens to come in too," said Head Porter. "She said something about a lecture, but I know she much prefers Portering these days. She can keep an eye on the front desk."

"Where's Porter?" asked Deputy Head Porter.

"He'll be along later," Head Porter replied. "Wedding whatnots. You know."

"We will have to close the Lodge," Deputy Head Porter said firmly. "This is important business."

"Close the Lodge? Bugger *that!*" The Dean marched into Head Porter's office, which was beginning to feel rather crowded. "The Porters' Lodge hasn't been closed in four hundred years!"

"Sir, we closed it for an hour last term because you wanted to tell us about a dream you had," replied Deputy Head Porter.

"Oh. Well. Yes. But that was very important indeed, Deputy Head Porter."

"I'll go and put the little sign up," sighed Deputy Head Porter, making her way to the front desk. On the way back she made a detour to the kitchen. Tea was going to be essential.

Dr Martens arrived as Deputy Head Porter was serving tea in Head Porter's office. The Dean had mentioned whisky but settled for a Viennese whirl, the consumption of which seemed to provide great inspiration for his vigorous re-telling of the events in Chinon. Dr Martens and Head Porter both agreed that it all sounded very exciting but were disappointed no one brought them anything from the gift shop. Ignoring this, The Dean paced the office slowly as he began his summing up.

"So you see, some Fellow as yet unidentified snatched the Holy Grail from Chinon decades ago," he said, adopting the lofty tones he employed for his students and other lesser mortals. "The Bursar's elaborate plan to plant a false Grail was, on the face of it, very cunning. But not cunning enough, looking at the bloody thing." The Dean tossed the unconvincing trinket up in the air and caught it again. "So! At present, we have no proper Grail to present to The Master. We cannot reveal details of the true scheme, as we would have to explain the disappearance of The Bursar. We can't give him this thing, of course. So! What to do, what to do?"

"Rats and a heifer," sighed Professor Fox. "I'm thinking I should have got him that earring when I first saw it, you know. Do you think the shop still has it? I'm going to check, the sudden."

"Stay where you are," instructed The Dean. "That kind of defeatist attitude isn't helping anyone."

"At least now we know what happened to The Bursar," said Head Porter, cheerily. "I was beginning to wonder. And you know who else we haven't seen in a while? The Master's Cat. You didn't happen to lock him in the dungeon too, did you?"

"I think I might have an idea," offered Dr Martens. "How about we put the fake Grail back in the hole and let someone find it. Once it is discovered to be a fake - which surely won't take very long - The Bursar will be completely discredited, and everyone will assume he is so ashamed that he has gone into hiding. Then we can try and find out what happened to the real Grail."

"Blimey, that is a very sensible and straightforward plan," exclaimed Deputy Head Porter. "Are you sure you're a member of The Fellowship?"

"You're a Porter now, aren't you, Dr Martens!" Head Porter enthused, grinning. "Oh, but there's a problem. All the Russians from the hole have gone away. Who will find the Grail? We might have to wait for someone to fall in there."

"It won't come to that," replied The Dean. "Now listen here. The Master will be expecting a report of some description about our extracurricular activities across the waters. I shall have to tell him that, regrettably, although we learned a great deal of interesting things about... things... our search was unsuccessful and to concede defeat to The Bursar. The fact that he is missing will arouse suspicion in The Master, who will no doubt send a gardening chap into the hole to have a poke about. And there we have it."

"And what say you, Mr Dean, about the rascally Fellow who stole the Grail?" asked the Professor. "Should we have words with The Master on that matter?"

"Absolutely not. We don't want the old bugger getting too interested in things. What if he decides to follow up matters with the Curator? No, we cannot risk it. We have, in effect, signed The Bursar's death warrant, remember. It might not look too good for us."

"Oh, I don't know," said Deputy Head Porter. "It's fairly traditional around here, isn't it? Fellows bumping each other off. You might even get a promotion or something."

"Even so." The Dean thought for a moment, then brightened. "It *is* jolly good that we are keeping up with traditions, though isn't it?"

"It is very good," agreed Dr Martens. "But The Master might want to release The Bursar. Which would be very bad. So better keep it quiet."

"Quite right, quite right," nodded The Dean. "We shall keep it under our hats. Now. You Porters must replace the Grail into the hole and don't hide it too well. The Professor and I shall meet with The Master this afternoon after lunch. The Bursar will be in the bad books by teatime, I tell you."

ABSENT FRIENDS

It had been two days since the return to Old College following the Grail quest of mixed fortunes. The place was in a state of heightened ebullience that Deputy Head Porter just couldn't bring herself to share. Despite the joyous undertakings of the imminent wedding of Porter and Detective Sergeant Kirby, her heart sat like a stone at the bottom of the murky waters of her very soul.

There was still no sign of Terry. Not a whisker.

On a more positive note, there had been no sign of The Bursar, either, suggesting that the Curator has remained true to his word and kept him locked deep in the Chateau's dungeons. Something remorseful nagged at the back of Deputy Head Porter's mind, whispering to her unthinking self that the disappearance of Terry was in some way retribution for the abandonment of The Bursar. She knew that it was nonsense. But it was there, nonetheless. She fidgeted at her desk in the Porters' Lodge, feeling absolutely wretched. *Where is my furry little man? Where can he be?*

She was roused from her morose reverie by the clattering of the Lodge door. Wearing a look that could sink a thousand ships, Professor Fox stomped through and dropped himself unceremoniously on her desk.

"Dear me," he said, looking carefully at her solemn countenance. "You're looking rather sad, I must say. I would hug you, but I am in no mood for it, myself. What is it? Still no word on Terry?"

She shook her head sadly, not daring to attempt speech in case tears came out instead. The Professor patted her shoulder kindly.

"Now, here's the thing: I'm sure Terry is off on an adventure - sorta like we did. See, he left because we left. Didn't want to miss out. Once he's had his fun capturing mice and boxing their ears, he'll return. All furry and quite happy. Besides, I need to be comforted at the minute. I am quite... blue."

"Well, I can put the kettle on and maybe find you a biscuit," replied Deputy Head Porter, only very slightly put out. "Aside from that, we shall have to see how it goes. What's the matter with you, anyway?"

The Professor sighed dramatically and shook his head with such vigour it looked as if his hat might topple.

"So the Gardeners - wicked things - have found the phony Grail and are parading about claiming all the credit," he growled. "The Master, of course, is beyond delighted. Completely taken in by the dadblame thing, can you believe it! He wanted to know how I enjoyed my 'holiday in France' and I'm getting rather cranky, you know. I'm this close

- and that's close - to telling him the truth, mind you."

"Don't do that," replied Deputy Head Porter, heading towards the Lodge kitchen in search of tea. "At least, not yet. There's still a very good chance the real Grail is in College somewhere! And, you know, it won't be long before he realises it's a fake."

"I know I know I know," he muttered. "But he's calling The Bursar a heroic genius! Can you believe? There was nothing heroic about how he hit the floor after the Thompson fellow socked him a good one! And there's nothing heroic about being locked in a dungeon."

Professor Fox shared some further choice observations about his fellow academics while Deputy Head Porter set about the business of preparing the tea. There was something gently salutary about that simple ceremony that she found remedial to both heart and soul. She didn't know if it was the preparation itself that was so calming, or the anticipation of the tea to come, but by the time they each had a mug of finest Assam in hand, they were both much chirpier.

"You know, I meant what I said about Terry," said the Professor, taking a generous slurp of tea. "If I was a cat, I'd be going off on adventures all the time, scaring the heck out of you. He'll turn up unexpectedly."

"Yes, I'm sure," she replied, almost meaning it. "I hope The Bursar doesn't turn up unexpectedly."

"Me too. That'd be just too scary. Nightmare inducing, in fact. You know, the other Bursar was bad enough. This one is positively awful. Must be a Bursar thing."

"You mean Junior Bursar?" asked Deputy Head Porter, thinking back to the sharp-faced little man who had caused her so many problems when she first arrived at Old College. "I didn't mind him, apart from when he tried to kill me twice. He was alright up until that point. And Senior Bursar was an admirable chap. I thought going from two Bursars to one would make life easier. Not the case, obviously."

"Not the case at all! One Bursar, twice as bad. And a Russian spy, at that. There is something cool about it all, but still, The Bursar is a rascal. Let's hope the Curator keeps a careful eye on him."

"I suppose you would keep a careful eye, if you only had the one."

This rather unkind remark at the Curator's expense caused them both to dissolve into fits of giggles, dribbling tea down their chins. As they mopped themselves with their sleeves, they were joined by a jovial Porter, grinning from ear to ear.

"There you are!" cried Porter. "I've missed you buggers, I don't mind saying. All alright, are we?"

Deputy Head Porter started laughing again, the sight of the usually dour Porter in such high spirits amusing her.

"You're chipper!" she said.

"Oh course I am, ma'am. Tomorrow I marry the woman of my dreams!" Porter's moustache bristled at the very thought of it. "Actually, ma'am, I wanted to speak to you about t'wedding. Well, stag-do, really. It's traditional, ain't it, have a few large ones before the big day. There's not really anything organised, as such, but I was thinking, maybe, we could go along t'Albatross after work, you know, in t'name of tradition and what not. I've asked Head Porter, he's up for it."

"Brilliant, Porter!" exclaimed the Professor. "Count me in twice!"

"I'm going to sit this one out," replied Deputy Head Porter. "Stag-dos are men only affairs."

"Don't be daft, ma'am," Porter replied, looking her up and down. "In that get-up you look just like a man anyway. I think you should come."

Never one to refuse an invitation from a friend, especially when accompanied by such a thinly veiled insult, Deputy Head Porter felt there was little else she could do but accept. Besides, someone needed to go along and keep things sensible. She couldn't rely on Head Porter and certainly not Professor Fox. No. She would go along to keep an eye on things. Tomorrow would be a big day, after all.

SOMETHING OLD, SOMETHING NEW, SOMETHING BORROWED, SOMETHING BLUE

Sitting somewhere near the back of Old College Chapel with only the merest hint of a hangover, Deputy Head Porter shuffled uncomfortably in her unfamiliar attire of a modest dress and pinching heels. At the head of the aisle stood Porter, fussing with the cuffs and hem of his morning suit, every inch the nervous groom. Although always reasonably smartly turned out in his Porter's suit, in tails and an embroidered waistcoat he was quite the sight to behold. The greying thatch of fuzz atop his head had been tamed into a neat side parting and some effort had been made to discipline his unruly moustache, which appeared to be fighting back against a thick layer of styling oil.

Deputy Head Porter was joined on the groom's side of the Chapel by an effusive Professor Fox, displaying high spirits and evidentially unabashed by the antics and carousing of the previous evening. Obviously more sensitive than he seemed, the Professor had sensed his colleague's continuing concern over the disappearance of her beloved Terry and had sought to comfort her by talking non-stop about anything and everything to keep her mind from it. In fact, he had lifted her spirits to such an extent that last night, combined with spirits of a more liquid form, Deputy Head Porter became convinced of his imminent return, quite probably bearing a clutch of small furry creatures as gifts. She was privately very grateful for the Professor's efforts and, really, being in his presence made anything less than mindless optimism practically impossible. Besides, he was quite the vision in his dashing white suit with matching top hat, the continual tap-tapping of his silver-topped walking cane providing a jolly diversion. And it just went to prove that he had at least one suit that wasn't blue, after all.

Not wearing quite so well was Head Porter. He sat awkwardly next to his Deputy, looking sheepishly at the floor and nursing a badly sprained ankle. For someone whose relationship with alcohol was so fleeting, he was surprisingly enthusiastic when such opportunities presented themselves. This invariably would lead to ill-advised acrobatic behaviour, followed swiftly and decisively by a plethora of injuries about his person. As impressive as last night's hip-thrusting, high-kicking tabletop dance had been at the time, it had left him rather disadvantaged the next morning. The shots of Pernod handed out by Dr Martens to guests entering the Chapel hadn't helped at all, although Professor Fox swore blind they had an invigorating effect. It was a slightly odd thing for the bride to request, certainly, but no one seemed put off at all. It was a promising start to a wedding. An even more promising start to a marriage.

Across the other side of the Chapel sat the bride's party. Deputy Head Porter could tell that a fair number of them were very obviously the Detective Sergeant's esteemed colleagues; she could spot a copper anywhere. There was something about the way they walked, the way they stood - even the way they sat. And she had spotted the suave figure of Detective Chief Inspector Thompson, reclining elegantly in the furthest pew, looking effortlessly dapper in an immaculate three-piece. His attendance was a surprise even to himself. He objected robustly - if privately - to matrimonial entanglement between a lowly College servant and a serving police officer. He objected even more strongly to Old College in general, headache-inducing as it proved to be on numerous occasions. But something about that time in Chinon had softened his resolve somewhat. He couldn't be sure quite what it was - his holiday was ruined, after all, and no one had seemed very grateful for his acts of heroism - but a grudging respect was blossoming. Fair enough, they were ridiculous and unreasonable most of the time, but they were gung-ho types and extraordinarily brave, when you thought about it. Or very foolish. There was an astonishing disregard for personal safety that one couldn't help but admire, at least. And there was probably nowhere else you would get given a shot of Pernod on the way into a chapel.

Right down the front was a lady who could be none other than the mother of the bride - a tiny woman with an enormous fuchsia hat and quite frankly the filthiest laugh ever heard on consecrated ground. She appeared to be directing ribald comments towards her future son-in-law, possibly in an attempt to ease his nerves. It did not appear to be having the desired effect. Porter's horizons had certainly been widened by the affections of DS Kirby, but probably not quite enough to accommodate the earthy humour of the sergeant's mother. The width of such horizons necessary for such a thing were probably impossible, due to the curvature of the earth and other metaphysical restrictions.

"I've got a question, Deputy Head Porter - where's The Dean?" Professor Fox whispered into her ear.

"Good point," she replied. "I haven't seen him all morning. He said he would definitely be here."

"He'd better come as greased lightening, or he'll miss things, I fear."

The Professor was right. Proceedings were gathering pace as Alex, the young Organ Scholar, flitted between the organ loft and the assembled choir, issuing instructions and advice in a manner that was becoming ever more urgent. He was often mistaken to be a quiet chap, the Organ Scholar, until you got to know him. He had a musical knowledge and ability that went beyond being simply gifted and skirted around the edges of genius. Unusually for one of such staggering aptitude, he was quite the most down-to-earth young chap you could hope to meet, especially in somewhere like Old College. He had recently launched a fledgling career as a DJ to supplement his meagre student income and had occasional late-night presenting spots on the local radio. And apart from anything else, he carried off the rather effeminate traditional red robes of his role very nicely indeed.

"I think I need another paracetamol," grumbled Head Porter.

"You just sit where you are!" hissed Deputy Head Porter. "They're going to start in a minute."

An almighty clattering, accompanied by a colourful selection of salty expressions, announced the probable arrival of The Dean. As a whole, the

Chapel swivelled collectively in their seats to stare at the flailing figure, suspicions confirmed. He had tripped on his way in, sending hymn books and sundries flying in every direction. He glared briefly at the stricken objects, before striding over to join Deputy Head Porter and company.

"It's these buggering shoes!" he growled, before anyone could say a word. "You see, in recognition of this most auspicious event, I have decided to side very much with tradition. These shoes aren't even mine!"

"There's a tradition about wearing other people's shoes at weddings?" asked Professor Fox.

"They're *borrowed*, old boy, *borrowed!*" The Dean jabbed a stubby finger at them to further accentuate the point. "Something old, something new, something borrowed, something blue. See, this tie is old. I've had it for simply yonks." It looked like it, too. "My undergarments are completely new, but I shan't show them to you here on consecrated ground, of course."

"Oh, quite right, please don't," the Professor replied. "Save it for the speeches. It'll make them much better."

"Well, if you say so, old bean, whatever you like. Anyway. These shoes are borrowed from Head of Maintenance, would you believe. His feet are perversely large, you know. And, of course, my trousers are blue."

Deputy Head Porter narrowed an eye suspiciously. She wasn't sure if The Dean didn't attend many weddings, or if he simply believed that he was to be the centre of attention whatever the occasion. Either way, he had made a cracking effort at being a bride.

Not quite as much of an effort as the actual bride, of course. Before further comment could be passed on The Dean's outfit, the opening chords of the Wedding March boomed from the organ loft and the soon-to-be Mrs Porter appeared like a vision at the Chapel doors. Beaming from ear to ear, her obvious delight radiated from the pinkness of her cheeks to the sparkly tips of her princess shoes, bathing the assembled congregation in a joyful glow as she passed by. Her dress was an elegant ivory silk, stylishly cut and displaying just enough bosom to be cheeky without being obscene. A glittering tiara sat upon her perfectly coiffured head and in her hand, she held a single white rose, and also an empty shot glass.

Deputy Head Porter was not personally given to romantic leanings and she often found the syrupy atmosphere at weddings only served to stoke her cynicism. But looking into the faces of Porter and his marvellous bride, the two of them brimming over with happiness and - dare she say it - love, it was all she could do to wrestle back a tear or two and hope that the lump in her throat cleared in time for the first hymn.

BUFFETS & PHILOSOPHY

"Deputy Head Porter, are you actually *crying?*"

The Dean looked at her, bemused, as they made their way from the Chapel and towards the buffet currently being laid out in the Armingford Room.

"No, Sir," she replied, quite possibly lying. "I've got confetti in my eye, that's all."

And she was indeed adorned with a light sprinkling of capricious confetti from the slipstream of the bride and groom.

"I might cry if we don't get to that dadblame buffet quick-smart," said Professor Fox, striding along with hands thrust deep into the pockets of trousers as gleaming white as his smile. "This Professor is as hungry as a termite."

He was not the only one. The wedding service was beautiful yet rather lengthy, in the opinion of

Deputy Head Porter. She imagined that these things were probably a lot more fun if you are actually taking part. But sat at the back with little to do but wait for the next sing-song, it was dreadfully tiresome. And even when it came to the singing, the choir cantillated at such a volume as to drown out the humble warblings of the assembly that it hardly seemed worth the effort. Still. Porter and DS Kirby appeared to be enraptured by the whole affair and that, surely, was all that mattered.

The enthusiasm held by The Fellowship for a decent buffet is well documented, but their zeal for a good feed pales in comparison to that of Her Majesty's Constabulary. The two factions headed towards their target with finely focused determination, whilst at the same time trying to give the impression of polite nonchalance. Even though Deputy Head Porter had every confidence that Head of Catering would have provided sufficient victuals to sink a battleship, she suddenly felt the need to quicken her step, in case all the best bits got snaffled up at once.

"Porter looks so happy, don't you think?" she said to her companions as they exited Old Court at something approaching a jog.

"He certainly does!" replied The Dean. "Anyone would have thought someone had given him a whippet or something. But in all seriousness, it was quite a touching sight all round, actually. Almost makes one want to take the plunge oneself, what do you say, Deputy Head Porter?"

She was not sure if this was a question or an actual offer, so decided to play it safe.

"I'm not sure I'm the marrying kind, Sir."

"I was married once," Head Porter joined in, wistfully. "It was a terrible, terrible thing."

"Oh?" said The Dean. "Perhaps you married the wrong woman."

"It wasn't that," he replied, a little sadly. "More like she married the wrong man."

"Listen, you piece of old fruit, here's the thing: When you fall off, you get back on, and start over again. Just like the song!" The Professor slapped Head Porter on the back by way of encouragement. "The right lady is out there... consider it like a search and destroy mission. You just have to find her, is all."

Deputy Head Porter was unnerved by the search and destroy mission. It suggested dubious things about the romantic life of Professor Fox. Rather than pass comment, she decided to make a helpful suggestion.

"Actually, weddings are supposed to be good places for romance. Everybody is already in the mood, aren't they?"

"Well, actually, I did mention it to The Headmistress," said Head Porter, brightening. "You must meet her, Deputy Head Porter. She's simply wonderful."

The flirtations with philosophies of the affairs of the heart took them all the way to the Armingford Room, where matrimonial merrymaking was already picking up quite a pace. Porter and his beaming new wife had taken their places at the top table, surrounded by their nearest and dearest. Deputy Head Porter noticed that Porter had only one discernible family member at his side; a round, noisy little gentleman with a fuzzy goatee beard. If she were a gambling woman, she would have bet on him being his brother, but whoever he might be, he had clearly wasted no time in sampling the free-flowing champagne.

The scene at the buffet was something akin to a well-mannered scrum. It was difficult to tell which set of guests had the upper hand. Although one might expect the police to be more experienced in subtle acts of violence, one can never discount the effectiveness of a determined academic elbow when a meal is involved. Aside from the bridal party, the only guest not currently engaged in combat was Detective Chief Inspector Thompson, who had wisely dispatched an underling to retrieve his supplies while he reclined with a glass of champagne, idly watching the string quartet who serenaded guests from the balcony above.

"I say, the Thompson fellow has the right idea," said The Dean, nodding towards the dashing detective. "Listen, you Porters need to go and fetch me some food at once!"

Head Porter and his Deputy returned looks that could strip paint.

"I don't think we actually count as being Porters if we haven't got our hats on," Head Porter replied, bluntly. "Besides, you're a fussy bugger and you'll only moan if we get you the wrong thing."

"I am not fussy!" snapped The Dean, his cheeks flushed. "I just don't eat things that are green. Or look like a leaf."

Before the argument could develop further, a sound like a thousand demons escaping from Hell suddenly ripped through the room. A sound that could only be caused by one thing - a thing that would soon chase off a thousand demons and eat a thousand more for breakfast.

THE MASTER'S CAT

Dr Martens looked up from her plate of satay chicken and squealed with delight.

"Look who it is! Whooosalovelypusspuss?"

Watched by the startled gathering of wedding guests, the malevolent mass of fur and claw streaked past, ears flattened against its head and spitting wildly. Something had certainly upset it quite drastically. The beast had never appeared so disturbed. Usually, it would be the cause of such a disturbed disposition. The Master's Cat hurtled headlong into the buffet, sending carefully crafted delicacies flying in all directions.

"What the bloody hell is that?!" cried an off-duty copper, halfway through a pork pie.

"Someone grab the bugger!" suggested another.

"I'm not bloody well going near that thing..."

Deputy Head Porter was worried. Anything that had had that kind of effect on The Master's Cat was something of note. Looking round desperately to discover what horror had so terrified the thing, it was not long before the cause of the consternation became clear. The Master's Cat was certainly *Terry*-fied.

Sauntering into the Armingford Room, tail swishing with self-satisfaction and whiskers cheerfully twitching, was none other than Deputy Head Porter's errant feline companion. Goodness only knows what he had done to The Master's Cat, well-known as being the most disagreeable creature in the whole of The City, but the mere sight of Terry entering the room was enough to send him leaping out of the window, worryingly close to the river beyond. A damp-sounding screech was inconclusive as to the fate of The Master's Cat.

"Terry!" exclaimed Deputy Head Porter, ecstatic at seeing her little friend again. "Where have you been? Naughty boy!"

Terry was perhaps the favourite surprise guest at the wedding.

But he was not the only surprise guest. Oh no indeed...

A VERY UNLIKELY VISITOR

Terry, seemingly oblivious to the heartache he had caused, was good enough to tolerate an inordinate amount of fussing and cooing from Deputy Head Porter, before deciding that he had had enough and hopped from her arms to saunter around the Armingford Room as if he owned the place. Amongst the small chaos of the disarranged buffet, he found a central spot and set about meticulously cleaning his rear end, leg thrust resolutely in the air.

Deputy Head Porter felt a twinge of shame that her small furry fellow was making such a spectacle of himself, especially as it was his pursuit of The Master's Cat that caused such wanton devastation in the first place. But she was just so very pleased to see him again that she didn't let it trouble her too much. Besides, the boys and girls of the thin blue line were taking the messy mishap in their stride with good humour, as one might expect. Some of the lower ranks of The Fellowship looked absolutely horrified at the culinary casualties splattered about the place, but Head of Catering had immediately despatched his best chaps to rectify matters as best they could. Luckily, the bride and groom were finding the whole thing uproariously amusing. Detective Sergeant Kirby, in particular, was enjoying herself immensely. With her head thrown back and mouth wide with laughter, her sleek dark bob bouncing with delight, her happiness lent her a beauty unparalleled by artificial glamour. Porter, too, seemed to have acquired a subtle sheen of spruce, afforded to him through the love and joy of the occasion. People are, perhaps, at their very best when they are truly happy.

Professor Fox and Deputy Head Porter were people-watching. They had found themselves a perch at the far end of the room which offered both comfort and a terrific view of proceedings. With ample supplies of slightly squashed offerings from the wedding buffet, they were settled in for an enjoyable evening. For the last half an hour, they had been observing a slightly tipsy Head Porter working his magic on a clutch of female friends of the bride.

"Now, an interest, the sudden," said the Professor, tapping his chin thoughtfully. "Head Porter is a totally different animal, when with the ladies! Look, they seem to hang on his every word. He has a way with women, I'm thinking. Why do you suppose he has been on his own for some time?"

"Well," began Deputy Head Porter, giving genuine and deep thought to the matter. "He's quite a difficult character at times, as you know. I think his problem is that he isn't so good at thinking about other people." She paused and had another think. "He is definitely getting better, though.

Didn't he say he had invited a woman along this evening?"

"If he has, she'll have to fight her way through the masses!" laughed the Professor. "And then there's The Dean, don't you know? He had quite the wild romantic past, DHP..."

"Really?!" Deputy Head Porter was most taken aback.

"Oh, yes and absolutely! Some very... excitable ladies. And ladies of all types and sizes."

"That surprises me. He always seems so... indifferent towards things of that nature."

"Aha, well, there is a reason for that." Professor Fox licked his lips and moved closer so that he might lower his voice. "You see, The Dean had his heart broken horribly and viciously... but I can so no more."

"What happens in Kuala Lumpa, stays in Kuala Lumpa?"

"Exactly, DHP! Now then, what about you? You are not so bad, for a lady. Is there no secret lover tucked behind the back of your drawers..?"

Deputy Head Porter spluttered, and her mind raced to even try to begin to answer such a question, when something far more concerning caught her attention. The shock of it caused her to eat three vol-au-vents in one go, which nearly chocked her. Professor Fox followed her gaze of startled fascination towards a slight but menacing figure gliding ominously towards them.

"I say!" he gasped. "Is that..? It isn't..?!"

"It bloody well is," replied Deputy Head Porter, swallowing hard on the last of the pastry. "The very nerve of the man! What on earth can he be doing here?"

"It'll be no good, I'll wager," murmured the Professor. "And probably murderous, knowing him. The beast."

Moving soundlessly through the oblivious throng, smiling faintly, was Junior Bursar. No one had seen him since he had fled to Tuscany during his retirement party, having revealed his pivotal role in the clandestine College organisation, The Vicious Circle. Junior Bursar had, both directly and indirectly, been responsible for the murders of numerous Fellows and associates over many years, but the crimes of this illicit order stretched back for centuries. Deputy Head Porter came dangerously close to becoming another victim when she uncovered the truth about The Vicious Circle and was even accused by The Bursar last year of being one of them. The Vicious Circle were not her favourite people.

Junior Bursar seemed quite pleased to see them, on the surface at least. Displaying the well-practiced visage of absent-minded bumbling that masked his understated threat, his face lit up us he greeted Deputy Head Porter and the Professor, conveniently ignoring the facts of their last meeting, when he tried to throw Deputy Head Porter off the flag tower.

"Well, well, Deputy Head Porter!" he cried, apparently ignorant of her shock and, it had to be said, slight fear. "How lovely to see you! And what a surprise to see you in a dress. Is it a special occasion? And Professor Fox! So, you *do* have more than one suit, I see. This must be an auspicious event indeed."

"This is Porter's wedding reception," replied Deputy Head Porter, her voice barely wavering. *I bet he can smell my fear, though. He positively thrives on it.*

"Oh, so that's what all this is?" replied Junior Bursar, every inch the doddery ageing academic. "I did wonder what all the fuss was about."

"Well," said the Professor, "Some might think it's obviously a wedding, since there's a bride and a groom and a cake. Those three are never together otherwise."

Junior Bursar's face crinkled into a thin-lipped smile.

"I thought, perhaps, it had something to do with the Holy Grail being discovered under Apple Tree Court?" There was an icy pause as he deployed that all-too-familiar stare that takes a firm hold of your soul by the scruff of its neck and gives it a good shake. "You wouldn't happen to know anything about that, would you?"

"We might know a bit more than you, can you believe," replied the Professor. "For instance, did you know that it isn't the real Holy Grail?"

"Well, of course I know *that*, dear boy!"

"How could you possibly know that?' asked Deputy Head Porter, wondering if the two Bursars were in cahoots.

"How, you ask? It really is quite simple, Deputy Head Porter. *I* have the real Grail. In fact, I have it right here."

A HAIRS BREADTH FROM THE HOLY GRAIL

For the second time in almost as many minutes, Deputy Head Porter was forced to consume things at speed to alleviate her shock. This time it was the full glass of wine she happened to be holding as Junior Bursar made his announcement. The complimentary champagne had been long since exhausted and she was now on to an undisclosed fizzy thing with an acidic after-taste. One glass was not enough. Nowhere near enough. She deftly snatched an identical glass from the unwitting hand of Professor Fox and downed that, too. Suitable fortified, she faced Junior Bursar, vainly searching for a flicker of humanity in eyes like frosted glass. *I never could get the measure of that man.*

"Ho ho, is this some kind of drinking competition?" The Dean sauntered over, a crystal tumbler of whisky sloshing merrily in his hand.

Noticing Junior Bursar, he looked him up and down, his distaste evident. "Oh, it's you, is it? I can't say it's a pleasure. However, I wouldn't try out-drinking our Deputy Head Porter if I were you, chap. She has quite the reputation."

Junior Bursar, ignoring The Dean, turned his hollow grin to Deputy Head Porter.

"Would you like me to get it out?"

"Good lord, man," cried Deputy Head Porter. "Not here, not where everyone can see."

"Who's getting what out?" slurred a staggering Head Porter, worse for wear and bumping into The Dean in his clumsy attempt to join the group. "Now, this sounds like my kind of party!"

Deputy Head Porter looked over to the gaggle of ladies Head Porter had left behind in order to come and join them. They were whispering and looking across, giggling behind their hands. *The last thing we need is them coming over to make friends.*

"We need to go somewhere more private," she whispered. .

"Wahay!" cried Head Porter, not grasping the gravity of the situation in the slightest. The Dean grabbed his arm to stop him toppling over.

"I don't know what's going on here," said The Dean, eyeing Junior Bursar. "But I'm not sure I like it. My rooms. Now."

***

Back in his rooms, The Dean was on a surer footing, pacing deliberately up and down his worn antique rug like a wolf patrolling his territory. He never once let his eyes wander from Junior Bursar, who maintained a countenance of doddery amiability. Quite why he insisted on keeping up the pretence of an eccentric old man when everyone knew him to be a creature of the utmost malevolence was beyond Deputy Head Porter. It only added to their suspicions, quite frankly.

Head Porter was rapidly feeling the effects of his excesses by way of an early onset hangover and was quietly dying on The Dean's red leather settee. The occasional soft moan reassured his colleagues of his continued presence in this world. Professor Fox had taken up station by the door, whether his purpose was keeping people in or out was something only he could know.

"Why have you come back?" The Dean's question was perfectly straightforward but posed in such a way that almost any answer would be incorrect. It's the lawyer in him. Junior Bursar returned the thinnest of smiles.

"A matter of honour, my learned friend."

"Pah!" snorted Deputy Head Porter, unable to stop herself. "Don't talk to me about honour. You tried to kill me twice, you bugger."

"Three times, in fact, Deputy Head Porter."

She mentally kicked herself. She always forget about the poisoned breakfast.

"But that is best left in the past. What concerns me now is very much in the present. The present Bursar. Ha! As if one man could replace myself and Senior Bursar..."

"I'm thinking we would be better off with no Bursars," said Professor Fox, curtly. "Fewer problems all round, see."

"I grant you, Professor, in such circumstances no Bursar might be better than the one we have. It seems my replacement is keen to grab false glory and claim my own great achievement as his own."

Junior Bursar fell silent to allow his words to take form in the minds of his audience. The Dean got there first.

"So. It was *you* that stole the Grail from Chinon all those years ago?"

"Yes! Who else could it be?" Junior Bursar allowed himself a little chuckle. "No one else could have the wits to solve the fiendish enigmas that led to the Grail!"

Professor Fox cleared his throat.

"Actually, we did just that, don't you know!" he replied, irritated. "DHP solved the riddle in the Crypt on her tea break. And in fact, I didn't find any fiendish enigmas, even though I looked hard."

"Well, well, well," tutted Junior Bursar, shaking his head. "I always knew there was more to you than met the eye, Deputy Head Porter. But I digress. I must speak to this cad of a Bursar at once. Quite apart from his spurious claims of discovering the Holy Grail, he has dug up Apple Tree Court for no good reason! Have you any idea how many years that turf has lain there undisturbed? I imagine Head Gardener must be incandescent."

"Oh, his is quite furious," replied The Dean, nodding vigorously. "And quite right too, I say."

"He always was such a fastidious fellow, Head Gardener..." Junior Bursar lost himself in nostalgia for a moment, before snapping back firmly to the present. "But, ah, again digressions. Tell me now - where is this blasted Bursar! I insist on seeing him directly. I have many a thing I wish to impart to him. Quite forcefully, I might add."

Worried glances were exchanged. No one especially favoured sharing the details of the nefarious deeds in Chinon with someone as duplicitous as Junior Bursar. To the relief of all concerned, The Dean took matters upon himself.

"Not so fast, my bean-counting friend,"

The Dean squared up to Junior Bursar, fixing him with the stoney stare he usually reserved for times of mortal danger, or when he had run out of whisky. It was a look so unnerving that even

Deputy Head Porter, adept at handling The Dean, had to look away for a moment. Whilst Junior Bursar might be the master of understated malice and unspecified threat, The Dean did overt belligerence quite unlike anyone else.

"How do we even know that you really have the Holy Grail, hmm? Answer me that. You expect us to believe you, just like that? I say you present the thing to us immediately. Junior Bursar - get it out, now!"

STUFF OF LEGEND

Gathered in The Dean's rooms, all eyes were fixed on the unassuming object placed with great care on the walnut coffee table. All eyes, that is, except for those of Head Porter - which were shut tight and watering slightly from the burden of inebriation. The ambiance was a strange, heady mixture of a thousand years of mystery charged with euphoric disbelief; the air tasted of electrified absinthe.

Deputy Head Porter tore her gaze momentarily from the quietly compelling item before her and glanced across at Junior Bursar. He sat with a smile of smug satisfaction displayed broadly across his angular features, openly gloating at his newly revealed status as the bearer of the Holy Grail. *And who could blame him?*

For centuries, the Grail had been ardently hunted by all and sundry, the apparent impossibility of the task pushing it ever further into the realm of myth. And yet there it was, right before their very eyes. Deputy Head Porter took several deep breaths. Somehow, it seemed almost more unreal to her now than when it was the stuff of legend. It exerted a magnetic vitality that drew them close; wordlessly it had gathered them to it in humbled awe. Professor Fox tentatively extended an exploratory finger.

"Don't touch it!" snapped Junior Bursar.

"But why not?' asked the Professor. "You've touched it, I'll warrant. I'm curious to see if it is hot or cold or both or neither. I want to know what it feels like."

"It's the Holy Grail, not a cashmere jumper," huffed Junior Bursar. "Besides, I do not wish for you to get your sticky fingerprints all over it. I shall be presenting it to The Master very shortly."

The Professor looked reproachfully at his hands and wiped them furtively on the hem of his jacket, scowling. "Not that sticky..."

"You will not be presenting this to anyone, much less The Master!" said The Dean, wagging a finger.

"I assure you that I will! Why, I cannot allow this so-called Bursar to come swanning in, taking credit for ruining a perfectly good lawn in pursuit of false idols!"

"Actually, The Bursar won't be swanning around anywhere anytime soon," said Deputy Head Porter, her satisfaction at the fact evident in her knowing smile. "We left him locked in the dungeons of the Chateau de Chinon. The Curator said that he would leave him there until we had forgotten all about him."

Junior Bursar's eyes twinkled with malicious glee. This was very much up his street.

"I say, Deputy Head Porter," he chuckled. "I am rather impressed, you know. I should recruit you to The Vicious Circle."

"I'm not sure I'm Vicious Circle material," she replied. "I'm more of a... perturbed oblong."

"Let's not speak of such things any longer," said the Professor, darkly. "We have enough dadblamery at Old College as it is, see."

Junior Bursar cackled.

"Says you, who are merrily dispatching Bursars left, right and centre."

"It was just the one Bursar," sniffed the Professor. "But I could be quite tempted to dispatch with more, don't you know."

"Enough of this!" thundered The Dean, waving an arm furiously. "There's a wedding in full swing over there and the buffet is still out. I don't need to be wasting time with this nonsense. Junior Bursar, you were an utter bugger then for taking the Holy

Grail from its rightful place and you are an utter bugger now for parading it about like a gaudy trinket."

"My dear Dean, you intended to do the very same thing!"

The Dean was momentarily thrown off-kilter. It was true, after all.

"Quiet, you! Don't argue with me. I'm The Dean."

Deputy Head Porter could tell that the threads of The Dean's rage were unravelling. He always resorted to telling people who he was when his arguments dried up.

The Dean squared up for another verbal assault on Junior Bursar when Head Porter made a belated and, it must be said, rather unpleasant, contribution to proceedings. A muffled gurgle drew attention sharply to his nesting place on The Dean's settee. This was followed by a sort of wet, rattling sound from the back of his throat and at once Head Porter was awake and wide-eyed. His heaving shoulders and swelling cheeks confirmed the worst.

"For God's sake, man - not on the settee!" The Dean looked aghast at the potentially unappetising scenario unfolding before him. "Deputy Head Porter - open a window!"

She rushed to the nearest window and flung it open. Professor Fox gamely leapt across to assist the struggling Head Porter - quite clearly on the brink of gastric explosion - which was very brave for a man wearing a white suit. The Professor managed to dangle the top half of Head Porter deftly through open window, just as what was not so long ago a wedding buffet escaped violently into the warm evening air. Said substance dutifully obeyed Newton and found itself artfully decorating the courtyard below, like something of a ventral Jackson Pollock.

"Goodness me," exclaimed the Professor, slapping Head Porter's back. "Ghastly business, this. Hope you're okay."

Head Porter replied with a weak nod and a gentle groan.

"I hope he didn't get any on the windowsill," mumbled The Dean.

Deputy Head Porter drew a sharp breath. A small, tiny panic suddenly crawled up her spine and nipped at the back of her brain. She spun round, looking wildly about the room. *Just as I thought.*

The door ajar and the coffee table notably emptier than before, Junior Bursar had gone.

BUGGER.

THE CHASE IS ON

As Deputy Head Porter was organising a choice selection of four-letter words in her head, Professor Fox was already heading for the door.. The Dean looked fit to burst with rage and confusion.

"Get after him!" he bellowed.

Deputy Head Porter joined the Professor in sprinting down the staircase and out into Apple Tree Court. Junior Bursar was surprisingly sprightly for a man of such advanced years and had circumnavigated the perilous excavation site and was already within reach of the far cloister.

"Stop!" cried the Professor. "Stop in the name of... the Professor!"

Junior Bursar flung a vicious glare over his shoulder and redoubled his efforts. Giving the archaeological crevasse a wide berth, they made after him. Panting heavily, they kept their quarry in sight but seemed unable to gain any meaningful ground. Deputy Head Porter could probably blame her pinching high heels, at a push, but the Professor really had no excuse, apart from, perhaps, too many sausage rolls.

As Junior Bursar continued onwards, ever snatching a peek at the progress of his pursuers, a moment of delightful serendipity came to pass. Emerging nonchalantly from the flowerbeds, paws caked in mud from some kind of digging, came a familiar black and white figure. Terry took one look at the unfolding scene and immediately deployed the classic feline attribute of being in the exact same spot as human feet are about to be. The result of which was to send Junior Bursar tumbling into the flowerbeds, with quite some grace, considering.

"Whoop! Whoop! Bursar down!" cheered the Professor, heading towards the scene at a great rate of knots, legs pumping wildly and top hat bobbing up and down with fearsome ferocity.

Deputy Head Porter followed behind, her stomach protesting at such robust activity while attempting to digest an ill-considered selection of food and drink. She had often lamented the frightful regularity with which College meals were interrupted by life and death occurrences (or things even more important than that), which caused her so often to abandon perfectly good meals in the name of duty. But hindsight is a wonderful thing and only now did she realise the expedient nature of such a thing. Giving chase on a full stomach was a miserable experience, indeed.

Junior Bursar sprang to his feet and, like a hunted animal, resumed his flight. Terry gave his departure a cursory glance before turning his attentions to the serious business of tail and paw grooming. He paid no heed to the Professor and Deputy Head Porter as they dashed past, diving into the cloister after Junior Bursar.

"He's heading into Old Hall!" gasped Deputy Head Porter, pointing towards the lithe figure vanishing through the ancient oak doors of one of the grander parts of Old College.

"Then so are we, I say!" the Professor replied, strangely chirpy.

The magnificent, towering wooden doors of Old Hall were slightly ajar and they slipped soundlessly inside, footsteps soft as whispers. There was a reticent hush about the Hall that didn't feel quite right to Deputy Head Porter. In a building with the age and experience of Old College, there was never what you might call a complete silence. The venerable stones of the walls themselves forever murmured with centuries of memories and a faint buzz of ancient life force trembled all along the elderly wooden beams and joists. If there was silence in Old College, it was because the place was holding its breath.

Stopping for a moment to catch her own breath, Deputy Head Porter looked around Old Hall. It was one of the original medieval parts of Old College and retained its grandeur with pride. The redoubtable iron fireplace - big enough to roast a hog - yawned on the far wall, an ominous portal to goodness knows where. Beneath her feet, well-trod tiles of red, white and black undulated like rolling fields, warped and worn with age. From every wall, oil paintings of academics long since passed gazed down with barely concealed contempt, retaining on canvass the pomposity they so treasured in life.

At the far end, bathed in the light of the late evening sun made kaleidoscopic by the stained-glass windows, stood three suits of armour; eternal sentries to the memory of times past. Their metallic limbs gleamed as splendidly as they had done the day they were forged, and Deputy Head Porter found herself thinking that she didn't envy the poor soul who had the job of keeping them that way.

"You know," whispered Professor Fox, eyeing the armour, "If this were a film, the villain would be hiding in one of those over there. I might hide in one too, the sudden."

"This isn't a film," Deputy Head Porter replied. "Films are more realistic than Old College."

"Let's take a look anyway, please."

They tip-toed across to the far end, watching the shadows furtively as they went. The silence was so thick it could make your ears bleed. Deputy Head Porter didn't like it one bit. She could hear her own heartbeat in her ears, but at least it went some way to blocking out the worrying noises coming from her stomach. They approached the suits of armour with care, studying them closely for any signs of interference. Nothing seemed amiss.

"A bit of a shame, really," remarked Deputy Head Porter. "I would have thought that would have been right up Junior Bursar's street, hiding in a suit of armour. You know what academics are like. Very fond of dramatics."

"These fine fellows can still be of service to us," the Professor replied, a worrying look of determined mischief in his eyes. "Here, he won't be needing this..." The Professor gently released the broad sword from the iron glove of the nearest hollow warrior.

"Is that even a real sword?"

Professor Fox handled it thoughtfully for a moment, before thrusting it towards Deputy Head Porter's rear area, poking her rather abruptly in the bum.

It is a real sword!

"Ouch! Why ever did you do that?!"

"It looked quite fleshy, I didn't think you'd notice too much. But I am sorry." Nonetheless, the Professor grinned from ear to ear, admiring the enormous blade and turning it this way and that, so it caught the light. "You should get one too - but no poking."

In fact, this was a very good idea. Junior Bursar may give the appearance of a weak and feeble geriatric, but Deputy Head Porter knew only too well what an effective agent of death the man could be. She looked to the next suit of armour and relieved it of a crossbow. *Nice!*

But then she saw it.

The final suit of armour was bereft of weaponry. It's empty glove hung redundant by its side.

Behind them, a voice...

"Well, well, well! I wondered when you might be joining me. Let us keep this brief, shall we?" Junior Bursar stepped from the shadows, wielding a pole-axe with frightening dexterity. The weapon sat so naturally in his hands, this could not have been the first time he had used one.

"If this dadblamery leaves a single mark on my suit, I tell you, *a single mark* - why, things will get spicy!" The Professor readied his stance and brandished his sword with surprising aptitude.

Deputy Head Porter looked forlornly at her crossbow. *How is it that these two are so comfortable waving about medieval weapons? I've never used a crossbow before. Which is probably just as well, as this one doesn't have a bolt in it anyway.*

Oh for goodness sake. I suppose it wouldn't be a proper wedding without a fight, would it?

VIOLENCE IS GOLDEN

The atmosphere in Old Hall was like ice laced with peril and cold, hard steel as neither Professor Fox nor Junior Bursar looked set to give way. Deputy Head Porter half-heartedly brandished her redundant crossbow in the vague hope that their adversary would flinch at the prospect of two against one. He did not. *Bugger.*

"Here, you chaps," she said quickly. "Let's think about this for a moment. Intellect triumphs over strength. Why are we fighting, anyway?"

"Well, I suppose," replied the Professor, "Because he's waving a gruesome-looking weapon. And I've got this other, cool-looking, weapon right here. Battle is bound to be done, now."

"*I* am fighting because the very reputation of Old College is at risk of being calumniated by the lies of The Bursar!" Junior Bursar squealed. "I cannot allow that to happen."

Deputy Head Porter sighed.

"Not that again. Listen. Have you ever thought, that just maybe, the reputation of Old College would be absolutely fine if it wasn't for the likes of you resorting to murderous methods every time someone so much as farts incorrectly..."

"There's actually a right and a wrong way to..?" mused Professor Fox. "I had no idea."

"The current footing can hardly be compared to a *fart*, Deputy Head Porter." It was difficult to tell if Junior Bursar was more annoyed by her comment, or by the fact he had been forced to say 'fart'. "We are faced with the infiltration of a foreign agent who is unrelenting in his vocation to make fools of us with a fake Grail, all the while plotting to make off with the real one to his confounded *motherland*. This is an affront to the decency of College and, yet again, I find you very much in my way. This simply will not *do*, Deputy Head Porter."

Deputy Head Porter had forgotten how difficult reasonable conversation with Junior Bursar could be. He was a man who occupied a space somewhere between incongruous and lunacy, particularly where the prominence of Old College was concerned. She had thought, once, that she had grasped the concept of handling Junior Bursar. It seems that she was woefully out of practice.

"Firstly, if you present the real Grail to The Master we will be forced to admit that we have left The Bursar trapped in a dungeon," she said, as reasonably as she could. "That won't look good for us and, even worse, there's a chance someone might try and release him. Secondly, he hasn't got the real Grail anyway, so I don't see what the problem is."

Junior Bursar tutted violently to himself and relaxed his grip on the pole-axe in order to wave a bony bunched fist.

"And *that* kind of thinking, Deputy Head Porter, is exactly what will keep you as a College servant whilst the likes of my good self are elevated to the grand heights of academia!"

Ah, yes. Those grand heights of academia, where everyone thinks like an absolute idiot. But with a great vocabulary, at least.

Taking advantage of the distraction of this brief oration, Professor Fox seizes his chance and strikes towards Junior Bursar, broad sword thrust boldly before him and emitting a terrible cry. Deputy Head Porter wasn't expecting that. She dropped her crossbow in alarm.

Junior Bursar was equally taken aback. The pole-axe quivered briefly in his grip and he stumbled several feet backwards.

"That's quite enough from you, I say!" roared the Professor. "Your argument is quite insufficient - just like you! Let us do battle!"

Deputy Head Porter realised that she had lost control of negotiations to the surge of testosterone as both Fellows took up arms with great enthusiasm. It crossed her mind to intervene, but the abundance of large, sharp pointy things ensured that the thought was quickly dismissed. After all, members of The Fellowship trying to kill each other was very much a traditional thing.

Professor Fox was surprisingly nimble with such a large sword and reigned blow after blow on the fearsome pole-axe, pushing ever closer to the soft and stab-able assailant at the other end. The business end of a pole-axe was no friendly thing, but the Professor barely flinched as it jabbed about his head and shoulders.

"Dadblamery to you and your giant toothpick!" he yelled at the increasingly frustrated Junior

Bursar. "I'll be poking you any moment - you'll see!"

The portentous echos of clashing steel and guttural gruntings filled Old Hall, as if a terrible battle was erupting within its walls. Heart in mouth, Deputy Head Porter could only spectate and speculate as to who might have the upper hand. Professor Fox was younger and stronger, but the reach of Junior Bursar's pole-axe gave him a considerable advantage. Every lunge of the Professor's broad sword was met with a deadly swish of pointed steel, only to be returned in kind by the flashing blade. This really could go either way.

But then...

The malefic sound of metal through air.

Swiftly followed by the sickening sound of metal trough something much more solid than air.

A haunting cry, like that of a stricken animal.

Her heart stopped. Time itself ceased to exist.

The Professor was *down*.

GOODBYE, OLD FRIEND

There was silence once more in Old Hall, except for the sombre sounds of the Professor's sword clattering morosely as it fell to the floor.

"Oh... Oh my..." gasped Junior Bursar, his face awash with pallid horror. "I mean, I didn't quite mean to... oh goodness..."

For a second, Deputy Head Porter was bewildered and frozen, unable to breath or move, her heart barely able to beat at all. In a moment she was detached from herself, floating listlessly to the roof, buoyed by a dreadful sense of nausea, looking down on an ugly scene that unfolded in crippling slow-motion.

All at once, the present came hurtling back in a vast, crashing wave of consciousness; the taste of metal in her mouth, the deafening rush of blood through her ears and a great thundering in her breast brought her bursting back to reality. A sound of whimpering came to her ears from a source unknown. It took another moment to realise that it was coming from her.

"Professor!" she cried, running to where he lay prone on the floor. She threw herself upon him, holding back frightened sobs but unable to prevent a determined tear from finding its way onto her cheek.

"Dadblameit! I'm vexed, you know!"

"Professor! Are you okay?"

"I really am very sorry..." Junior Bursar shuffled contritely nearby.

Professor Fox sat up abruptly, flinging Deputy Head Porter to one side as he did so. His face was a vision of pure rage and his eyes burst with fury and the colours of a thousand stars. He turned a cold, dark stare to Junior Bursar. If looks could kill, this would be nuclear war.

"LOOK WHAT YOU'VE DONE!"

The Professor held aloft a sorry-looking object that appeared to have once been his top hat.

"My dear fellow, I really am..."

"MY HAT! IT IS... NO MORE! Well, it's here, it's just a shadow of its FORMER GLORY!"

Deputy Head Porter gave the Professor a quick once over and found that the white suit remained immaculate and there was not a scrub or bump anywhere about his person. The bits she could get at, anyway. The only casualty was his beloved topper. Whilst this was obviously something quite clearly approaching a tragedy, she was surprised by the almost harrowed remorse displayed by Junior Bursar.

"Professor Fox - boundless apologies - it might be one thing to kill a man in cold blood, but the desecration of his headgear is quite unforgivable. Might I..?" Junior Bursar reached out to the mangled millinery, but his hand was slapped smartly away.

"Don't touch me!" the Professor spat. "I don't want to end up like my hat, you heathen! You have done quite enough damage already. Look at it! I've had this hat since forever..."

"I didn't mean it. I was aiming for your face."

The Professor's response was barely intelligible and would probably be unrepeatable anyway. Snarling and rabid, he launched himself at Junior Bursar, grappling at his throat and sending both of them tumbling across the tiles in a bundle of mortal combat.

For cripe's sake. Here they go again.

"Ho ho, what's this? A fight! Bravo!"

Deputy Head Porter turned to see The Dean swaggering through the doors, followed by a peaky-looking, but nevertheless upright, Head Porter. She clambered to her feet and joined them, the three of them watching the ensuing battle with varying degrees of enthusiasm.

"Is this about the Holy Grail?" asked Head Porter, scratching his head.

"No, this is about the Professor's hat," replied Deputy Head Porter. "They were fighting about the Grail, now they're fighting about the hat. Junior Bursar ran it through with a pole-axe, look."

She offered up the tattered remains as evidence. There was a collective intake of breath and anguished expressions.

"Rum business, that," said The Dean, shaking his head. "No wonder the little chap is so angry. Go on, Foxy! Give it some welly!"

"He really doesn't need any encouragement, Sir," she replied. This was true. In fact, Professor Fox was getting worryingly close to causing the old fellow some serious damage. "You know, I think we should probably stop him."

The Dean let out an irritated sigh and looked generally disappointed.

"Well, I suppose you're right, Deputy Head Porter," he huffed. "There does seem to be some blood coming from somewhere. It's a bugger to get out of those tiles, Head of Housekeeping will be furious."

The Dean and Deputy Head Porter tackled the Professor, who by this stage was a veritable pummelling machine. They grabbed an arm each and, with quite some difficulty, hauled him away from a dazed and bloodied Junior Bursar, who himself was dragged to his feet by Head Porter. Still growling and spitting, Professor Fox reminded Deputy Head Porter of Terry when she pulled him off his latest kill. This was probably why she began to stoke his hair and ears. It seemed to work.

"Now see here, Junior Bursar," said The Dean, approaching him slowly with the beadiest of looks in his eye. "I like a good rumpus as much as the next man. But you have completely savaged this man's hat! That, old boy, is not only uncalled for but also ungentlemanly. Hardly behaviour befitting a member of Old College."

"Hmmm" is all Junior Bursar could offer in reply.

"Now. In order for honour to be upheld, I suggest you hand over the Grail at once and resume your retirement in Tuscany. If you do this, no more shall be said about the hat, do you understand?"

"I... I seem to have mislaid the Grail, Dean. Perhaps in all the excitement."

"Don't believe a word of it!" cried Head Porter, pointing a finger. "You can't trust him!"

"No, no, really, I..."

"I'm not going to shake the man down," sighed The Dean. "If he won't uphold his honour, that's his business. But mark my words - I *will* tell the

Curator all about you. You must sleep with one eye open from now on, Junior Bursar. Now go!"

Junior Bursar said no more, but nodded stiffly at each of them before turning towards the great wooden doors, placing his cuff carefully under his bleeding nose and walking away with slow, painful steps.

"Do you think he will return to Tuscany?" Head Porter asked, once Junior Bursar had gone.

"Oh, I should think so," replied The Dean, nodding vigorously. "He might be a murdering, Grail-stealing sociopath, but he knows a smack on the nose when he sees one."

"My poor, dadblame hat," mumbled the Professor, glumly turning the battered remnants over and over in his hands.

"Do you know, I have an idea," said Deputy Head Porter, tucking her arm in his and giving it a squeeze. "Come with me."

Dusk had thrown her velvety shawl across the evening and the warm night air was sweet with the smell of night flowers as they stood at the edge of The Bursar's hole in Apple Tree Court.

"Whatever are we doing here, Deputy Head Porter?" asked The Dean, keen to return to his whisky and whatever was left of the wedding buffet.

"I thought this would be a fitting resting place for the dear departed hat of Professor Fox," she replied, smiling. "Down here lies the most ancient parts of Old College. These foundations have definitively sustained the very heart and soul of our esteemed establishment for centuries. I thought that if the hat were to be interred here, a little bit of the Professor would forever be part of Old College."

Professor Fox beamed with delight.

"I'm thinking that is rather brilliant, the sudden," he said. "I think we're all glad, now, that my hat obviously feels no more pain. You know, I'm thinking it died immediately. Which is the best death to be had for a... hat. Now, the little brute will rest in peace - forever." He gave his favoured headgear a final pat, before casting it gently into the exposed bowels of Old College. "Goodbye, old friend."

"We can always go hat shopping tomorrow," cooed Deputy Head Porter. This did not go down well.

"I'm thinking it's too soon..."

"I say, what's going on over there?" remarked The Dean, pointing over towards the flowerbeds by the cloister. "That looks like Terry. Is he... digging?"

"He's probably burying a poo," replied Deputy Head Porter, helpfully.

"I bet not," said the Professor. "If he is, it's a strange way to go about that. He looks rather excitable about something. I think we should investigate."

CAUSE & EFFECT

Ralph Waldo Emerson once said that shallow men believe in luck or circumstance, while strong men believe in cause and effect. He makes a good point, although while Old College could now be said to be the subject of a stroke of good fortune, the cause could indisputably be accredited to Terry. And the effect?

Well.

Languishing before them in the flowerbeds of Apple Tree Court was none other than the very thing they had been searching for; in fact, the very thing that has been searched for by so many before them - knights, adventurers, crooks and scoundrels aplenty.

The Holy Grail.

Deputy Head Porter concluded that it must have fallen from Junior Bursar's person when he tripped over Terry during the pursuit into Old Hall. That was rather too much luck for anyone, although she wasn't knocking it.

A peculiar hush fell about them as they stood transfixed with the fantastically innocuous object nestled gently amidst the begonias. But yet, it seemed almost impossible to look right at it, as if it spurned the gaze of mortal eyes. It's colour could not be described, for it seemed to have no colour at all. Or, at least, it was a colour that lay somewhere on the spectrum beyond understanding. The familiar magnetism it exuded in The Dean's rooms remained and the urge to be ever closer to it, indomitable. Deputy Head Porter's head began to swim a little and she realised that she was hardly breathing at all.

"By Jove, I don't believe it," murmured The Dean, uncharacteristically subdued.

Terry pawed furiously at it, hoping for it to roll away and become a plaything, so Deputy Head

Porter deftly swept him up into her arms, to restore some decorum befitting of the circumstances. Professor Fox patted his head, but Terry's great green eyes never wavered from the Grail. Head Porter bent down and, with a shaking hand, carefully clasped it.

"Unbelievable!" he said, his voice barely a whisper. "This is it, it's the Holy Grail!"

"I think we should hide it," said Deputy Head Porter. She didn't know why she said that. It felt like the right thing to say.

"I shall take care of that," The Dean responded, returning to his authoritarian demeanour. "It must be removed from public view at once, or things could start to get tricky."

"What's do be done with it, I wonder?" asked the Professor.

"I don't know, I don't know," snapped The Dean. The enormity of the situation was burdensome, even for him. "Something dreadfully cunning, no doubt. In the meantime, you chaps should get back to the wedding. It is rather rude to abandon a party without any kind of explanation, you know."

"Oh, I do that sort of thing all the time," said Professor Fox. "They wonder for a bit, get cranky for some bits, then forget about it - forever."

"Obviously, no one can know the real reason for our abstraction," continued The Dean. "No. It is of the utmost importance that the existence of the real Grail is concealed. We gave our word that it should be returned to Chinon and that it exactly what we shall do, when circumstances allow. We shall let College continue with its smug self-congratulation about the thing dug up from The Bursar's hole. Maybe they will realise it is a fake, maybe they won't. Some will claim it as real, others as a fraud. The unexplained disappearance of The Bursar will neatly add to the nature of its discovery and the thing will forever remain swathed in myth, which is quite as it should be."

"Surely The Master will realise it is a fake," muttered Head Porter.

"Quite so, quite so," replied The Dean. "But after lauding the great success of its discovery, will he admit to it? More likely he will lock it away to save face, I'll wager."

"But do you think he knew about The Bursar following you to France?" Head Porter's brow was furrowed with the effort of all this thinking.

"Highly unlikely!" barked The Dean. "Why would The Bursar tell him about that? It was imperative to his plans that everyone was fooled by the fake Grail. No, his vanishing will become another great mystery of Old College. As if we didn't have enough of those as it is."

"I think I could do with a stiff drink," said Deputy Head Porter, never so sure of anything in her whole life. Head Porter groaned at the very mention. "You should get some water or something. And maybe get back in there with the ladies. They did seem quite taken with you."

Deputy Head Porter's suggestion perked up Head Porter considerably and he joined her and Professor Fox back in the Armingford Room, where the wedding reception had evolved into the type of party that the police guests were more likely used to shutting down. The string quartet were nowhere to be seen and a raucous sound system, manned by entrepreneurial Organ Scholar Alex, had been employed to recreate something reminiscent of a nightclub from the early nineties. The bride had hitched up her dress and was performing some kind of tap dance routine atop the buffet tables. Her new groom, Porter, was enthusiastically applauding and his moustache - as well as a great deal of the rest of him -was in glorious disarray. The elegant Detective Chief

Inspector Thompson was perched as far away from the music as possible, reclining with polite irritation whilst reading a small book and sipping a large sherry. Deputy Head Porter decided to have a quick word.

"Good evening, Chief Inspector," she had to shout above the thumping music, but attempted to remain respectful.

"Ah! Deputy Head Porter. Enjoying the party?"

"It's been... eventful!" she replied. "I hope your holiday wasn't too thrown off by rescuing us."

"It was completely ruined, Deputy Head Porter, as I'm sure you know very well."

"Oh. We are very sorry about that, Chief Inspector."

"I'm sure." The Chief Inspector closed his book at smiled at her. "They say the Holy Grail was found here at Old College after all. Seems like you had a wasted journey?"

The presence of a question rather than a statement was not lost on Deputy Head Porter. She returned his smile.

"Well, they do say that travel broadens the mind, Sir," she replied. "And what with that business with The Bursar, well, perhaps you can say some good came out of it all."

"That's a peculiar system of morality, Deputy Head Porter," and he winked.

"About that. I shouldn't ask, but I really would be very grateful if you kept the events in Chinon to yourself. I mean - strictly speaking nothing illegal happened. Not counting The Bursar, of course, but... you know what I'm getting at, don't you?"

"I do," the Chief Inspector nodded. "And you don't have to worry. As far as The Bursar is concerned, well. He was never quite on the level, was he? And anyway, I really cannot recall any Bursar, now you come to mention it."

"Thank you, Sir."

"Would you care for a sherry?"

The evening wore on and many of the more sensible-minded guests returned to their beds, but there were still a good many hardy souls determined to make the happy couple's night something to remember. With Head Porter happily reunited with his gaggle of admirers - who appeared more amorous following a bout of vigorous imbibing - Professor Fox and Deputy Head Porter circled the impromptu dance floor. It was well known that the Professor was quite incompatible with dancing, so she didn't suggest they joined in. Instead, they watched and laughed and passed comment on their fellow guests.

"Now here, for example," the Professor continued. "See that guy there? He must have gotten dressed with the lights out. How else can you explain it?"

"Hang on a minute," said Deputy Head Porter, squinting at the chap in question. "Don't we know him?"

For a moment they concentrated on the gentleman, flailing wildly in the midst of rhythmic expression. As they continued to stare, he noticed them. They obviously did know him, as recognition lit up his face and he waved frantically at them both.

"Goodness me! That's the fellow from the Antique Shop!" exclaimed the Professor. "He began this whole dadblame thing. What's he doing here, now?"

"Ask him yourself. He's headed over."

The Shop Keeper was indeed delighted to see them, although that could have been partly to do with the inexpensive and plentiful rum on offer. News of the discovery in Apple Tree Court had seeped out to certain factions of the community and when he came to Old College to seek out Deputy Head Porter and the Professor, he found celebrations in full swing. He assumed it was all in honour of the Grail, but when he discovered otherwise, he thought he might as well stay anyway, seeing as no one had explicitly asked him to leave. He was confused, at first, by the tale of the ancient monastery under College, but the Professor reassured him with a carefully redacted account of the events in Chinon.

"So, we really were right all along?" he gasped, eyes wide with excitement. "The clues and everything?"

"Quite right, my man," replied the Professor. "It was just such a shame that someone had already gotten there before us. By the way, I think whatever that is you're wearing works rather well. I'm sure you definitely put it on with the lights on."

"How ill-fated it should be that you were too late," agreed the Shop Keeper, shaking his head and choosing to ignore the comment about his outfit. "I wonder who it could have been?"

"Could have been anyone, I imagine," said Deputy Head Porter, rather more quickly than she meant to.

"Hmm, yes, I suppose so," he was thoughtful for a moment. "Nonetheless - a party is a party and we cannot let such things stand in the way of a good time!" With that, he snatched up another drink and whirled away to join the sweaty mass on the dance floor.

"You know, DHP," said the Professor. "I think he has a few good points. A party is a party after all."

"What do you mean, Professor?" Deputy Head Porter could only hazard the wildest of guesses as to where this might be going.

"All the excitement of quests and knights and... weddings. It has got me having thinks a bit. There is something we just must have speaks about..."

ALL GOOD THINGS

Stood at the edge of the dance floor, where now only the hardcore of dervishes persisted in an increasingly erratic display of alcohol fuelled carousal, Deputy Head Porter awaited with interest the pearls of wisdom Professor Fox seemed intent on sharing with her. Despite his previous urgency at garnering her attention, he appeared to have drifted into abstraction, perhaps forming his thoughts into something approaching clarity.

Most of the wedding guests had since beaten a wobbly path to their beds, leaving a cluster of die-hard detectives and several battle-hardened relatives gamely sustaining the dying embers of the party. They were making an admirable attempt to remain a raucous troupe, but there was a sense that they too would soon succumb to the need of slumber. The Professor turned towards Deputy Head Porter and looked her straight in the eye.

"I think... I think our adventure has taught me something, DHP. Something about people and their minds."

"Please do tell, Professor."

"So, here it is, and I shall tell most of it. Junior Bursar is quite insane. Mad, in fact. Madder in the head than anyone's ever been before."

An astute observation but hardly a revelation, thought Deputy Head Porter.

"And we might as well add the Curator to the list. I think he's mad too. But in a very different way. How horrid, but true."

"Yes indeed," she replied, nodding. "Perhaps it's just us. maybe we attract a certain type of person."

"Nah, I bet not!" he replied, amused. "But... you might have a point, in an around and about way. Anyways and a few - both these fellows were guardians of the Grail. It was a great passion for them both, I think. And the Shop Keeper - he has dedicated his life to the search for it and he is quite unstable, you must admit."

"And you think that the Grail has driven them mad?"

"I actually do, can you believe. The Grail, or the love of the Grail, either or." The Professor thought to himself for a moment. "That, or what it represents, you know. A kind of secret thing. A love for the secret, but not the thing itself. There."

The Professor seemed happy with this, for the time being. He tousled his hair, feeling quite naked without his hat. He continued.

"There is always some madness in love and, although love is without reason, there is always some reason in madness. There, I think that explains it better. Now you probably think *I'm* mad."

Deputy Head Porter looked over to their weary-looking hosts, Mr and Mrs Porter, swaying languidly together in a dance that plays to music no one else could possibly hear, sweet nothings whispered between them, dreams and promises flourishing from their newly seeded vows.

"And what about them?" she asked, smiling and nodding over. "Do you suppose that they are mad, then?"

"Oh, without question!" the Professor replied, adamant. "But you know, Madness is no bad thing, I am thinking, if you can go willingly into it of your own choosing. And who can say what is madness in any case? It's just a different way of thinking about things, I say. And love - well - that is an elective madness."

Deputy Head Porter knew at this point that she had had far too much to drink. The Professor was making perfect sense.

"Take Head Porter, for instance," he continued, pointing to where their friend was in the dying throes of seduction. "He looks quite ready to jump headlong into enamoured insanity if you ask me."

"Poor chap. He always ends up scaring off the ladies, somehow."

"He should get a bit madder, then try his luck again, I say!"

"Talking of mad people," said Deputy Head Porter, something suddenly coming to mind. "We should check on The Dean. I want to know what he has done with the Grail."

They found The Dean in his rooms, large whisky in hand and a self-satisfied smirk upon his face. He was fairly pleased to see them.

"Aha! I wondered if you chaps might pop up. Cheers!" He raised his glass by way of a greeting. "Head Porter not with you?"

"He's making a last-ditch attempt at seducing one of the bride's friends," replied Deputy Head Porter.

"Really? Which one?"

"Anyone, I think."

"Hmm! Good tactic, I say. Drink?" The Dean did not wait for a reply but began filling the chipped Arsenal mug he kept for guests with his finest Scotch. The Dean didn't really like sharing his whisky and the insalubrious vessel was a means of letting people know so.

"I say... you wouldn't have any cherry brandy, would you?" asked the Professor, eyeing the decanter with deep suspicion.

"No, not at all," The Dean replied. "But you can have some of this and just pretend."

"Rats and a heifer. It will do."

Suitably furnished with unnecessarily expensive whisky, Deputy Head Porter tackled the elephant in the room.

"Sir, where did you hide it?"

"Hmm? You mean the Grail?" As if she could mean anything else. "Ahh. Well. I have deployed the usage of such sly chicanery you wouldn't believe. I've hidden it where no one will think to look."

"Good for you," said the Professor, wincing as he sipped tentatively at his whisky. "I always hide my important stuff where everyone looks first, dadblameit. Now, where is it?"

"In plain sight, of course!" The Dean replied, with a flourish. "It is right in front of your eyes and neither of you spotted it at all. You may now bask in the awe of my genius."

Seeing an excellent excuse to rid himself of the unwanted beverage, Professor Fox sat down his mug on the coffee table and began to search around. Deputy Head Porter felt obliged to join the hunt, but didn't get much further than the Professor's discarded whisky. As it happened, her assistance was not required, as the Professor's eagle eye fell upon the elusive object before she had even had a chance to take a sip.

"Aha! I found it!" The Professor grinned and pointed to the Grail, nestling comfortably on The Dean's writing desk among the usual conglomerate of odd articles that, for some reason, were essential to his everyday life. "And... I see you've filled it with paper clips."

"Well, it might as well make itself useful while it's here," said The Dean, dismissively.

Well, quite, thought Deputy Head Porter. *Although it seems to be a somewhat humble engagement for a thing of such undoubted legend.* But the more she thought on it, the more she felt that a peaceful and unassuming existence - quietly going about its business without the need for pomp and circumstance - was rather more apt than one might imagine.

As she let the burning amber liquid slide down her throat and fuzzy her head, Deputy Head Porter idly pondered the venture now behind them and thought that they might now declare themselves knights, having followed with such fortitude in the footsteps of the Templar. The acquisition of the Holy Grail might seem like quite the prize, but that was a simple treasure hunt compared to the forbearance of friendship that seemed to her to be the real reward. This called for a dramatic gesture of some kind. She clapped her hands together to gather the attentions of her colleagues.

"Gentlemen!" she began grandly and feared that she wouldn't be able to keep it up. "Gentlemen. We have solved puzzles, cracked codes, got into fights and travelled all the way to France. The upshot of which is that we have discovered the Holy Grail!"

"But it was Junior Bursar who actually discovered the Grail," the Professor pointed out.

"Well.. yes.. but we had the right idea and we got it off him in the end."

"Wasn't that the dadblamed Terry that did that?"

This wasn't going particularly well. It had sounded absolutely brilliant in her head, as well.

"Look, the point *is,*" she continued, determined not to be put off. "This is the first time we actually have something to celebrate at the end of an adventure. Quite remarkable it is, too. With that in mind, I think we should have a bit of a dance."

The Dean and Professor Fox looked doubtful, but she put on her very best pleading face and they were powerless to resist. The Dean broke first.

"Very *well,* Deputy Head Porter," he huffed, turning to his elderly record player with the wobbly needle. "But you know I only have one record."

"Goodness. What is it?" asked the Professor. "I only dance to certain things, it is said."

"It's the theme tune to *Minder*."

"That... will have to do."

As The Dean fiddled with the rickety device and the Professor took her hand in anticipation of the victory rollick, Deputy Head Porter couldn't help but think that there couldn't be anything else quite so perfect for that exact moment in time; the perfect end to the perfect quest. Things were certainly good.

And you know what they say about all good things, don't you?

The End

SECRET DIARY OF TERRY

Part One

Good day to you all, creatures. No doubt you all know me as the undisputed hero of everything and also as the owner of the creature who wears a bowler hat. I know she has a name but that does not interest me so much. She smells of onions and flowers, so I think of her as Onion Flower. She feeds me well and has a fabulous looking tail, but she keeps it at the back of her head which is very odd. Still. It is not for me to understand such primitive creatures as yourselves, rather to guide you as best I can in your life's work of serving catkind. But I shall save that for another time.

Quite recently Onion Flower went away somewhere, she did tell me beforehand, but I wasn't really listening. There was something climbing up the wall at the time and it was a lot more interesting that Onion Flower, but quite soon I rather regretted not paying some attention. I saw the travel box being placed in the hallway and I became very wary. Last time I went in there I was taken to a strange smelling place. I did have a nice sleep, however, but when I woke up, I discovered that my gentleman's area had been decommissioned. Quite an embarrassment for any beast, although it is one less thing to worry about, I suppose. I was determined not to be fooled twice.

Regrettably, Onion Flower deployed a plan of the utmost deviousness against which I was quite powerless. She threw my most favourite mouse-rattle right into the box and I was straight in after it without even a thought. I do so hate it when she takes advantage of my natural hunting abilities in such ways. But anyway. Any hopes of receiving replacement kitten-makers were dashed when I was finally released at a place where another creature was lurking.

I recognised the smell of this creature - a powerful aroma of elderly bacon, when it has turned green - he had been to my lair before. I specifically remember him coming over as Onion Flower had made me a shepherd's pie but for some reason, she didn't seem very happy when I ate it. She is a curious beast.

Green Bacon seemed very pleased to see me and was telling me what a wonderful time we would have together. I was doubtful. A quick sniff around his lair suggested a distinct lack of things to kill and at first it was unclear as to where my sleeping quarters were to be. Of course, I allow Onion Flower to share my nest at home as she needs to be close by in case I need feeding, or letting out or reassurance of my place at the centre of the universe. I am not so sure about sharing with Green

Bacon. I am rather particular about what I allow in my nest.

Luckily, I soon locate what must be my quarters - a fair-sized room at the top of the stairs with a barely adequate nest. As with any new nest, it is important to place my own scent upon it and experiment with its suitability. I was diligently going about this business when Green Bacon shooed me off quite abruptly. I can only assume this was because he wanted to warm the nest for me first and I decided to forgive this intrusion due to his obviously untrained nature. I pity the poor cat that decides to take him on, I tell you.

When I returned downstairs, Onion Flower had gone. She regularly leaves the lair, of course, but I admit to feeling quite uneasy that she had left me here. For example, I hadn't been shown the facilities, nor had I been reassured that Green Bacon had received adequate training in chin scratching and tummy rubbing - essential elements of my upkeep, you know. Suddenly, I felt a little perturbed. I debated doing a wee near the television to relieve the tension, but settled on nibbling between my toes instead. It always helps me think.

With impeccably clean paws and, after a time, a tummy full of tuna (well done, Green Bacon) I felt able to consider my predicament somewhat more clearly. I decided that I simply cannot allow my creature to go wandering off willy-nilly. Only one thing for it! I must track down Onion Flower and insist that she return us both back to the lair.

Part Two

My night spent at the lair of Green Bacon was not too awful, although he is a poorly trained creature. The back door was left ajar for me to explore what passes for his outside territory, but I wasn't much in the mood. There were smells out there I wasn't all too sure about, to be honest. I passed some time sniffing about his lair and did find three spiders, which was encouraging. Some kippers appeared on a small plate in the kitchen, which I ate. I thought they might be to keep me from starvation until the steak had finished cooking on the stove, but this vanished quite mysteriously. I made a note to put in a formal complaint with Onion Flower.

The upstairs nest which I had chosen for myself was strangely shut away behind a door when I went up to have a snooze. I suspect that Green Bacon had got in there himself, which was very rude. I had to make do with a makeshift nest I found downstairs. It was kind of Green Bacon to wash and iron his clothes in anticipation of my arrival, although the pile needed some degree of rearrangement before it met my needs. Although I slept quite well, I was unable to announce myself first thing as the door to the nest room was still shut tight. Luckily for Green Bacon, I can make quite a racket when I have a mind to and he was soon up and about, getting my breakfast.

This creature was pleasant enough but very simple. His lack of training was endearing at first, but I could see that things would soon become problematic. His feet seemed to be everywhere that I needed to be and I barely had time for three brief groomings before he hoiked me outside among the strange smells. This was no good at all. I decided to follow Green Bacon in the hope that he might lead me to Onion Flower.

I followed Green Bacon through an unusual and bustling territory, the likes of which I could never have imagined existed. My lair is situated amongst rolling fields and lazy little lanes and I am rarely bothered by the hairless creatures, except for when Onion Flower holds one of her inexplicable gatherings (the noise! Oh goodness...) This territory is teeming with the things, swarming like bugs between buildings the size of battleships. They cannot surely be lairs. I dread to think what they are. I certainly would not like to nest in them, that's for certain.

My brief foray into foreign parts turns out to be very much worth the fleeting vexation. Before too long at all we arrived at a place that reeked of a vaguely familiar aroma. It is the smell that sits lightly on Onion Flower whenever she returns each evening. This must be Old College! And I don't mind admitting that I found it to be quite remarkable, even by my extraordinary feline standards. The myriad of scents that assaulted my senses were thick with multi-faceted richness; it is not just the variety that excites my nose but the very quality.

But you must realise that smells are just the surface layer of a place, or thing. The basic senses can only tell you the most superficial things about a place, or thing. It is the extra sensory perceptions that a fellow must properly pay attention to. It is a tricky thing to explain to you creatures, although I believe that there are those among you who have a rudimentary grasp of such things. It is when you think with your mind, not your brain and your gut sees things that your heart is blind to. Old College deafened me with its unheard chorus and dazzled my eyes with the unseen. My hackles twitched with something that was neither fear nor malice, rather an ancient thing that spoke from one wise beast to another. When a lair such as this has been around so long, it acquires a vitality all of its own.

Green Bacon scurried off into a hut of little interest to me but at least I knew I was in the right place. I found a quiet spot beneath a strategically placed bush and took a moment to tidy up my tail. I could not quite smell Onion Flower yet but this was definitely her territory. She must be lurking somewhere. It also struck me just then that this is a very fine lair indeed and much more befitting of a cat of my standing. There were many, many creatures here that would no doubt be delighted to serve me.

Yes.

I decided to locate Onion Flower immediately and inform her that we now had a new lair.

Part Three

You see, the biggest difference between human creatures and cats is that humans are never satisfied. This is what makes the feline breed a significantly superior species. Whilst you destroy yourselves chasing ambition and greed, we furry gods recline in our smug satisfaction; beautiful, wise and eternal.

Never more did I feel this anomaly of human nature than during my explorings of my new lair, the estimable Old College. It is true that cats view the world very differently from you hairless fellows, for you only see the things allowed by your limited faculties; you see only the things that are there. We can see the things that were, the things that could have been and the things that are yet to come. My investigations of the new lair revealed not only an abundance of excellent hunting and snoozing spots, but also an air thick with the echoes of triumph and disappointment, secrets and lies and ignorance wrapped up to appear as wisdom. It seemed to me that this was a place where humans come to be better. Not better humans, sadly, just better than other humans.

The scent of Onion Flower was faint throughout the lair and I began to think that perhaps she had not been here all that recently. The stench of Green Bacon permeated completely, giving the impression that he was everywhere at once. At the places where his niff was most potent, I added my own scent with the intention of exerting a bit of authority. He is a nice chap but he needs to learn his place. It was about this time I began to feel rather worried. I could detect a hint of another feline in this territory. The marking was not strong, as if she (for the scent of a lady cat is unmistakable) did not maintain regular patrols. A fine territory such as this would require vigorous attention, perhaps she was unwilling or unable? I thought to seek her out and inform her politely of my intention to install myself and Onion Flower at the earliest opportunity.

Seeing as the scent of lady cat was so very vague, I thought it best to place my own, much more potent markings about the place so that people might be aware of my arrival. No doubt they would want to find a fitting way to welcome me and it is only fair to give them the opportunity to make preparations. I buried little piles of my waste material around and about, taking great care to spread it as far and wide as possible. I would have hated for anyone to have missed out on my announcements.

My endeavours completed, I took to higher ground to better survey my new home. I scaled the ancient stone with surprising supinity. I had prepared myself for a little crumbling here and there as I made the walls and window ledges my playground, but not a movement beneath my little paws. The fierce underpinnings of pious pomposity must reach to the very tops of its towers. From up here, the lair looks very beautiful indeed. The courtyards are laid out in neat little squares of green, framed with the delight of bursts of pinks and purples. The cloisters echoed with the sounds of a thousand footsteps, the music of long forgotten laughter and somber laments of fallen tears. My new subjects scurried from place to place with such a sense of purpose that I could not help but think that they must have already noticed my little announcements. Oh yes, this lair would work out just wonderfully for Onion Flower and I.

Up here, the smell of lady cat was much more evident. I followed it to a dear little window that had been kindly left ajar for me and slipped through, testing the air with my whiskers as I went. Inside, the small but opulent quarters seemed smothered with a polish that tickled my nose quite rudely. Almost every surface, from floor to ceiling, was adorned with a heavy dark wood. There were shiny things scattered about but they did not smell of interest to me. In fact, all I could smell at this point was her.

Her thick, velvet fur.

Her claws like polished steel.

Her aura - masquerading as fear, but actually something else... something... vicious?

Part Four

"Who disturbs my slumber?"

The husky mew of a fellow feline drifted up from beneath an over-stuffed sitting chair in the corner of the room.

"It is I, Terry" I replied, a little puzzled that she did not already know who I was. "Surely you have noticed my announcements?"

An over-stuffed cat of epic proportions languidly sashayed into view. I would like to have said that she was quite a beauty, but that would have been something of an untruth. Indeed, her fur was wonderfully thick like smoked velvet and her big green eyes shone like bedeviled glass. But her snout was rather squashed and her cheeks so fat that they almost swallowed her eyes. A disconcerting *swish swish* indicated an impatient tail flicking across the floorboards as unsheathed talons caught themselves on the polished wood.

"I do not trouble myself with such things," she replied, exposing needle-sharp fangs in a gaping yawn. Her coat rippled and bristled as she awakened her massive bulk.

"Right. Well, I am here now and no doubt the creatures will soon be making great preparations for my welcome proper. If you intend to remain in my lair I should inform you that anything above the size of a vole is mine and you will be expected to limit your requests for tummy rubs to occasions when I am asleep." I thought my terms were more than fair. I did not want my new subjects exhausted by fussing such a porcine puss.

"Your lair? This is my lair." Lady cat narrowed her eyes and stretched herself to her full length, like a great velour sausage. "I am The Master's Cat."

This came as something of a shock. I had heard much talk of The Master's Cat, of course, from Onion Flower and Green Bacon. I knew it as a vicious beast, fierce and unfriendly. And certainly not a lady.

"You do realise that everyone thinks you are a chap, don't you?" I retorted, trying to keep my whiskers straight. "And it is no small wonder. You look like a fluffy pig."

"How rude you are!" she replied with outraged indignation. "I shall have you know that I am magnificent. All my creatures say so. In any case, I have no gentleman's equipment to speak of."

"Well, neither do I these days, so that proves nothing."

"No doubt that is because you are not a gentleman!"

"But at least I am not a pig!"

She hissed at me but I was not perturbed.

"Listen. I am claiming this lair for myself and Onion Flower. You had best make yourself scarce."

"... Onion Flower? Oh." The Master's Cat was suddenly on the back paw. "You know she is not here, don't you? She has gone adventuring with Shouting Whisky and that one in the hat... Cherry Noodle."

She spoke this name with a great tremble in her voice. I know this Cherry Noodle. He does indeed wear a fine hat that I plan to leave an announcement in just as soon as I can. He will be delighted, no doubt.

"Do you know when she will return?" I asked, trying not to show my concern. I do hope she will be back.

"They are looking for a thing. I don't know what it is. But Green Bacon seems to think they will be back very soon indeed."

Excellent news! I would have just enough time to prepare the lair and ensure that everything smells as it should - namely, of me.

"Good, then" I said to her, nose proudly in the air. "I shall let you share a spot with Cherry Noodle, seeing as you two are both rumbunctious beasties."

This suggestion seemed to cause quite some upset. The Master's Cat made the most hideous noise - like a human singing or some such thing.

The mewlings she uttered were not discernible to me, but she leapt - claws a-flash - right towards my very nose...

Part Five

The fight that followed was one of such epic ferociousness that I hesitate to share details so grisly with you delicate human creatures. Although, perhaps I indulge my feline flair for the dramatic rather too feistily. There is little cause for alarm, although it was a somewhat spectacular event.

The Master's Cat flung the full fury of her considerable weight right at me, accompanied by sounds that were reminiscent of Onion Flower singing a song. It was hideous. But a pampered paunch that size was no match for a lithe and athletic parcel of sinew and muscle such as my good self. I leapt up like a flash, alighting on the surface of a nearby bookcase in relative safety. I believe even this piece of furniture, quietly existing for centuries undisturbed, was stunned at the speed of my alighting. As for my tubby assailant, she careened along the polished wooden floor like a furry juggernaut, her wildly scrabbling claws unable to slow her inevitable expedition which ended rather abruptly when she collided with the underside of a cabinet at great speed. To my great delight, at least two-thirds of her vile bulk became hopelessly trapped between the furniture and floor, leaving her little fat legs and tail flailing furiously behind her.

There followed a brief period where I learned several new words which sounded very rude indeed - even worse than some of the ones Onion Flower uses when she is particularly irked. The vigorous and urgent flicking of The Master's Cat's tail put me very much in the hunting mood and I spent quite some time pawing and nipping at it, something which perturbed her greatly. As delightful as this past time undoubtedly was, I had rather more pressing matters to attend to and I left her in situ to pursue the urgent task of finding something nice to eat.

As it turned out, my new lair had all manner of delicious specimens to tantalise my appetite. There was the common ground food, of course - mice and voles and even a plump little rat down by the river. Rats have a much stronger flavour than mice - rustier, in fact - but once one gets used to it they are a real delicacy. But better than the moving food was the warmed-up food that seemed readily available in large quantities.

I discovered an entire building in my lair, completely dedicated to the production of my meals. You see, this is what comes of leaving good quality announcements - people really do take notice. The rich variety of aromas was of such torrid emanation that the shock of it nearly knocked off my whiskers. This was surely the finest fare in the land, and would you believe that it was right here, in my very lair! I could have filled my tummy a hundred times over, which led me to believe that maybe some of this food was meant for Onion Flower too. Well, I have no quarrel with that matter. She can take her fill upon her return. She will return, won't she?

The creatures in the food building were at first a little alarmed at my presence, but that is only to be expected. When faced with such a noble beast such as myself for the first time, it can be a lot to take in. Nonetheless, they soon remembered themselves and furnished me with some wonderful victuals, the quality of which could not have been better if I had hunted them myself. I left soon after, not wishing to cause too much of a commotion on a full stomach.

My next task was, naturally, to find a cosy spot in which to curl up for a while, to allow my burgeoning belly to get about its business. After such a prodigious meal there would no doubt be the opportunity for the making of many more announcements and for that I would need to be well refreshed. I found a wonderful spot up high in the organ loft where the air was warm and the smells uninteresting. The last thing one wants when trying to find repose is the distraction of fascinating flavours exciting the nostrils.

I slept the sleep of the Gods, but that was nothing compared to my delight upon awakening. The lair was a-buzz with activity and excitement, with all manner of rushings about and, evidently, fine preparations. The creatures rushed from one place to another, carrying beautiful things and fussing with sparkling fripperies that had something of a ethereal air about them. Well, this must be it! The great celebration to mark my arrival at the new lair. The creatures were clearly beside themselves with delight. And quite right too.

Final Chapter

My lair was indeed alive with the most lavish of preparations for the great celebration of my arrival. People were really making quite the effort – I even saw a lady creature dressed as a princess in a big white dress. For all I knew, an actual princess had decided to take up residence with me. I'm not sure how Onion Flower would feel about that, but I am sure she would get used to it in time.

Speaking of Onion Flower, her scent had definitely returned to my new territory. Shouting Whisky and Cherry Noodle's, too. She has returned! I imagine she and her friends simply could miss my festivities. The vaguely repugnant creature smells were not the only thing to grace my nostrils, either. My food building was emanating the most fantastic aromas know to cat. This was indeed going to be a wonderful time.

It was whilst idly hunting for Onion Flower that I became somewhat distracted. But what a distraction! I was in the courtyard with an apple tree in it when it caught my eye. Like a fallen star, it nestled in the grime of the gutter, glinting with the remnants of fading hope. A Shiny Thing!

And what a Shiny Thing. It was perfectly round and almost luminous. In its centre was a swirl of colour, like a tiny galaxy dwelling within. Of course, all I could think was that this precious item must be a gift for yours truly. A princess and a Shiny Thing. It almost brought a tear to my eye.

But all was not to be well. Barely moments later, a familiar voice disturbed the moment.

"What have you got there?" came the unmistakable growl of The Master's Cat. "Get away from it – it is mine!"

"I think you will find that it is very much mine!" I replied with as much indignation as I could muster. Being a cat, that's quite a lot. "My lair, my Shiny Thing."

"Foolish boy! This is my lair!"

"Was your lair. My lair now."

The Master's Cat twitched her tail and rose her flabby hackles. Her hiss was rather vicious, although a little too wet-sounding to be truly chilling. Her cold, green eyes stared through mine and straight into the back of my brain as she extended a defiant paw, reaching for my Shiny Thing. I unleashed my well-practiced and blood-curdling professional hiss, being sure to showcase my fine fangs. The paw did not retreat. In fact, it inched a little closer.

Well, I wasn't having any of that.

Determined to see the back of this foul fiend for good, I launched my attack. With claws drawn and teeth a-gnashing, my hind quarters unfurled their full kinetic capabilities and I flew at her piggy face, landing a direct hit right across her nose. Wailing like a toddler with a scrapped knee, she turned and fled.

I decided to mount a pursuit, keen to see her off my territory once and for all. She moved with surprising swiftness for such a waddling beast. I tore after her, my ears flattened against my skull and tail rigid with determination. I was barely aware of where I was running, focused entirely on my quarry. She darted into an open doorway and I followed rapidly after.

And how lucky that I did – for she led me straight into the middle of my arrival celebration! The room was full of delighted human creatures, eating and drinking in my honour. Even the princess lady in the big white dress was there and she looked happier than anyone. Marvellous!

The Master's Cat headed straight towards the huge tables, upon which was laid my own feast. The very nerve of her – first she wants my lair, then my Shiny Thing and now my feast! But her abject terror was evident as she leapt from the tables and straight out of an open window. There was a pause, followed by a low growl and finally, a sort of desperate splash. And then, I heard no more.

Well – even I could not have predicted the extravagance my creatures would go to in order that I might be welcomed to Old College. I was rather taken aback. But I quickly remembered my dignity and hastily began the grooming process, in order to be at my very best for my adoring public.

A minor event – I was briefly reunited with my beloved Onion Flower, but the weightier matter of the Shiny Thing was sitting quite heavily on my mind. I allowed myself a modicum of fuss before politely making my excuses and slipping away. Groomed and feeling very special (it must be said), I returned to find my treasure happily untouched. But I was sure that it would not stay that way for long and decided upon my intent to hide it very carefully.

I experimented with various places of seclusion, an endeavour that took up a good portion of my precious time. But this was an important matter. Eventually, I settled on the cunning ruse of burying the Shiny Thing in one of the few flowerbeds that I had not used for my announcements. Although digging is not a tradition feline activity, I am rather good at it. But just as I was covering over my cherished find, my whiskers detected the unmistakable waft of danger in the air.

Looking up, I saw an evil-smelling elderly gentleman hurtling across the courtyard. He was headed in my general direction and it was most obvious to even a fool that he was after my Shiny Thing! The beast! My suspicions were confirmed when I saw that this creature was being hotly pursued by none other than Onion Flower and Cherry Noodle, evidently intent on putting a stop to this heinous crime. At this point, I deployed the most mysterious and maligned of the feline attributes; an esoteric skill of which even I am not entirely sure of the inward machinations.

With deft nonchalance, I placed myself in the exact position required for tripping the chap, whilst at the same time being in the exact position not to be stepped on. He tumbled with considerable grace into the flowerbed, but it was not to detain him for long. He was soon up and running again, my favourite human creatures shouting after him ferociously.

But he left something behind. What it was, I could not tell you, but it had the appearance of a drinking vessel. Its odour I could not distinguish but it spoke to me, in a way - it spoke to me from many, many centuries past. This thing spoke to me of beauty and power, of salvation and of redemption. Although it had a physical form, it was not something of the human realm, I think. Not even the cat realm. Possibly it was something greater even than cat.

How long I gazed at it, I cannot say. Time did not seem to exist in its presence. All I can say is that by the time I thought to get about hiding it (with my Shiny Thing, of course) Onion Flower and her friends had returned. The wicked old fellow was not with them and they all seemed as entranced with the object as I was. Not quite as entranced as they were with me, quite naturally, but they seemed very pleased to see the thing.

Now I had my Shiny Thing and my Onion Flower, there seemed little left to pursue that could make this wonderful day any better. Cherry Noodle had furnished me with a wonderful chin scratch and several pats and even Green Bacon had paid a degree of reverence to my good self. After all the excitement, the only thing I desired now was some peace and a little slumber. Returning to my favourite spot in the organ loft, I soon slipped into a tranquil doze and dreamed the dreams of one very happy kitten who anticipates further great adventures at Old College.

ABOUT THE AUTHOR

Lucy started writing from the age of ten when her primary school teachers were at a bit of a loss as to how to contain her effervescent personality.

They tasked her with writing stories for the younger children in a bid to keep it from disrupting her peers.

Lucy developed her skills throughout her teenage years, when she was inspired to read the words of Homer, Livy and Virgil. These formative years also saw her develop her other great passion of music, where she threw herself into several years of misbehaving and playing bass guitar in unsuitable rock bands.

She widened her literary horizons through the works of Terry Pratchett, Oscar Wilde and Flann

O'Brien - the latter of which remains to this day her favourite writer.

Lucy develop a penchant for the unusual and the absurd, something which was exacerbated by her time serving in the Police where the many varied experiences and characters she met had a profound effect on her outlook on life.

After seven years on the front line and driven by fascination with Inspector Morse, on a whim Lucy applied for the job of Deputy Head Porter at one of the foremost colleges of Cambridge University. To her great surprise, and that of many others at the time, she landed a role as the first female to don the iconic bowler hat in the college's six-hundred-year history.

Having left formal education at the tender age of sixteen with little to show for it, being thrown amongst the academic elite was something of an eye opener. Documenting the quirks and fables of College life on social media, Lucy was soon persuaded to start a blog – Secret Diary Of PorterGirl. Acutely aware of the dim view taken by College officials of any slight upon their reputation, she wrote anonymously and in such a way as to disguise the true identity of the now notorious Old College.

However, being quite possibly the worst Deputy Head Porter of all time made her decide to hang up her bowler hat and peruse her dream of becoming a writer. Lucy considers this is the best decision she has ever made.

Printed in Great Britain
by Amazon